Sonata for a Killer
(A Miranda and Parker Mystery)

Book 17

Linsey Lanier

Proofread by

Donna Rich

Copyright © 2021 Linsey Lanier
Felicity Books
All rights reserved.

ISBN-13: 978-1-941191-68-2

Copyright © 2021 Linsey Lanier

All rights reserved. Without limiting the rights under copyright reserved above, no part of this publication may be reproduced, stored in or introduced into a retrieval system, or transmitted, in any form, or by any means (electronic, mechanical, photocopying, recording, or otherwise) without the prior written permission of both the copyright owner and the above publisher of this book. This is a work of fiction. Names, characters, places, brands, media, and incidents are either the product of the author's imagination or are used fictitiously. The author acknowledges the trademarked status and trademark owners of various products referenced in this work of fiction, which have been used without permission. The publication/use of these trademarks is not authorized, associated with, or sponsored by the trademark owners.

SONATA FOR A KILLER

Okay. Their last case was an unintended surprise, but now it's time for Miranda and Parker to relax and get back to retirement.

Except Curt Holloway, Miranda's old buddy and teammate, has other plans. When he decided to leave the Investigative Agency, Parker put Holloway in his place as acting CEO.

Now Holloway wants out.

Well, just for a week.

Or so he says.

His ex-wife needs him, he says. He has to go, he says. Looks like he might walk for good if Miranda and Parker don't say yes. And so they do. It's not so bad. Everything is hunky dory for a while.

Until attorney Antonio Estavez shows up and tells them a convicted felon he once defended in court has escaped from prison.

And he's coming to kill him.

They have to find this dangerous fugitive before it's too late.

So much for retiring.

THE MIRANDA'S RIGHTS MYSTERY SERIES

Someone Else's Daughter
Delicious Torment
Forever Mine
Fire Dancer
Thin Ice

THE MIRANDA AND PARKER MYSTERY SERIES

All Eyes on Me
Heart Wounds
Clowns and Cowboys
The Watcher
Zero Dark Chocolate
Trial by Fire
Smoke Screen
The Boy
Snakebit
Mind Bender
Roses from My Killer
The Stolen Girl
Vanishing Act
Predator
Retribution
Most Likely to Die
Sonata for a Killer
Fatal Fall
Girl in the Park
(more to come)

WESSON AND SLOAN FBI THRILLER SERIES

Escape from Danger
Escape from Destruction
(more to come)

MAGGIE DELANEY POLICE THRILLER SERIES

Chicago Cop
Good Cop Bad Cop

For more information visit www.linseylanier.com

Linsey Lanier

CHAPTER ONE

He opened his eyes and listened.

His keen ears waited for the clomp clomp clomp of the guard's boots against the concrete floor in the hall.

Every night for the past three years he had heard that sound in the various institutions where he'd been kept. A steady, intense rhythm, like the driving bass line in Chopin's *Prelude No. 24*.

He raised his hands and studied his fingers. He could still play it, couldn't he? Yes, of course he could. And he would soon. Soon he would never hear the guard's boots again.

He listened.

There was no sound of boots now. Only the familiar cough of the inmate on the other side of the block and the steady snoring of his cellmate.

It was time.

He rose, found the tiny flashlight he'd been hiding under the mattress, and put it in the breast pocket of his jumpsuit. Then he quietly stuffed his pillows under his sheet and blanket, shaping them with his hands until it looked like he was lying there. Just as she'd told him to do.

Good enough.

He moved over to the sink, bent down, and pulled out the loose brick from the wall. He'd discovered it a few weeks ago, just when he'd needed it. Just when she had agreed to help him. When she'd given him the pocket light.

And there they were.

The two keys she had smuggled to him in his mashed potatoes. He had had to be careful not to swallow them that day.

He took them out of the compartment, put them in his pocket, and wedged the brick back in place. Straightening, he smiled to himself.

He was ready.

As quietly as he could, he moved to the door of his cell. He removed the smaller key from his pocket, put his hands through the bars, and inserted the metal into the keyhole.

He gave it a turn, and the door opened.

It was so easy. Too easy?

Holding his breath, he stood and listened. Still no guard. He stepped out into the hall, grateful he was on the first floor. The concrete balcony on the second floor hid him from the cameras a bit. She said the guards wouldn't be watching them now.

Still, he had to be perfectly quiet. He took the flip flops off his feet and held them in his hand while he made his way over the cold floor and past the dozen cells to the corridor that led to the kitchen. When he reached it, he turned down another passageway. And there it was.

A narrow door with a thick chain and padlock.

The Devil's Hole.

It had once been a cell, but was no longer in use.

He stared at it for a long moment. Was it true? Was this the way out?

She had told him this passage had been dug by a prisoner twelve years ago. The rumor was that the officials had left it intact so the inmates would realize escape was futile.

It didn't matter. Escape was his only option.

Yes, yes. I'm hurrying.

He took the second key out of his pocket and inserted it into the lock. He gave it a twist. It opened as easily as his cell door had.

He pulled on the door, stepped into the narrow dank space behind it. Working quickly, he put the two ends of the chain back together and locked it again behind him. He was inside.

Now what?

He turned around and felt a tingle in his stomach. It was as if he had ended up in the same place he had started. The walls felt as if they were closing in on him. But there was no cell here now. No inmates. No beds. No latrine. It was just an empty space.

But at the far end, there was the hole the prisoner had cut into the wall.

After his attempt to escape, that man had been found and shot.

Would that be his fate, too? It might. Still, he had no choice.

He crossed the floor, bent down at the opening, and peered into the darkness. It smelled damp and foul.

He took out the pocket light and ran it over the drain pipe behind the wall. He reached into the hole and touched the metal. His fingers felt the moist cold of it.

All he had to do was follow that pipe, and it would take him to the outside. To freedom.

He had no choice.

With a shudder, he took a deep breath and forced his body through the hole.

He had to bend awkwardly to get inside the hollowed out space. There wasn't even enough room to crouch here. He had to lie down on the ground.

The pipe was as wide as his own body. The area around it was just large enough to breathe in. He would have to crawl along it on his back all the way.

You're taking too long.

Hurry. Yes.

He had to go now. Holding onto the pipe, he pulled with his arms and pushed with his feet as he dragged his body over the dirt. Push and pull. Push and pull. He began to sweat. Soot fell into his eyes and mouth. He spat it out. He had always hated dirt. His studio had always been spotless. He'd insisted on it. He had insisted on so many things he no longer could.

Keep going.

He did. As fast as he could, though it seemed like an eternity. Push and pull. Push and pull. After a while, he wondered if he had died in his sleep and this was the everlasting purgatory he'd been sent to as punishment for his crime.

He hadn't meant to do it. He hadn't meant to kill her.

He'd loved her.

That night was a hazy fog in his mind.

Rosalynd, my darling. If the guards shot him outside, at least they would be together soon.

Keep going, I said.

Yes. Yes. Push and pull. Push and pull.

After two more eternities, at last he came to the ninety degree bend in the pipe where it reached the grounds outside. Struggling, he maneuvered his body until he was partially erect. A manhole cover formed the lid to the hole just above his head. He could see the night sky through its slots.

She had told him it would be unlocked. Was she right?

Stretching out his hand, he touched the cold metal. He put his fingers through the holes and dared to give it a push.

The cover moved. She was right. But it was heavy.

He pushed harder. The lid slid across the grass and he felt fresh air on his face. Finding a foothold in the pipe, he climbed up and out of the enclosure.

He was out. He was out.

He lay on the grass, breathing in the smell of it, feeling like a child. He wanted to roll around in it. He wanted to laugh. He wanted to weep, but freedom wasn't his yet.

He turned over and raised his head. Behind him rose the guard tower and the prison wall topped with barbed wire. Before him lay a short patch of mowed grass.

He had to get across that grass to the field and the road beyond. That was where she had told him to go.

He got up and ran, half crouching until he reached the field.

He plunged in, limping over the uneven ground, pushing his way through the tall weeds like an Olympic swimmer doing breaststrokes. He had lost his shoes and his feet stung with debris from the ground, but he couldn't stop.

Panic drove him.

Air. Air. He was breathing harder than he had in his life, but he couldn't get enough air. His heart pounded hard in his chest.

Lights? Were those lights? Barking. Dogs? Had they set the dogs on him?

He knew this wouldn't work. Why had he even attempted it?

Because I told you to.

Yes, he had to keep going no matter what. Even if they killed him.

But at last he reached the side of the road where the grass had been cut again. He burst out of the weeds and stood on the pavement, gasping for breath.

Don't stop. Keep moving.

Yes. Move. He had to find it. Where was it? Where? Had she lied to him?

He stumbled over the pavement. There were no cars on the road. Could he walk?

He stumbled along for what seemed like a mile. And then he saw it.

An old white Buick.

He hurried to it as fast as he could. It had a dent in its side, just as she'd described it.

Quickly he moved to the driver's side and got in. He tore open the glove compartment and fumbled inside it. There it was.

He pulled out the envelope and peeked inside. Yes. A bus ticket, just where she'd told him it would be. And in the backseat was a duffle bag with clothes and food and water. That would come later.

He turned back and stared at the keys in the ignition. Everything was here. Everything. She had kept all her promises.

Why wouldn't she?

Jolting, he glared at the passenger seat.

There sat Ludwig, his old mentor from Julliard, with his rumpled brown coat, his long matted hair, and his glasses on the end of his nose.

"Wh-what?" he stammered.

Why wouldn't she keep her promises?

He didn't know what to tell him.

His teacher shook his head and laughed. *You never did know when a woman was in love with you. But then, most of them were.*

What was he saying? "Ludwig, should I go back? Should I beg for forgiveness? Throw myself on their mercy?"

Ludwig's thick brows became a thunderstorm as he scowled in disappointment. *Of course, not. You're innocent, after all.*

Yes. That was true. He was innocent.

Come now. The voice from the backseat startled him. He turned and glared at the dark figure sitting there next to the backpack.

Get on with it, or all this practice will be for naught.

A shudder went through him. He would always say that before a performance. He had always been terrified of displeasing him.

"Yes, Papa. You are right, as always."

He touched the pocket of his prison shirt. Tucked inside were the pills. The two small blue ones and the large pink one. He needed them, but he couldn't take them now. He had to save them for later.

Of course, I am right. Now get going. We have to be in Atlanta by morning.

"Atlanta?"

Yes, of course. Where else would we find that lawyer? You remember what we have to do, don't you?

"Yes, yes. I do." And drawing in a deep breath, he turned the key.

The engine started, he pulled onto the deserted road, and feeling as if he were going mad, he drove off into the night.

CHAPTER TWO

Miranda Steele sat on the fifteenth floor of the Imperial Building in the corner office that used to belong to Parker.

Sunlight streamed in through the tall windows, giving the glassy furnishings and the blue-and-silver decor its familiar ethereal glow.

The sight of the space had made her stomach flutter when she first walked in a few moments ago.

Had she missed it? A little, she decided.

Not being in charge—she'd never miss that—but she did miss all the Parker Agency had meant to her. Everything she'd learned here. And especially the joy of working with her handsome husband—who just now was seated next to her on the window side of the glass top meeting table.

Across from them sat her old buddy, Curt Holloway, dressed in his typical brown suit and matching tie.

The suit looked new, his buzz cut was military, and his face stern. He was in charge of the Agency now, but he hadn't felt comfortable sitting at Parker's former desk while they were in the guest chairs.

She could relate to that.

"What is it you want to speak to us about, Curt?" Parker said in a low tone.

They'd both decided Holloway was the right choice to manage the Agency when they'd retired a few weeks ago. But yesterday, he'd called them while they were in Chicago on their way back to Atlanta.

They had arrived at Hartsfield yesterday afternoon. But they'd decided to go straight to the penthouse and make Holloway wait until this morning for the meeting he'd requested with Parker.

After all, they'd needed time to get settled into the place again after spending the last two weeks in a luxury cabin in the North Georgia mountains. They had found the penthouse spotless, of course, thanks to Parker's top notch cleaning service.

So they'd lounged around in the sunken tub and the huge bed.

Holloway turned his head and looked at the door as if making sure it was shut, though he'd closed it himself just a few minutes ago.

He cleared his throat. "Well, sir, ma'am. We seem to have an issue."

Miranda tensed. It must be a whopper of an issue for Holloway to call her ma'am. Had the Agency been asked to track down another murderer? A serial killer? Or did this have something to do with Santana?

"What sort of issue?" Parker said in his boss tone.

Holloway cleared his throat again and shifted in his seat like his pants were too tight. Had he screwed something up?

"Well." He adjusted his tie. "Actually—"

"What?" Miranda snapped.

He started to give her a glare, like old times, then caught himself. He blew out a defeated breath. "It's Audrey."

Miranda felt her brows shoot up. "As in your ex-wife Audrey?"

"Yes."

Audrey Wilson. Holloway's movie star wannabe ex-wife. Not one of her favorite people. "What about her?"

"It's good news, actually. She's written a book."

"A book?"

"It's called *My Ordeal*. It's about what she went through last fall. You remember."

Did she ever. She could feel Parker wince at the memory of that experience.

"The thing is," Holloway continued, "Audrey needs to go on a book tour."

Miranda grimaced. "Isn't she in jail?"

The woman had nearly killed Holloway during the bank robbery she'd been charged with. Plus she'd totaled Parker's midnight blue Lamborghini. Miranda didn't know if she'd ever forgive her for that. She'd loved that car.

Okay, Audrey had been under the influence of some pretty hefty mind control drugs at the time—stuff she and Parker had also experienced—but the DA wasn't buying that story, as far as Miranda knew.

Holloway cleared his throat again. "Well, yes. Audrey's awaiting trial in Fulton county prison. But somehow her publisher got a judge to agree to releasing her for the tour."

Parker drew in a breath. "And what does this have to do with us?"

Holloway gave Parker a steady look that must have taken all the courage he could muster. "Audrey asked me to come with her on the tour, sir. As a bodyguard."

Say what?

Miranda just stared at him. "Won't the prison send a guard with her?"

"Two, actually. The publisher got them to clear me as one of them. Audrey insisted on it."

Just as brazen as Miranda remembered her.

"It'll only be for a week," he added.

Parker leaned forward. "What exactly are you asking, Curt?"

Holloway took a deep breath and spat it out. "Detective Judd is on vacation. So is Detective Tan. I'm shorthanded."

"And so?"

Parker was making him say it out loud.

"And so I was wondering if you could help me out. Both of you."

He gave Miranda a silly boyish grin she'd never seen on him.

"Curt, are you asking us to come out of retirement?"

Holloway swallowed. "Yes, sir."

"And to fill your position while you're away?"

"Yes, sir."

Oh, brother.

Miranda sat back and folded her arms with a smirk. "Why did you sign off on Judd's vacation if you had this conflict?"

"Detective Judd's vacation was approved weeks ago. Long before I, uh, before you put me in charge."

Parker nodded. "Judd's niece is getting married in Iowa. I approved his leave."

"I didn't know about the book tour until yesterday. Audrey called me and begged me to do this for her."

"Why don't you send one of our very capable bodyguards?" Parker said.

"She wants me, sir."

She wanted to use him. And Holloway just let the woman wrap him around her little finger. Same as she did before. It was disgusting.

"We'll have to think about it," Parker said firmly.

Holloway made a squeaky sound of frustration. "Well, uh, sir, the tour starts tomorrow."

"Tomorrow?"

"In fact, we have to be at the airport in a few hours. The first stop is Austin."

Miranda could tell Parker was fuming. But composing himself, he turned to her. "Are you all right with this, Miranda?"

He wasn't going to say yes without her okay. She appreciated that, but they were kind of stuck. Neither of them could walk away from the Agency with no one in charge.

She raised a shoulder. "I guess I'm okay with it."

Pointing a forefinger, Parker turned back to Holloway. "One week, Curt. Or there may be someone else sitting behind that desk when you get back. Do you understand me?"

Holloway bobbed his head as if he were doing an imitation of Dave Becker. "Yes, sir. I understand. Just one week."

And before they could change their minds, he got to his feet and rushed out of the room as if it were on fire.

Miranda stared after him. "I think he's glad to get out from under that glare of yours. It's pretty scary."

Scowling, Parker ignored her attempt to lighten the mood as he rose and went to the desk. "This is highly irresponsible. I expected so much more of Curt."

"It's Audrey. She's got him tied up in knots."

"Apparently." He sat down and began working the laptop Holloway had left running.

Getting used to the idea, Miranda scooted over to the desk and put her butt on it. Then she leaned over and grabbed Parker's classy red silk tie. "You know the power some women have over a man, don't you?"

His gray eyes grew hungry as they studied her. "You're making me regret this decision already."

She snickered. "It's been a while since we've made love on this desk."

"Let me see what Curt has been up to first."

She dropped the tie and stood as Parker hit the keyboard. Fun and games would have to wait. "You could have pulled rank, you know."

"Pulled rank?"

"Put your foot down and said no. Tell him Audrey would have to fend for herself."

"I could have. But I didn't choose to go that way. Yet."

She felt a sudden tug in her gut at that word. Was Parker missing the Agency, too? The work? Not that they had been away from it for long.

"Hmm," he grumbled in a low tone that was somewhere between annoyed and angry.

She came around the desk and peered over his shoulder. "What is it?"

"Holloway's schedule."

She scanned the spreadsheet. "Looks like he's got everybody in nice little slots."

"Except Detective Tan is supposed to be teaching the new IITs."

IITs. Short for Investigators in Training—the rigorous training all new hires went through when they joined the Parker Agency.

"Who's doing that if she's on vacation?"

"It doesn't say. Do you think you can fill in for Tan?"

"Teaching the new IITs?"

"Yes."

Miranda never thought she'd be doing that. "I guess so."

Here's a list of the names of the students and the current lessons. Parker printed them out and reached for the papers. After the machine finished whirring, he handed them to her. "They're in the gym."

Man, he sounded like a boss.

So much for playing around in the office. It was back to work. She took the papers from him and sighed. "Okey dokey. I guess I'll see you later."

And she dared to lean over and pop a kiss on his cheek before she turned to go.

"Miranda?"

"Yes?"

His gray eyes gleamed as his lips rose in a half smile. "We'll find time for your suggestion soon."

She smiled back. "Hot dog."

CHAPTER THREE

Oh, brother. What had she gotten herself into?

Dressed in sweats and holding a counter and a clipboard with the list of names Parker had given her, Miranda watched the new recruits rumble around the gym's perimeter, pounding the slats like a herd of rhinos in heat. The memory of doing the same with Holloway and Becker flanking her sides flashed in her head, making her feel nostalgic.

"Move it!" she yelled at them. "The bad guy's already in Nebraska." Her imitation of the tough-as-nails Detective Tan fell flat.

There were a dozen new recruits in the class now. Soon that would be down to nine or ten. The Agency's rigorous training was too much for most candidates, and they dropped out before the final exams.

She clicked the counter as the herd passed her again. Five more to go. What a bore this was. Almost as bad as doing background checks.

While she loved working a case, hunting down a killer and all, Miranda had forgotten how tedious the Agency's day-to-day operations could be. Plus, she felt awkward standing here, supervising. She didn't mind running around the gym herself, but pushing a class of recruits to do it?

Not her style.

Her gaze went to the hanging bags where she used to work out her frustrations. She nearly sighed at the sight of them.

Being back in the office was doing things to her insides she hadn't expected.

She really had missed coming here to work every day, wondering what was in store for her. Whether she'd be hunting down a killer, searching for a kidnapping victim, tracking a stalker—or facing a stack of paperwork.

Surely Parker had to feel the same, at least a little bit. What would happen if Holloway ran off with Audrey and never came back? Would they come back to their old jobs?

And then she thought of the days she'd spent behind Parker's desk, mourning the loss of him. And the things he'd suffered during that time.

No, they were done with this work. They had made that promise to each other, and it was firm.

This gig was only temporary.

One of the IITs came up to her and stood with his hands on his knees, gasping. His red hair was wet with perspiration. "Ms...Steele?"

"What is it, uh…?" She scanned her paper, but it didn't tell her which face went with which name.

"Larry. Larry Cutler."

Larry Cutler was messy and sweaty, but he had a nice smile. "Okay, what is it, Cutler?"

"We're supposed to break for lunch now."

Miranda looked down at her counter. The class had passed her several times, but she hadn't clicked it.

Good enough for her.

She turned a page on her clipboard and studied the schedule. Lunch at noon. Next class at one-thirty. They'd be going over the tests the recruits had taken last week. Ugh.

She checked her phone. It was ten past noon. She was late.

She blew the whistle around her neck. "Okay, everybody. That's enough for now."

But everyone had already stopped running and were staring at her as they cooled off.

She cleared her throat. "Hit the showers and grab some lunch. We'll meet back in the classroom at two."

To make up for the ten extra minutes—and to give her time to figure out what to do with those tests.

Off to a great start, wasn't she?

As everyone headed toward the locker room, Miranda tucked her clipboard under her arm and started for the door, deciding she'd see what her sexy husband had in mind for lunch.

"Ms. Steele?"

She turned around to see Cutler was still standing there, sweat still staining his running clothes, his red hair still as disheveled.

"What is it?"

"It's a real honor to have you for a teacher," he said with a shy grin. Then he trotted away to catch up to his peers.

An honor, huh? Cutler was in for a shock when classes got going.

Still, Miranda felt her cheeks go red. And as she headed through the door and back upstairs, she couldn't help but smile.

CHAPTER FOUR

After changing back into her dress slacks and blouse, Miranda was back on the fifteenth floor, making her way through the cube banks when one of the detectives rose from her desk to stretch, and she spotted the familiar head of short sunflower blond curls.

Immediately they locked gazes, and Miranda stared into Cindy Smith's wide electric blue eyes.

"Miranda. What are you doing here?"

The Southern accent made Miranda smile. And to think, this woman used to be one of her worst enemies when they were IITs.

She strolled over to her cube. "Holloway needed some help. It's just for a little while." No need to go into the annoying details.

Smith looked surprised by that answer. "Is Mr. Parker here, too?"

"In his office."

"Wow." She sat back down.

Miranda stepped into her cube and took in the decor. Potted plants, family pictures in pretty frames, and neat piles of pastel colored sticky notepads. A little too girly for her taste.

Miranda eyed the pile of manila folders. "What are you up to?"

"Oh, the usual background checks."

"Kind of boring, huh?"

"Not always." Smith picked up a paper from an open file. "There's this deadbeat husband I found three hidden bank accounts for."

"Really?" Miranda took the paper and looked it over. Impressive. But Smith had too much talent for routine work. She glanced at her laptop screen where an autopsy photo was displaying. Had to be a murder vic, and she was in bad shape. "That's not a background check."

"Oh, no. I'm following a slasher case up in Chicago."

"Chicago?"

Smith adjusted the photo and the headline appeared. "Serial Killer Claims Another Young Woman."

That sounded like the case Detective Templeton was working up there. The one she'd wanted Miranda and Parker's help with.

The one they'd turned down.

"That lead detective is sharp. She's going to make a name for herself on this case."

Miranda knew Smith longed to make a name for herself, too. In her mind, she'd already done that, but evidently she still had a bit of insecurity. "Let me see that picture again."

Smith pulled it up and Miranda leaned in to study wounds on the body. Sure enough, it was one of the photos Templeton had shown her yesterday. She took the mouse and scanned the article.

They had identified the victim. She had been a pre-med student at the University of Chicago. She'd been missing since last Friday. Her roommate said she had a habit of jogging in the park every morning. The police suspected that was when she'd been nabbed by the killer. But she'd been taken somewhere and returned to the park after the sicko was through with her.

The press was speculating this murder was connected to another in Kenwood last week. Templeton hadn't mentioned that. Maybe she didn't think there was a connection. Probably too early to call it a serial killing. But that was news reporters for you.

Smith rubbed her arms as if the A/C was too cold. "It's just awful. That creep reminds me of—you know. The creep back home."

She meant the killer on the Outer Banks that they'd gone after last November.

Miranda let go of the mouse and straightened. "Not enough artistry to be Jay Charles York. Besides, he's gone."

His boat had been lost at sea, and he had gone down with it, either drowning or already dead from the bullet wound Miranda had given him.

"I know, but still." Smith pulled on the sweater that hung from the back of her chair.

They'd both been through a terrorizing nightmare at the hands of that psycho.

"I sure do miss Janey," she sighed.

For a second Miranda thought she was talking about her friend in Chicago, Jane Anderson. Then she realized she meant Wesson. "Yeah, have you heard from her?"

"Not a word."

Smith and Wesson had been inseparable at one point, so much so that everyone had made a joke of their names.

But that was before Santana.

Shortly after that ordeal, Wesson had sent Miranda a text saying she was taking an extended vacation.

She didn't say when she'd be back, but she indicated she'd be gone at least a month. That gave her a little more than a week before she had to be back. Miranda was regretting she hadn't told Wesson to check in once in a while before she'd okayed her sabbatical.

But who knew? Wesson was probably taking in the Grand Canyon or shopping at Gucci's somewhere. Maybe she'd gone to see her sister in LA. Or maybe Simon Sloan had gotten her to join the FBI. Would be nice to get some notice if that was the case.

Miranda handed her the paper. "Let me know if you hear anything."

"Sure will." Smith turned back to her file.

She ambled away and looked down at the schedule on her clipboard. Test results, then Principles of the Legal System. The lecture material had already been written.

Looked like a pretty dull afternoon.

Suddenly, a quotation came to her. It was from a business book she'd forced herself to read when she was in charge of the Agency.

"The first rule of management is delegation."

She turned back. "Hey, Smith. How would you like to help me out?"

Smith's blond head popped up over her cube wall again. "Sure, Steele. What do you need?"

"I need someone to take over the IIT class this afternoon."

Smith blinked in surprise. "Detective Tan's class?"

"Yeah. She's on vacation. You'll just be going over a test they took last week and then reading a lecture about legal stuff. It won't be hard." She shoved the clipboard into Smith's hands. "All the answers are there."

"Are you sure?" Smith's eyes filled with anxiety.

"Of course, I'm sure. Go for it. If you have any questions, just give me a call." And she hurried away before Smith mustered up the courage to say no.

CHAPTER FIVE

Taking a detour around the cube banks, Miranda made the mistake of passing by the office belonging to Parker's daughter, Office Manager and general PITA at the Agency.

She'd almost made it past the open door when she heard Gen's shocked voice. "Miranda?"

Okay. She couldn't just snub her.

She turned back and stuck her head in the door with as happy a smile as she could muster. "Hi, Gen."

Her posture military rigid, Gen sat behind her ultra neat desk in one of her usual charcoal business suits. Her short, nearly white-blond hair looked like it had just been styled. Her eyes were as piercing as her father's could be.

Though not nearly as sexy.

"What are you doing here?" she demanded.

"I work here."

She raised a sharp brow. "You mean you *used* to work here."

Miranda opened her mouth to reply, but Gen didn't let her get a word out.

"You didn't answer my text about the baby shower."

Text. Baby shower. She'd gotten it yesterday in Chicago—and had promptly forgotten about it. "Oh, yeah. I'll get back to you. I'm on my way to see your father."

Gen jumped to her feet. "What is he doing here?"

She wanted to say, "He works here, too." But Gen didn't let her.

"Never mind. Get in here and sit down." She grabbed Miranda by the arm and ushered her to her office.

IITs didn't call Parker's daughter "The Little General" for nothing.

But Miranda knew she had to face the woman sometime. Straightening both her clothes and her dignity, she took a seat in the cushy guest chair. "Okay, Gen. What do you need from me?"

"Ideas."

"Ideas?" She wasn't exactly the party planner here. "About the baby showers?"

"Baby shower," Gen corrected. "I've decided to combine them. There isn't time for both."

Okay. "So it's a double baby shower?"

"Exactly. Normally, I'd rely on Coco for ideas about the decor and Joan for ideas about the food. But obviously I can't this time, since they're the ones having the babies." Her tone couldn't have been more condescending if Miranda had been a misbehaving twelve-year-old.

Gen sat down across from her like she was interviewing her for a job. She reached for a pen and tapped it on a small pad of paper. "So. What are your ideas?"

Nonexistent. Miranda twisted in the chair. "Well—"

Gen held up a forefinger. "First, there's the venue. I thought of Parker Towers, but we've done that so often before. There's Luigi's or The Village, but neither of those places seems quite right for a guest list of one hundred."

Miranda's mouth flew open. "A hundred people? For a baby shower?" Even if it was a double.

The few baby showers Miranda had been to in her life consisted of five or six women in a trailer.

Gen spread her hands. "Joan knows everyone in our circle and so does Coco. People will be offended if they're not invited. Besides, it's less than fifty couples."

Couples? "You're inviting the guys, too?"

"It's done these days. Dave and Antonio will be there as well."

That might be okay, but Miranda didn't think Fanuzzi would go for a big crowd. "I'm not sure—"

Gen held up two fingers. "Second, we need a theme."

"A theme? For a baby shower?"

"Of course. We can't do mermaids or cowboys because we don't know the gender of either baby. Rubber Ducky is just so plebeian." She rolled her eyes and shuddered.

Miranda almost agreed with her on that one.

Exasperated, Gen waved her pen-less hand in the air. "And then there's the catering which has me all in a dither. That's the main reason Parker Towers is out. Joan and Chef Basardi don't see eye to eye over cuisine."

Miranda didn't even know Fanuzzi knew who Chef Basardi was.

"I really would love to throw two separate parties, but time is so short. I'm going to have to send the invitations by email. Besides, Joan hasn't been feeling well lately."

"She hasn't?"

"It's the swelling again."

That didn't sound good. Miranda cared a lot about her friend. She felt bad for not checking up on her.

"Coco's doing fine, as usual. She's still helping Joan with her catering, but she's another problem. How am I going to find musicians to meet her criteria? She's as picky about music as Joan is about food. What am I supposed to do?" She held her hands up in desperation.

At least she'd finally stopped talking. But Miranda had no words to fill the dead air space.

Parker. He'd know what to do.

She started to get up. "Uh, I think I'll have to get back to you on this, Gen."

The woman's look turned so ferocious, Miranda sat back down.

"Do you really expect me to drive all the way to the North Georgia mountains?" Gen growled.

With a smug look, Miranda crossed her legs. "No, I don't. Your father and I will be around the office for the next week."

Gen's dark eyes flashed. "Why?"

She hadn't let Miranda explain before. "Because of Holloway."

Slowly a crease formed on Gen's forehead. "Because of Curt? What does that mean?"

"He asked your father and me to fill in for him for a week."

One of Gen's brows began to quiver. "Why?"

"Because Audrey wants him to be her bodyguard on her book tour."

Gen drew in a breath of sheer shock. "Book tour?"

Patiently, Miranda explained about the new book and the warden and the editor and the tour.

Gen sat back in her chair as if Miranda had just punched her in the chest. "Oh." Her voice took on a shaky, girlish tone. "Curt didn't tell me that. We—we've been working on the budget for next quarter. He didn't say a word."

"He didn't know until yesterday."

Anger flashed across her face. "And he just dropped everything? Just like that?"

"Well, yeah. Like I said, he asked me and your father to fill in for him. It's just for a week." That sounded lame.

Gen's eyes began to tear up. She swallowed, reached for a tissue on her desk. She pressed it to her face and shot to her feet. "Excuse me," she blubbered and rushed out of the room.

Uh oh. Miranda had hit a nerve.

When she agreed to put Holloway in charge of the Agency, she hadn't thought about Gen's feelings for him. But how could she still care for him after he dumped her for his ex? Miranda thought about the night Gen came to the penthouse and cried her eyes out on Parker's shoulder.

That had been months ago. She should be over him.

Maybe having him for her boss had rekindled Gen's feelings for him.

Sheesh.

Miranda got to her feet. She didn't know what to say to Gen, and she probably wasn't coming back anytime soon. Now was a good time for her and Parker to sneak out and get lunch. She'd talk to him about this then.

She stepped out into the hall and headed for his office.

CHAPTER SIX

Parker sat in his former office staring at the spreadsheet before him, more irritated with Curt Holloway than ever.

The young man had always been a good investigator, he had a fine military background, but when it came to his ex-wife, he lost all discernment. And Parker wasn't happy with Holloway's financial judgment either. He sat back in his chair and rubbed his chin.

It was tempting.

The prospect of coming back to the Agency, falling into the old routine, taking up a case or two. But he had determined to retire. He and Miranda would be taking no more risks. What happened in Chicago was an anomaly.

The last one he would allow them to give in to.

He was certain he could stick to their agreement. But Miranda was a different story. Being back at the Agency might be an enticement his headstrong wife wouldn't be able to resist.

Perhaps he should show her this.

He pressed a key on the laptop, and a photo of his arch nemesis appeared. It was a newspaper article from Gulf Shores, Alabama, a resort community along the Gulf Coast. The article featured an interview of a young couple who said they'd seen a speedboat wash up on shore at the beginning of the month. It was mostly hyperbole and speculation. Nothing much in the way of proof or clues, but the locals were fascinated with the rumors of the businessman who had become a notorious criminal and his possible escape.

Though the military had attempted to suppress the story, a few details had leaked out to the public and had been elaborated on as they were passed about, as such stories do.

But Donovan Santana was a very real person. Or had been.

That man was the reason Parker and Steele Consulting was no more. And once Parker found him, it would stay that way. The only question was whether he'd find him dead or alive.

The office phone rang. He picked it up. "Yes?"

"Mr. Parker?"

"Who is this?"

"It's Alex Witherby. I was calling Mr. Holloway."

Alex Witherby was one of the Agency's best bodyguards. Parker had always been impressed by his work. "Curt isn't in at the moment, Alex. What do you need?"

"I'm manning the front desk for Sybil. There's someone here demanding to speak to the top person in charge."

Curt put a bodyguard at the front desk? A little over two weeks away and the entire Agency seemed to be falling apart. "I'll be right there."

With a low growl, he hung up and hurried out the door.

CHAPTER SEVEN

Miranda stepped into Parker's gorgeous sunlit office for the second time that day and found it empty. Had Parker stepped out to get something to surprise her for lunch?

She smiled. Of course, he had.

The open laptop caught her eye. Curious, she swung around the desk, plopped into the chair, and gave the mouse a shove.

At the photo on the screen, she sucked in a breath.

Santana.

Back when he was still a multi-billionaire businessman in Boston. And an article about the search for him along the Gulf of Mexico in Alabama.

Parker must be out of practice. He never left his secrets open like this. But she'd known he'd been trying to find out what happened to that bastard, just as she had.

"Miranda."

She jolted at the sound of his voice.

He stood in the doorway, a coffee cup in his hand. No food.

For a long moment, his piercing gaze met hers. He knew what she'd seen on the laptop. And that she knew he knew, as well. And since they knew each other so well, she decided to pretend she didn't know anything.

As she rose, she gave him a big smile. "There you are. I was wondering what we were going to do for lunch."

He took her hand and smoothly pulled her away from the desk.

She wanted to call his bluff, have it out with him right then and there. Or float into his arms. Instead she floated into a guest chair, and he took the one beside it.

He continued to study her intently. "Don't you have to be back for class soon?"

"I gave them until two for lunch. Plus I handed the class off to Smith."

"Smith?"

"I think she can handle it. For one afternoon, anyway."

He shook his head. "Probably better than Curt has been handling his duties."

Something else was wrong. She knew it. Holloway wasn't ingratiating himself to Parker in his new position at all, was he? "Is there a problem?"

"Not yet. At this point, it's more of an annoyance."

"What kind of an annoyance?"

"Assigning a bodyguard to the receptionist desk for one thing."

She spun to face him in her chair. "He did what?"

"A bodyguard who can't tell a pushy insurance salesman from a real client."

She had to laugh at that, but Parker wasn't smiling.

He gestured toward the laptop. "I had a look at Curt's notes and discovered he was about to initiate a round of serious cutbacks next quarter, including layoffs."

"Layoffs?" Miranda recalled Gen had said they'd been working on the budget together. She decided not to mention that to Parker just now. "Why is he doing that?"

"I don't know. It's not necessary at all."

She thought a moment, and a pang of guilt hit her. "Uh oh."

"What?"

She tapped her fingers on the arm of the chair. "Uh, that might have been my fault."

"Your fault? How?"

"Because I thought we were broke, remember?" She had confessed as much to Parker when they'd come back from Santana's island adventure, and he had explained his sneaky accounting tricks to her.

His brow rose in surprise. "You told Holloway the Agency was broke?"

Miranda raised her palms."I told the whole team. They were expecting luxury suites when we went to Boston to look for you. I told them we couldn't afford more than a cut-rate hotel and cheap meals."

Parker rose and went to the window, his face taking on a pensive look as he stared out of it.

Memories of Boston and what they'd both been through were no doubt cavorting through his mind. He hadn't gotten over it. He might never get over it.

She might not, either.

But surely they could get through a week of management together. Parker would fix the budget, she'd do her administration thing, and then they could get back to retirement.

And to figuring out what to do with the rest of their lives.

She brightened. "Hey, didn't you promise me dancing lessons?"

She was relieved to see him smile. "I did."

"We can discuss it over lunch."

"An excellent suggestion." He pulled her to her feet, and she was just about to give him a kiss when she heard footsteps in the corridor.

She turned around and saw Antonio Estavez standing in the doorway, his dark eyes blazing.

The good-looking young man had on his typical dark blue lawyer suit and power tie, accompanied by the long jet-black hair he always tied back in a ponytail. He looked very distressed.

"Papa. Miranda," he gasped in his slight Hispanic accent. "What are you doing here?"

"It's a long story, son. Have you come to see Curt?"

"Yes. I need his help. Actually, I was hoping he could contact you. Both of you." He sounded thoroughly rattled.

All thoughts of lunch went out of Miranda's head. "What's wrong? Is it Coco?"

"No. Not yet. I don't think so." He put his face in his hands.

Parker hurried to the door and closed it behind Estavez. "Sit down, son, and tell us what's wrong. Do you need coffee? Water?"

He shook his head as he settled into the chair Miranda had vacated a moment ago. "He's out. He's escaped. I cannot believe it."

Miranda had never seen Estavez like this. He always oozed oceans of confidence. "Who's out?" she said.

"Enrico Bagitelli."

"Who's that?" Sounded like a gangster from the forties.

She went to the fridge hidden in the cabinets on the opposite side of the room and got Estavez a cold bottle of water anyway.

"He's a classical pianist. Rather famous in his day."

She put the bottle in his hand and eyed Parker, who had settled in behind the desk. His face said he was as worried as she was.

She sat down in the other guest chair. "Why are you afraid of a piano player?" Especially since he was married to one.

"Let me explain." Estavez opened the bottle and took a deep swallow from it. Then he drew in a breath. "A little over three years ago, Enrico Bagitelli hired me to defend him against an attempted murder charge."

"Obviously, you lost." Parker's voice was gentle. Estavez was very proud of his win record in court. Losing a case would be a sensitive subject.

But he shook his head. "No, Papa. I never got to try the case."

Parker sat back and folded his arms. "Go on."

"I prepared as diligently as I could in the limited time I had, but Mr. Bagitelli was difficult to work with. I spoke to him only once. He was distraught, and it was hard to get the facts from his perspective." He took another sip of water.

Miranda was getting impatient, but she didn't dare press him.

After another moment, Estavez continued. "It happened the day of the pretrial. I was set to ask for a continuance because my client was upset and confused about the facts. And—"

Bracing herself, Miranda glanced at Parker. "What happened?"

"The prosecution told the judge it was very clear what happened, and he had all the evidence the court needed. He was out of order. We hadn't even finished discovery. But the judge let him play the video anyway."

"What video?" Parker said.

"I don't have the original with me now. But I have a video of the video a news reporter filmed."

Miranda scratched at her hair. "Estavez, you're not making much sense."

"It would be easier for me to show you."

He pulled his cell out of his pocket, brought up the video, and rolled it back to the beginning. He must have been viewing it.

Parker came around the desk and stood behind them to watch as Estavez pressed Play.

A courtroom appeared on the screen. The judge was an older looking woman with wispy dark hair and a sour look. Beside her bench was a projector screen. A man in a suit stood to the side of the screen holding a remote control. The prosecutor, Miranda assumed. He pressed a button, and the video inside the video played.

The image was dark and seemed to have been taken at night. But Miranda could make out a small parking lot surrounded by maple trees casting shadows on the pavement. A wrought iron fence marked the edge of the lot, and the Atlanta skyline appeared in the distance.

Parker bent over to squint at the picture. "Is that outside Atlanta Symphony Hall?"

"Yes, Papa. This is footage from one of ASO's security cameras."

"ASO?" Miranda asked.

"The Atlanta Symphony Orchestra," Estavez explained. "This is a lot used by the musicians."

Miranda turned to the screen again. Two cars were parked in the lot, spread out from each other some distance. The only person to be seen was a woman in a dark dress walking down the middle of the pavement with her head down.

Too far away to identify her.

Suddenly a sports car came roaring in from the bottom right side of the screen. The woman on the pavement froze as she looked back in terror. Then she tried to scamper to the side of the lot.

But the car didn't slow down. It seemed to be aiming straight for her. She started to run, but she was no match for whoever was flooring the accelerator.

The front bumper struck her hard with a sickening thud, and she disappeared under it.

The sports car screeched to a halt and backed up, rolling over her. It disappeared from the screen for a moment, then reappeared so that you could see just the hood and part of the front door.

The door opened. A man's foot appeared under it. The shout of the same man came from offscreen. The door closed and an instant later, the man appeared, running toward the lump on the ground that had been the woman he'd hit.

"Rosalynd. Oh, Rosalynd. No, no, no. This is impossible. Impossible. You cannot leave me." His voice was deep, but panicked, and he had a slight Italian accent.

As he bent down beside the body, another voice came from the courtroom. "No! How dare you? That film is a lie."

The same voice with the same panic in it.

The camera in the courtroom turned to the defense table. Estavez stood next to a good-looking middle-aged man with long wavy dark hair.

His face was livid. "How dare you do this to me!" he screamed at his attorney with that bellowing voice.

And then he rushed at him and grabbed him by the throat with his long-fingered hands.

Screams erupted.

Shock on his face, Estavez tried to fight him off, but he needed help.

As the judge banged her gavel for order, the bailiff and another officer rushed to the pair and pulled the defendant off of him.

The video ended.

Sitting back, Miranda let out a breath. "Wow. That was your client, Enrico Bagitelli?"

"That was him." Estavez's face was grim.

"Who was the woman he struck?" Parker said in a tone that said he was as angry at this man for attacking his son as he was for his running over an innocent person.

"His sister-in-law. Rosalynd Rose Allen."

"And you couldn't get him off after that video, right?" Miranda said.

"I didn't have a chance to defend him. He fired me right away. I didn't follow the case after that, but I heard he was convicted of attempted murder."

Attempted. "The woman didn't die?"

"No. She was taken to the hospital and fell into a coma. I suppose that's still her case, or he would have been charged with her murder."

"You said he escaped. Did you mean from prison?"

"Yes. It happened last night. I just heard it on the radio on my way to lunch. You have to find him, Papa."

Parker's brow creased. "Why? If you weren't his lawyer."

Looking pale, Estavez reached into his pocket and drew out an envelope. "Because shortly after the trial proceeded, I received this letter from Mr. Bagitelli."

The paper looked old and had a ragged edge where it had been torn open. Estavez's fingers shook as he drew out the letter inside and handed it to Parker.

Parker opened it. His brows rose as he read it aloud.

"*Mr. Estavez,*

As you well know, I am being tried for a crime I did not commit. I did not try to kill Rosalynd. I loved her more than my own life. Nonetheless because of you and that video, I am here. I will never forget that. I will never forget you.

If I am convicted, I will escape. And when I do, I will come after you and your family and kill every one of you. Don't think I won't.

Enrico Bagitelli"

Miranda blinked at Estavez in shock. "But you didn't show the judge that video. The prosecutor did."

"I had never seen it before. As I said, the prosecutor did not follow procedure."

"Did you tell Mr. Bagitelli that?" Parker asked.

"I tried to, but he was upset and irrational. It was obvious he was having some mental health issues, but he denied he had psychological problems when I questioned him, and I didn't have the chance to research the matter."

Parker returned to his desk and reached for his keyboard. "What prison did he escape from?"

"Bibb County Correctional Facility. It's near Macon."

"Yes, I know it." He found a local news station covering the story, and turned the screen for Miranda and Estavez to see it.

Classical piano music filled the air as an intense looking dark-haired man in a black tux and tie attacked the keyboard of a grand piano.

The man in the previous videos.

A reporter's voice overrode the music. "Renowned pianist Enrico Bagitelli escaped from Bibb County Correctional Facility early this morning, according to officials at the prison. Three years ago, Mr. Bagitelli was convicted of attempting to kill his sister-in-law by running her over with his vehicle. A manhunt is now underway."

The screen morphed into an overhead shot of forests and fields, with officers and bloodhounds combing through the area.

Without much success apparently.

Then a familiar face came on screen. Lieutenant Hosea Erskine. He was standing in front of APD headquarters, and it was still dark. He must have been interviewed hours ago. Miranda noted the intensity in his brown, marble-like eyes.

"Since the original incident occurred in the metro area," Erskine told the reporters, "the Atlanta PD are involved. I assure you the unit assigned to the case is committed to aiding in the capture of this dangerous criminal."

"Do you believe Mr. Bagitelli will return to the scene of the crime?" a reporter asked.

"We don't know yet, but we're not ruling that out. Right now, we're working in complete cooperation with the GBI and the authorities in Macon."

With a grunt Parker stopped the video and picked up his cell phone to dial. He put it on speaker and laid it on the desk as it rang.

After a moment, the familiar, Darth Vader like voice came through. "Lieutenant Erskine."

"Hosea, it's Wade Parker. I'm calling to ask about your progress on the manhunt for the prisoner who escaped from Bibb County Correctional Facility."

"Enrico Bagitelli?"

"Does the facility have more than one fugitive?"

Erskine let out an annoyed cough. "No, it does not. And the manhunt is progressing as expected."

"So you have him in custody?"

"No, we do not. Why are you so interested in the case, Parker? Aren't you supposed to be retired?"

Parker glared down at the phone. "I'm interested because that man threatened my son and his family."

There was a pause. "He threatened Attorney Estavez?"

"Yes."

"How did he do that?"

"Antonio was the initial representative in Mr. Bagitelli's case. The pianist is under the impression Antonio is the reason he went to prison."

There was silence for a moment. Then Erskine coughed again. "Do you have any evidence to that effect?"

"I do." Parker picked up the letter from Bagitelli and read it to Erskine.

After another long silence, Erskine barked, "Send me a copy of that."

"I'll deliver it in person. Miranda and I are coming to headquarters to assist your unit."

"Stay where you are, Parker. We don't need assistance from civilians. Email will be fine."

Miranda wanted to chew through nails. She couldn't stand that Erskine considered them "civilians" after they'd helped him solve so many cases.

Parker's voice was low and quiet. "I have a right to protect my son, Hosea."

"Then I suggest you use some of those pricey bodyguards you have in your stable. Go back to your retirement, Parker. We've got this."

He hung up.

Miranda watched Parker's jaw go tight.

"That's not a bad idea about the bodyguards," she said, trying to sound hopeful.

Parker nodded and drummed his fingers on the desk. "Most likely, Bagitelli is traveling on foot."

"Unless he jacked a car."

"That should have been reported by now."

"Maybe."

"He may still be in the area of the prison." He turned to Estavez. "Macon is two hours away. Do you still have that Cessna?"

Estavez sat up. "Of course, I do. And my license is current."

Miranda's brows popped up. Estavez had a Cessna?

Parker didn't wait for more discussion. He rose from his desk. "Let's go."

"Sounds good to me."

And with that, she and Parker grabbed some supplies from his desk—including her old Beretta and Parker's Glock, and hurried out the door.

CHAPTER EIGHT

In the Agency's Mazda, the three of them drove out to DeKalb-Peachtree Airport.
While Estavez did the standard flight check on his shiny white Cessna with its teal-and-navy stripes, Miranda stood on the tarmac and listened to Parker call in to the office they'd just left.
After explaining the Holloway thing, he asked Kay Carson, one of his top investigators, to stand in for him for the afternoon, and then he assigned bodyguards Bill Taylor to watch the Parker estate, and Amir Khan to keep an eye out for anyone suspicious at Chatham, Grayson, and McFee, Estavez's law firm.
Miranda recognized the names.
She'd been IITs with both Taylor and Khan, and she thought either of them could handle the situation if their escaped convict showed up.
When the flight check was done, they climbed aboard the craft, and after some chatting with the control tower, they were in the air.
An hour and a half later, they were cruising over the same expanse they had seen on the news.
At about a thousand feet, Miranda could make out the outline of the prison and its surrounding area. Police and hounds were still combing part of it, but the grounds around the facility were huge and filled with vegetation, thick trees, and grassy fields in various shades of green and brown.
If he'd made it through those dense weeds and forests, Bagitelli wouldn't be there. He would be gone.
Still, how far could he get on foot?
In the distance, small subdivisions and clusters of houses dotted the landscape. Miranda knew more officers would be going door-to-door there, in case Bagitelli was holding some poor family hostage.

If the authorities didn't get a lead soon, they'd spread out farther and wider, and whatever trail they had would go cold.

Miranda was determined not to let that happen.

"Where would you go?" Parker said from the rear seat.

Miranda peered through the binoculars Estavez had handed her when they took off.

"Not many roads that go anywhere." By design, she assumed, so there wouldn't be an easy escape route. "The main road runs right in front of the prison, so he wouldn't have taken it, or the guards would have seen him."

"Unless the prisoner picked up the road a mile or so north of the prison."

She peered down at the spot Parker had suggested. "He'd still have to make his way through some nasty terrain. But say he did. What did Bagitelli do then? Hitchhike from there?"

"Possibly."

"Maybe he had someone pick him up," Estavez offered. "An accomplice."

"Another possibility."

She pointed down at the line of asphalt curving through the woody area. "That road leads into the city and connects to a highway that heads north. Is that I-75?"

"It is."

"Which could take him back to Atlanta."

"Or farther south."

Nerves rippled through her stomach. They might be wasting time with this trip.

"Let me get a little lower." Estavez banked the Cessna, and they circled the northern part of the roads.

Again Miranda peered down hard. And then she spotted something.

Sitting up straight, she squinted through the binoculars.

"What's that, there?" The road was a country lane now. But she could see a small patch of white alongside it. "Is that a car?"

She handed the binoculars to Parker and he studied the spot for a long moment. "It could be a vehicle."

"I say, it's worth checking out."

"I agree," Estavez said and made another turn.

###

After about twenty minutes, they had landed at the regional airport, rented a dull brown Corolla—instead of one of the luxury rides Parker used to book when they were on a case—and were headed for the spot in question.

It was another twenty minute drive from the airport, but traffic was light.

Parker zoomed down the rough two-lane roads, making Miranda's heartbeat kick up as she fed into his intensity. They were going to get this guy.

They had to.

After what seemed like an eternity of uneven asphalt and dense trees, Parker turned left onto the route that ran in front of the prison.

Jericho Road, Miranda noted on the GPS screen.

It, too, was a two-lane country road that needed repaving. And it, too, was surrounded by tall pines that did little to block the sun from bearing down on the asphalt. They drove along, passing clusters of small homes, open fields, and a lot of pickup trucks.

After another few miles, they passed the prison, which was marked only by a solitary brick sign. At least they had a better idea of where Bagitelli had started. The car she'd spotted should be around here somewhere.

They rumbled over a small stream called Muddy Creek, according to the sign, turned right at a fork, and went down another few miles. Here, too, the sides of the road were nothing but mounds of grass and red Georgia clay with more forest beyond.

It didn't look like it had from the air.

Miranda let out a sigh of disgust. "Maybe I was seeing things."

"No, you were not." Parker pointed out the windshield. "Look there."

She turned her head.

On the right side of the road, the trees opened revealing a dry patch of ground that extended out a good ways. Overhead, telephone wires stretched between weather-beaten poles.

And there beside one of them sat an old white Buick.

Parker pulled over to the shoulder, and they all got out of the rental. With the two men on either side of her, Miranda walked up the dusty path to the Buick, the sound of rustling trees in her ears.

When they were a few feet from the rear bumper, Parker stopped and held out a hand. "Let me check it out first."

Miranda held her breath as he drew his Glock and approached the vehicle's side. Her own hand went to the butt of her Beretta. If Bagitelli was sleeping in the backseat, this could be an easy apprehension.

If he wasn't armed.

Parker bent over to peer inside the windows, then he took a step back and holstered his gun. "It's abandoned."

Moving her hand to her pocket to pull out a rubber glove, Miranda walked toward the vehicle, noting it had a dent in its side.

"It doesn't make sense. This is what? Seven or so miles from the prison? Why did he stop here if he had a car?"

"Perhaps it broke down," Estavez suggested.

Hard to tell that without trying to start it, which wouldn't be a good idea.

Parker already had his gloves on and was trying the driver's door. "Unlocked. No sign of anyone here." He went around to the passenger side while Miranda took the backseat.

She opened the vehicle's rear door and looked inside.

It had a musty, old leather smell and was littered with typical junk.

A plastic cup, an empty bag of chips, a blanket, a toy truck. Had Bagitelli jacked a car with a kid in it?

And where was the kid now?

Raising her head, she saw Estavez walking alongside the road, peering into the thick weeds.

"I don't see any signs of a body," he called out.

"Good to know."

She bent down to study the floorboard, and saw a bit of fabric tucked under the seat. After reaching for it with her gloved hand, she pulled it out and let out a yelp. "Jackpot."

"What is it?" Parker said from the front.

"Orange jumpsuit. Neatly folded and left on the floor under the seat."

Peering over the seat, Parker scowled. "Not very well hidden."

"Except you couldn't see it from the road."

"True."

Miranda took out her phone and began snapping photos of the suit and the backseat. Then she took some more of the exterior, including a good shot of the dent and the license plate.

It was local.

Looking up, she noticed Parker was rummaging through the glove compartment.

"Hmm."

She turned to him. "What is it?"

He held up papers. "This vehicle is registered to a Dixie Sawyer. Her address is listed. I believe it's near here."

A chill went down her spine. "Do you think this Dixie Sawyer had something to do with the escape?" Her mind was going in that direction.

"It's possible."

Or she was a victim. Miranda closed the door and came around to where Parker was working. She took her phone again and snapped photos of the registration as he held it out for her.

While Parker put the papers back into the glove compartment, she stared at the vehicle. "We should call Erskine or the locals and report this."

Narrowing his eyes, Parker peered down the empty road. "Let's pay Ms. Sawyer a visit first."

Good idea. Parker could get more information out of the owner of this car than the police could.

She had to smile. "I still love how your mind works."

He smiled back. "Likewise."

CHAPTER NINE

Dixie Sawyer lived in a small trailer park south of the city.

After another thirty-minute jaunt over the country roads, they hit a residential area and finally reached the place. It was marked by a sign reading, "Mossy Acres."

Homey.

Parker turned in the drive, and they rolled past a neat row of evenly spaced units in assorted colors. He pulled up to one near the back.

Miranda eyed the dirty-yellow single-wide with brown shutters. In a far window, the A/C ran noisily. The porch looked like it needed replacing, but was nonetheless decorated with hanging plants and wind chimes. During her sojourns around the country before she'd met Parker, she had lived in a few places like this.

As she got out of the car, she spotted a beat up old gray pickup near the door and wondered if it was a second vehicle. She definitely had mixed feelings about whoever this woman was.

Had she aided a dangerous criminal? Or was she a victim? And who would they find inside that trailer?

With Estavez behind her and the tinkling of the chimes in her ears, Miranda followed Parker up the rickety wooden steps of the porch.

After evading a low hanging tomato plant, he rapped on the metal door, making it sound like a tin can.

No answer.

Miranda could hear a TV inside. Sounded like a game show. Somebody was home.

Parker rapped again.

This time Miranda heard voices. Seemed like two women. Arguing, maybe.

Finally the TV switched off, and she heard footsteps cross the trailer floor.

The door opened, and the thin face of a woman appeared. Lots of makeup. Fake eyelashes and deep navy shadow that matched a metallic blue band atop her head she'd stuffed her straw-like blond hair into.

"Yeah?" she said in a distinct smoker's voice with a Southern accent.

And then she blinked at Parker in the open-mouthed way most women did when they first saw him.

He smiled graciously. "Excuse me, ma'am. Are you Dixie Sawyer?"

Her look went from awestruck to defensive as she eyed Miranda and Estavez. "Maybe. Why?"

Parker laid on more charm. "We're sorry to disturb you, Ms. Sawyer. I'm Wade Parker of the Parker Agency in Atlanta and this is my partner, Miranda Steele, and our associate, Antonio Estavez. We're investigating a matter in the area and would like to speak with you a moment. May we come in?"

The woman's lip curled in an expression Miranda was all too familiar with. "Investigating? What sort of a matter?"

"A local one."

The way Parker said the word "local" had the woman looking even more uncomfortable.

She took another glance at her visitors and shook her head. "I don't think so. I'm busy. You'll have to come back another day."

She started to close the door, but Parker moved fast and wedged a strong arm against it. "I assure you we won't be long. It's very important."

Another female voice came from inside the trailer. "Let them in, Dixie."

Dixie glared at Parker.

"Do it," said the voice. She sounded annoyed.

The pressure was too much. Dixie rolled her eyes and opened the door. "Okay, okay. Y'all come on in. Excuse the mess."

Miranda stepped onto a well-worn carpet and took in the matching well-worn flower-pattern couch with a messy brown throw strewn over it.

On the narrow side of the room, a small table held the TV she had heard. The window behind the couch was decorated with thin flowery curtains, pulled back to reveal the greenery of dense trees. In the air was a scent that smelled like vegetable soup and cornbread, reminding Miranda she'd never gotten that lunch with Parker.

Dixie went over to the sofa and reached for the blanket. She had on tight white capri pants with a form fitting red lace top, hoop earrings, and open-toed basket weave sandals revealing toes painted in the same deep navy blue as her eye shadow and nails.

Pretty dressed up for a day at home.

Dixie lifted up the throw, and Cheerios scattered onto the floor in front of a tiny coffee table. There were toys on the floor, too. A game and a couple of little trucks like the one Miranda had seen in the back of the Buick.

"Oh, crap," Dixie groaned.

"Oh, that's from Little Travis," sang the other woman as she hurried out from behind the counter of the typical trailer kitchen with a broom and dustpan.

This woman seemed like the homespun type. Just the opposite of Dixie.

She wore a plaid pastel blouse with short puffy sleeves and loose-fitting jeans. Her hair was a rich chocolate brown, cut under the chin. Her face was plump as opposed to Dixie's skinny one, and her expression was troubled.

She trotted over to the spot and began sweeping up the mess.

Parker raised a hand in protest. "There's no need to clean up for us, ma'am."

The woman just kept sweeping and putting the toys on the table.

Dixie tossed down the blanket and moved away from her guests. "You heard him, Dolly. Stop it."

Dixie and Dolly. Cute.

Dolly looked up at Parker with big brown eyes. "Oh, I'm sorry. Force of habit. Travis is my four-year-old. I'm always cleaning up after him." She laughed nervously.

Miranda was getting impatient. "And you are?" she said to the woman.

"That's my older sister," Dixie said.

Sisters. No wonder they answered for each other.

"Travis is my nephew. He stays here sometimes. He's taking a nap in the back now." Dixie waved her hand in the general direction behind the living room.

Uh huh. Miranda wondered if Bagitelli was back there, too. "Does Travis ride in your car a lot?"

Dixie shifted her weight. "Sometimes. Why?"

Miranda glanced at Parker. He gave her a look that said, "Go for it."

She gave the woman a dead stare. "Is your car missing, Ms. Sawyer?"

Dolly's back went straight. "No."

Dixie gave her a dirty look, then turned it on Miranda. "Why do you think that?"

She was evading the obvious answer.

"Was it stolen?"

"Stolen?" Dixie rubbed her arms and looked around the room. Big sis wasn't helping out with this one. "As a matter of fact, yes. It was."

"When did you first notice it was missing?" Parker asked in his smooth-as-velvet tone.

"When? Uh...when I went outside this morning." She waved toward the window. "I usually park it in front of the porch. And it was just...gone."

Miranda folded her arms. "Were you on your way to work?"

"No," Dolly said again.

Dixie turned to her with an I-wasn't? look.

"Where do you work, by the way?" Miranda said.

The question took her off guard and she blurted out the answer before she could catch herself. "At Bibb County Correctional. I'm a cook in the commissary."

The place where Bagitelli had escaped from. Now wasn't that interesting?

Dolly took the dustpan and broom back to the kitchen, talking as she went. "We were supposed to go shopping this morning. Dixie called me and said her car was missing, so we went in my truck instead. It's parked outside." She washed her hands and returned to the side of the counter.

The pickup they'd seen. That story was smellier than a Southern fish fry. Miranda took a step toward Dixie. "When did you report your vehicle missing?"

Dixie's eyes went so wide, her fake lashes nearly touched her brows. "Report it?"

"It's typical to report a stolen vehicle once one notices it's missing," Parker said with just a touch of sarcasm in his voice.

Dixie looked at Dolly. Dolly looked at Dixie.

Miranda folded her arms. "Actually, we just found your vehicle a little while ago on Highway 80. A few miles from Muddy Creek."

"You did?" Dixie seemed honestly stunned.

Dolly was defensive. "How did you know it was her car?"

"Old white Buick with a dent in the side?"

Dixie sucked in her breath.

"Her registration was in it," Parker said flatly. "That's how we discovered your name and address, Ms. Sawyer."

Miranda took another step toward the woman. "Do you know what else we found in the vehicle, Ms. Sawyer?"

Stepping back toward the wall, Dixie began to rub her throat as she swallowed hard. "I can't imagine."

"Prison clothes. Neatly folded and placed under the backseat. Did you know a convict escaped from Bibb County Correctional last night? Pretty coincidental, huh?"

Dixie blinked at her, then at Parker. Finally she opened her mouth in defiance. "He was innocent."

"Shut up, Dixie."

Dixie glared at her sister, then at her visitors, whom she suspected were about to arrest her. Then she flopped into the recliner in the corner, put her face in her hands, and began to bawl.

Dolly hurried over and put an arm around her sister. She turned to Miranda. "She didn't do anything wrong."

"He was innocent," Dixie moaned.

"Who was innocent?" Miranda pressed.

"Enrico Bagitelli."

Bingo.

"He's a famous concert pianist," Dixie whined. "He oozes talent. He doesn't belong in prison."

Miranda's palm went to her Beretta as she glanced toward the narrow little hallway. "Is he here? Is he in the back with Travis? Is he threatening you?"

Dixie blinked up at her in shock. "No, of course not. If he were here, my car would be here, too."

"Are you saying you let him use it?"

"Yes, yes," she sniffled.

Parker pulled up an old-fashioned wooden chair with a straw seat from near the door and sat down next to Dixie. "Why don't you start at the beginning and tell us what happened?" He was using his smooth soothing tone now.

After another look toward the back, Miranda settled in at the edge of the couch, while Estavez remained at the door, keeping his distance and not saying a word, though she could tell he wanted to shake this woman.

"At the beginning? Okay." Dixie pushed the hair out of her eyes and took a deep breath. "It was at work, oh, about three months ago. Right after the holidays. There was a new guy among the inmates, and I noticed him right away. Part of my job is to watch the detainees while they get their food. You know, to make sure everyone gets the right portions, and no one steals anyone else's. At least not until they get to the dining hall. So I get to know the faces. Most of the men are really hardened criminals. Gang members, killers. That sort. It's scary. But every once in a while, there's someone different. Enrico was like that. I knew it the first time I laid eyes on him. He was a gentle soul."

She turned her head and stared out the window.

Had Dixie Sawyer fallen for an inmate?

"What happened?" Parker prodded softly.

"I found out his name and read up on him. He's famous. I have a lot of his recordings now. Never was one for classical music before, but Enrico, he touched my soul. Anyway, we developed sort of a relationship. A friendship. It was purely innocent."

Miranda raised a brow. "How did you manage that?"

"Oh, there are nooks and crannies inside the prison walls. The library, the laundry. I have a second cousin who's a guard. He got me the job in the kitchen. I told him I wanted to meet Enrico, and he arranged it."

"You never should have gotten Lester involved," Dolly scolded.

Dixie gave her a sneer.

Evidently Dixie had confided all these details to her sister along the way. "Go on."

"We met several times. We talked, got to know each other. I read in the news that he had tried to kill his sister-in-law. He told me that was a lie. He said his lawyer had framed him."

Miranda resisted the urge to look over at Estavez, but even from her spot on the couch, she could feel Parker tense.

Dixie pressed a hand to her chest. "Deep in my heart, I knew Enrico was telling the truth. He'd never hurt anyone. And he was so sad. He wanted to play the piano again. He wanted his life back. I decided he deserved that."

He seduced her.

"And so, I came up with a plan."

"Which involved your car," Miranda said.

"Yes." She drew in a breath. "I need a cigarette."

She got up, opened a drawer in the coffee table and took out a pack. Then she came back to the recliner and sat down.

"There was a secret passage in the prison."

"Secret passage?"

"Oh, it isn't really secret. All the inmates know about it. They can see it when they walk to the commissary. It's a door to a cell with a locked chain around it. They call it The Devil's Hole. About ten years ago, a man tried to escape from that cell through a hole he'd dug in the back of it. It led to the water system, and he followed the pipe. He got out, but he was found and shot. So the warden decided to make an example out of him. Sort of a warning to the prisoners. You know, that trying to escape is futile."

She tapped a cigarette out of the pack and held it between her fingers without lighting it.

"Lester told me all about it. He said that fugitive would have made it if he'd had a decent getaway plan. He also said he had a key to the lock. He knew where the keys were for each cell, too. And so…"

She put the cigarette in her mouth and took it out again.

"And so what happened?" Miranda prompted.

"And so I got Lester to make me copies of those keys. The one to The Devil's Hole and the one to Enrico's cell. And I gave them to Enrico."

Pretty incriminating. But Miranda didn't dare say another word just now for fear Dixie would clam up. She waited, and after playing with her cigarette a bit more, Dixie went on.

"Last night I parked my car alongside Jericho Road. I had told Enrico where it would be if he could get to it. I guess he did. I left him food and clothes and money in a duffle bag."

She put the cigarette back into the pack. "I left him a bus ticket, too. He was supposed to drive to the station in Macon and leave my car in the lot. That's the real reason Dolly's here. We didn't go shopping. She drove me to the station to get my car. But it wasn't there. We drove around the lot three times, but couldn't find it. I couldn't imagine what had happened. We watched the news and—" With a sob, she pressed a hand to her forehead. "They showed a video of what Enrico did to his sister-in-law. It was so vicious. Oh, God. What have I done? What have I done?"

She began to cry again, and once more Dolly comforted her.

"Where was the bus ticket to?" Parker asked in a quiet voice.

"Tallahassee."

"Florida?"

"Yes. He said he had a friend there. An orchestra conductor."

"What was the friend's name?"

"He never told me that."

Miranda's stomach flinched. Was this guy in Florida? And where did he go from there? "How much money did you give him?"

"About three hundred dollars. It was all I could spare."

Not enough to leave the country, but enough to get lost in a crowd. They might never find him—until he popped up on some street in Atlanta, ready to take his revenge.

Parker waited a moment for the woman to grow calm again. Then he spoke with a sharpness in his voice that said he was growing impatient. "Ms. Sawyer, evidently Mr. Bagitelli didn't go to Macon. Instead he left your car just a few miles down the road from the prison. Why would he do that?"

Blinking, Dixie glanced around the room as if trying to find the answer. Then she shrugged. "I guess he went with my first plan."

"Your first plan?" Miranda wanted to shake the information out of the woman.

"There's a Food Mart about a mile down the road from where you said the car was. It's on the corner of the first light you come to."

"What about it?"

"It's a bus stop. The first early bus to Florida stops there at one in the morning. I thought it would be easy for Enrico to get there on foot, so he wouldn't need my car. But he insisted it was too risky."

"He wanted your car."

She nodded. "When I told him about the bus station in Macon, he insisted that was a better idea."

"Why did he change his mind last night and abandon your car?"

"I don't know. He could be a little impulsive. He was sort of strange." Her shoulders sagged.

"Strange how?"

Dixie made a circle with her hand as if trying to find the right words. "He'd talk to himself. Almost as if he thought there was another person next to him, listening. Maybe he talked himself out of going to Macon. The Macon bus didn't leave until six a.m. I said the police would be looking for him by then, and someone might recognize him. He said he was willing to take the risk. I guess he decided I was right, after all."

Parker rose. "I think we have enough information for now. Thank you for your cooperation."

Her makeup smeared, Dixie looked up at him in desperation. "Can I get my car back now?"

"I'm sorry, Ms. Sawyer. I'm afraid we'll have to report it to the police." Along with everything she'd told them.

With a dazed look, she nodded. "All right. I understand. I'm truly sorry. Will you tell them that?"

"You'll have to do that yourself."

"But what's going to happen to me? What's going to happen to Lester? And Dolly? She didn't do anything. She tried to talk me out of it."

Parker gave the sisters a look of as much compassion as he could muster. "I suggest you all find yourselves a good defense attorney."

CHAPTER TEN

Back in the rented Corolla, Parker dialed Erskine's number and told him everything they'd learned.

Erskine said he'd forward the information to the locals, alert the GBI, and contact the authorities in Florida. "I see you haven't lost your touch, Parker," the crusty police Lieutenant added. "But we'll take it from here. Go back to your retirement."

Parker nearly growled into the phone. "We are not dropping this case, Hosea."

"I would advise you to reconsider that."

Parker's jaw tightened. "We will not be reconsidering anything. And Hosea?"

"What?"

"If anything happens to Estavez, his wife, or anyone else in this family, there will be hell to pay."

Parker made a sharp tap on the screen to hang up.

Whoa, he was irritated.

But Miranda couldn't blame Parker for being irked with Erskine. She'd thought of a few choice words for the man herself, but had decided to hold her tongue. Though she didn't quite understand Parker's and Erskine's love-hate relationship, all she knew was that there was too much testosterone and male ego wrapped up in it.

Deep down they respected each other, but each always took the opposite approach. Erskine went by the book, while Parker was more of a color-outside-the-lines kind of man.

She'd always liked that about him.

And looking out the window, she realized where they were headed and saw he was doing that right now.

"We're going to that food mart, aren't we?"

"We are indeed."

"Again, just what I would have done. At least *we* think alike."

He reached over and squeezed her hand. "I prefer your company over Hosea's any day."

The gesture made her stomach flutter, despite the situation.

Parker didn't even seem to mind that Estavez was in the backseat.

But as Miranda glanced over her shoulder, she saw the lawyer wasn't paying any attention to them. Instead he was gnawing on his knuckle and staring out the window.

"If Bagitelli went to Florida," he murmured, "we may never find him."

"We'll find him, son. I promise you."

At Parker's words, new determination roused in Miranda's gut. She wasn't about to let that piano playing killer get away.

She grabbed her phone and did some research. Tallahassee was a hundred and eighty-eight miles away. Five hours by bus. Estavez was right. Bagitelli could be anywhere by now.

Especially if he stopped at a friend's house and borrowed some cash.

They motored back down Jericho Road and past the prison once again. When they had turned onto Highway 80 and passed Muddy Creek and the spot beyond it where Dixie Sawyer's white Buick sat, Miranda noted a police car had pulled up behind it.

She wondered if another car was at Dixie's trailer, its driver slapping the cuffs on her.

About a mile farther, just as Dixie said, there was a stop light. They found the Food Mart on the corner.

Parker pulled into the lot and drove right up to the door.

Miranda steadied herself. "Should we pretend to be shopping or go for the direct route?"

"Direct would be best."

"Okay, then." She got out and followed him inside, with Estavez trailing behind, looking more anxious than ever.

Inside they were greeted by the smell of brewing coffee and a skinny young man at the counter who couldn't have been much past twenty. With wispy red hair and a matching bit of fuzz on his chin, he was dressed in a red clerk's cloak with a "We ID" badge on one front pocket and the name "Coy" on the other.

"Can I he'p ya?" he said with a smile in a rich rural accent.

Parker took a business card out of his pocket and handed it to him. "Good afternoon, Coy. I'm Wade Parker from the Parker Investigative Agency in Atlanta and these are my associates, Miranda Steele and Antonio Estavez. We'd like to speak to you for a moment if we may."

"To me? Shore thing. What about?"

"We understand you sell bus tickets."

"Shore do. We're an official stop of the bus company." He grinned proudly.

"We're interested in a passenger who might have gotten on the bus last night."

He frowned, "Last night? Oh, I wasn't here then."

"Actually, it would have been early this morning. Around one."

"I don't get in until noon."

This guy wasn't much help. Miranda peered out the window. "Is that where the bus picks up its passengers?"

"Yes, ma'am. Right out there."

"So if someone already had a ticket, he might not even come inside the store, right?"

"No, he wouldn't have to. But most folks stock up on drinks and snacks before their trip."

Bagitelli wouldn't have. Dixie Sawyer had made sure he had food.

Miranda was just about to give Parker a this-is-a-dud look when a bell jingled and a door in the back of the store opened.

After a moment, the newcomer appeared at the end of the chips and crackers aisle.

It was a gray haired black man with dark rimmed half glasses. He was hunched over and seemed to be in his early seventies. And even though he wore overalls under a striped shirt, he had the air of a college professor.

Coy began to straighten his coat, then his counter. "Hello, Mr. Holt. I wasn't expecting you for another hour."

"Couldn't sleep, Coy. You know I always like to keep an eye on this place."

"Mr. Holt's the owner," Coy said by way of introduction. "These are some folks from Atlanta asking questions about the bus, Mr. Holt."

"About the bus? I wasn't informed there would be an inspection."

Parker gave the man a grin. "We're not from the bus company." He drew out another card and did another round of introductions.

"From Atlanta?" the man said, studying Parker's card through his glasses. "Investigators? What are you investigating in these parts, if I may be so bold?"

"There's been a local incident we're following up on, Mr. Holt."

"Call me Jebediah. What sort of incident?"

"A serious one. What we need to know, Jebediah, is whether you saw a man boarding the bus to Tallahassee last night around one in the morning. Were you here then?"

"Yes, I was. I'm usually here for the night shift. Usually, it's pretty quiet." He rubbed his chin and fell silent.

Miranda was ready to head out. They'd make more progress with an online search.

Then Mr. Holt pursed his lips thoughtfully and nodded. "But, yes. There was a man in the store around that time and he did have a ticket to Tallahassee."

Her heart nearly stopped. "He did?"

"Yes. And you're looking for this man? Why?"

"We believe a prisoner from the local county prison may have boarded that bus," Parker told him.

Coy's brows shot up. "You mean that escaped killer?"

Sudden shock on his face, Jebediah turned to him. "What escaped killer?"

"Haven't you heard, Mr. Holt? It's been all over the news."

"You know I stay away from the news, Coy. It upsets the equilibrium."

Coy turned toward the TV on the wall. "Why, there it is now." He reached for the remote and turned on the sound.

A woman in a red power outfit was speaking. "According to the GBI, the former classical pianist escaped from Bibb County Correctional Facility around midnight last night and disappeared into the woods. There is reason to believe he might have made his way to northern Florida."

A mugshot of the prisoner appeared on the screen.

His longish hair was dull and flat. The creases in his face made him look old. And the intense look in his dark, deep-set eyes sent a chill down Miranda's spine.

Jebediah let out a low-pitched whistle. "As I live and breathe."

"What is it?" Parker said.

As if trying to keep his balance, Jebediah pointed at the screen. "That's the man I sold a ticket to."

"Sold? We were told he already had a ticket."

"Yes, he did. A ticket to Tallahassee, Florida."

Parker scowled. "What are you saying, Mr. Holt?"

"That man didn't go to Tallahassee. He exchanged his ticket for the bus that was in the lot about to take off."

"And where was that bus going?"

"Atlanta."

CHAPTER ELEVEN

As soon as they were back in the car, Parker was on the phone to Erskine again.

"I told you to stay out of it, Parker," the Lieutenant barked.

Parker ignored him. "Bagitelli went to Atlanta."

"What?"

"He took the one a.m. bus from a food mart outside Macon this morning. He's in the city now."

"I thought you said he was at a conductor's house in Tallahassee."

"He changed his plans. The man who exchanged his ticket just identified him."

Erskine was silent, processing the news. At last his bark sounded through the speakers again. "I'll put out a BOLO and contact the news stations. Do you need security?"

Erskine was taking that letter from Bagitelli seriously.

"I already have men at the estate and at Chatham, Grayson, and McFee," Parker told him. "You might add an extra patrol to the penthouse. And to Carlotta's restaurant."

"I'll do that. And Parker?"

"Yes, Hosea?"

"My advice to you is to go home and stay put."

Now it was Erskine's turn to hang up.

"He's right, Papa," Estavez said from the backseat, sounding shakier than ever. "We need to get back to Atlanta."

But Miranda could see from the road signs Parker was already headed for the local airport.

###

It was dark when they touched down again at DeKalb-Peachtree.

After Estavez took care of the Cessna, they drove back to the Agency and dropped him off at his car.

Then Parker took the liberty of following him home to the Parker Estate.

As they reached the winding lanes of Mockingbird Hills, Miranda gazed out the window at the majestic castle-like structures that made up the neighborhood. Under the lamplights stood the stalwart forms of chimneys and stone staircases and fancy arched windows surrounded by flowing, perfectly manicured lawns filled with trees, shrubs, and flowers.

They swung around the familiar curve of Sweet Hollow Lane, and Miranda felt the knot in her stomach tighten. But then it had been twisting and churning all day.

She felt for her Beretta for reassurance.

A few empty cars were parked along the curb in front of a neighbor's house. And then, at the top of the rise, the Parker estate appeared.

As usual, the sight of it took her breath.

The majestic live oaks standing guard over the gables of the mansard roof, the rambling stone balustrade that stretched across the front of the huge edifice, the regal front door.

She couldn't help thinking of the first time Parker had made love to her here. She remembered coming here after she and Parker had broken up to discover Parker's father had decided to give the house to Estavez and Coco. She recalled the couple giving a party here to announce they were having a baby. And she remembered the house being full of family and friends after she and Parker returned from their excruciating ordeal on that island.

This place wasn't her home any longer, but it held more memories than anywhere she'd ever lived.

They watched Estavez turn into the stately drive and turn off the Lexus. Parker slowed and waited until the defense attorney got out and gave them a signal to move on.

The Agency's late shift bodyguard was parked down the street keeping watch, so Parker didn't argue with his son.

Instead, he drove slowly away.

"Do you feel like Thai for dinner?" Parker said once they had turned onto the interstate.

Of course, when they had a break his first thought would be about feeding her.

"Actually, I was thinking of Italian."

His brow rose. "Like our fugitive?"

She lifted her shoulder. "Maybe he stopped for a bite somewhere."

"Very well. Italian it is."

Miranda didn't think Bagitelli would go to the high end place Parker picked. Too pricey for a man on the run. But Parker surprised her. Instead of dining inside, he ordered two gourmet chicken Parmesans to go.

This was going to be a working meal.

They headed back to the penthouse, and he had a word with the guard on duty before they rode up the elevator.

Inside the luxurious thirty-fifth-story former bachelor pad, Miranda watched Parker spoon the saucy, cheesy creations onto the fine China he'd placed on the granite countertop in the kitchen, and then carry the plates into the dining room.

Far be it from a Parker to eat out of Styrofoam.

As soon as they were seated at the massive glossy table surrounded by blue-and-slate modern art, Miranda took the plastic container of red pepper Parker had set out, and dumped the whole thing onto her plate. Then she reached for the fine silverware and cut off a bite of chicken.

A big one.

She put it in her mouth, the exquisite flavors began to blend with the pop of the spicy peppers, and she let out a long slow moan of satisfaction.

With an elegant gesture, Parker opened his cloth napkin and put it on his lap. "I'm so sorry we didn't have time for lunch."

Miranda wiped her mouth and took a sip of the rich red wine he had poured. "We were too busy to stop to eat. I'm a big girl, Parker. I can handle missing a meal. I just wish we had something to celebrate."

His face growing dark, Parker picked up his wine glass. "It was too optimistic to think we'd find Bagitelli right away."

That was an understatement.

Instead of commenting, Miranda dug into her food.

They ate in silence, their thoughts seeming to crisscross one another in the air, or at least she thought so by Parker's expressions.

When they were finished, they put the leftovers away, shoved the plates in the dishwasher, and headed side-by-side past the blue marble support beams in one of the penthouse's classy sitting areas to the sleek onyx desk near the windows.

And the computer on it.

They pulled up chairs and got to work.

Miranda watched Parker's deft fingers fly over the keyboard, then let her gaze drift to his handsome face.

The worry lines she saw there struck a note of sorrow deep in her heart. Parker was as troubled about the boy he'd taken off the streets years ago as if he were his own flesh and blood. Maybe more so. She felt it, too.

It awakened the familiar call of her destiny more than ever. Loud and clear.

They would find this piano playing creep and put him back where he belonged before he got to Estavez or Coco or anyone else.

"Here's something." Parker's voice pulled her out of her thoughts.

"What is it?"

"A bio of our fugitive." He began to read from the screen. "Enrico Giovanni Bagitelli was born in Naples, Italy and started playing piano at three."

Miranda blinked at the text. "Three years old? Is that a misprint?"

"Not at all. Quite a few virtuosos start that early."

"Wow." She didn't know that. "Couldn't have had much of a childhood."

Parker ran the cursor under the next lines. "Bagitelli was under the tutelage of his father, Giovanni Bagitelli, who was the head of his own prestigious Academy of Music in Naples. The boy won a rigorous National Piano Competition at four and gave his first concert at five."

"At five?"

"It's indeed an impressive curriculum vitae."

Miranda picked up reading where Parker left off. "'Bagitelli's father passed away when the young man was thirteen, and his mother moved to New York where Enrico was accepted into Juilliard's Pre-College Division. There he trained under the renowned piano teacher, Ludwig Kraus.' Never heard of him."

Parker regarded her tenderly. "Not exactly your cup of tea."

She smiled back at him and kept reading. "'From there Bagitelli went on to graduate Juilliard and begin a long career of touring, recording, and taking on the occasional prodigy. He became a beloved icon in his field.'"

She sat back. "He was popular."

"Yes."

"And had an ego to match."

"Evidently." Parker read further. "'Unlike the strict methodology of his father, under Ludwig Kraus, Bagitelli was free to develop his own style, a mixture of bombastic explosion and tender emotions. Audiences loved it. Women adored him. He received an abundance of fan mail. Tickets to his concerts abroad sold out in minutes.' Ah, here's a link. This is one of his most memorable performances of Chopin's *Prelude No. 24*."

Parker clicked the link and an image of a younger Bagitelli appeared in a black tux sitting at a shiny black grand piano. Music flooded the room as the virtuoso attacked the keyboard with a ferocity and vigor that had Miranda's gut tight again.

It was a fierce, heavy tune, with a lot of anger, or so she thought.

She watched the intensity on his good-looking face. His eyes were closed—didn't need to look at his hands or the notes, she guessed. His black brows were twisted in an expression of near pain as his head bobbed up and down to the steady rhythm, his long wavy hair flopping this way and that. She thought she saw a bit of sweat fly from his forehead.

But the music was moving. Almost as driving as a rock song.

And then it finished, and the final thunderous chord hung in the air until the performer turned to the audience for applause—which was just as thunderous.

Miranda sat back and let out a breath. "Wow."

Parker seemed impressed, too. "I would say 'bombastic' is an understatement."

"Emotional dude."

"Yes."

"The type who could easily fly into a fit of rage and try to kill someone?"

"Apparently."

She scanned the text of the bio again. "It doesn't say anything about how Bagitelli's career ended."

"No, this is a publicity piece written before the incident. Let's see what else we can find." Parker clicked around some more. Then went to his emails. "Here's the video Antonio showed us earlier today. He found the original."

"That's good. Let's have a look at it." Miranda scooted up to get a closer view of the screen as Parker started the video.

The iron gate alongside the lot appeared, protecting pedestrians and drivers from the drop-off. Tall Atlanta bank buildings twinkled in the distance.

Once again, the lone woman in the black dress strolled down the dark pavement of the Atlanta Symphony Orchestra parking lot.

Once again, an engine roared and a sports car appeared.

Parker paused the video just before the vehicle struck the woman.

"Can't see the driver." Miranda leaned in closer and peered at the shape of the hood on the frozen screen. The sports car was a shiny candy apple red. "Is that a Maserati?"

"A Gran Turismo," Parker confirmed.

He pressed Play again, and the video continued the gruesome scene. The car hit the woman and she disappeared under it. The car squealed to a stop, backed up, and Bagitelli got out of the car and ran over to her. His anguished cries came through the speakers.

Not wanting to hear them again, Miranda grabbed the mouse and paused the image. She shook her head. "Something isn't right about this, Parker."

"I agree."

"Wait a minute. There's sound. And color. This isn't surveillance video."

Parker frowned. "No, it wouldn't be. Antonio must have been mistaken."

"Surely Bagitelli's new lawyer must have figured that out."

Parker took back the mouse, returned to the email from Estavez, and read the last part of it. "'It wasn't surveillance video, though the prosecutor claimed it was that day.'"

"Hmm. It must have been taken by a bystander." Miranda squinted at the screen. "Not many people in that lot."

"There could have been some behind the Gran Turismo."

"True."

As she chewed on that idea, Parker did another search and came up with a newer article.

She scanned it quickly. "This one's more personal than the bio. Bagitelli had a wife. Fiona Delacroix who studied at the Paris Conservatory and who was coming into her own as a musician when she became a student of Bagitelli. Interesting. They met at Juilliard, where he tutored her during his senior year."

"One of his occasional prodigies."

"Yeah. 'They were married after Fiona's third year of touring, and often played together.' Are there any videos of that?"

Parker searched again and found one. "Schubert's *Marche Militaire*."

This was a peppy, happier tune. Miranda watched the couple smile at each other, as they sat side by side on the piano bench, leaning back and forth together, while their hands danced over the keys.

Fiona was thin and a little taller than Bagitelli, but Miranda caught a bit of strain on the face of the dark-haired woman in the black sequined dress. As if she were trying too hard to keep up with her husband.

Still, the music was beautiful.

Bagitelli's touch was softer now, not as "bombastic." She wondered if this Fiona had tamed the beast in him.

The video finished and Parker found another one with Bagitelli and Fiona at a keyboard. He began first, playing the low notes slowly, three at a time. Dum da duh, dum da duh, dum da duh.

Miranda snapped her fingers. "I know this one."

"*Moonlight Sonata*," Parker said after she couldn't come up with the name.

"Yeah. That's what I meant."

Smiling he pointed to the text under the video. "This piece seems to be their most requested."

Miranda frowned. "Kinda boring."

"It's Beethoven."

"Excuse me. I prefer something snappier."

Shaking his head, Parker clicked on another video.

This time the pair were at separate pianos. They looked older, and Fiona's playing seemed more fluid.

Bagitelli was playing the lead with his "bombastic" style. Between his notes, Fiona's fingers flew all over the keyboard. And then they broke into a lovely melodious tune.

Miranda sat up. "Hey, I know this one, too."

"Tchaikovsky's *Waltz of the Flowers*," Parker said. "From *The Nutcracker Suite*."

"A ballet, right?"

"Yes."

Suddenly she had a vague memory of sitting beside her father in a downtown Chicago concert hall while the orchestra played that tune, and beautiful ballerinas floated over a big stage. He must have taken her to see it one holiday.

She shook off the memory and got back to work. "So was it Fiona's sister Bagitelli tried to kill?"

Parker eyed her knowingly, but didn't comment on her reaction. "It doesn't say, but nothing indicates Bagitelli had siblings."

Miranda's gaze went to the text under the video. "'We will miss them.' What does that mean?"

"Let's find out." Parker found another short article on Bagitelli from years ago. "Enrico Bagitelli mourns the death of his beloved mentor, Ludwig Kraus."

"His teacher at Juilliard."

"Yes."

There was a photo of Bagitelli and Fiona in mourning clothes outside a New York cathedral. Miranda noted again that Fiona was a few inches taller than her husband.

She read from the screen. "'A member of Enrico Bagitelli's staff announced today that he and Fiona will stop touring for a period of mourning.' How long ago was that?"

"It doesn't say." Parker followed a link to another article, then another.

None of them gave them any more information about Bagitelli and Fiona. There wasn't even anything much about Bagitelli's arrest and conviction.

Some publicist had taken care of that, no doubt.

Her eye went to an interesting paragraph. She pointed to the words on the screen. "Hey look at this. Bagitelli was worth thirty million."

Parker scanned the article. "Again, not unusual for someone of his fame."

"Hmph. Still, it smells like motive. The sister-in-law might have been blackmailing him for money, and so he got rid of her. Tried to make it look like an accident, but failed."

"Also failed in killing her."

"Right." Until she eventually passed away from the injuries he gave her. "Still, he can't access his money now. He knows the police will be watching his accounts."

"And so we should assume for now that he will go only as far as a few hundred dollars will take him."

"Unless he's got a friend he can press for a loan. Or he steals some cash."

"That would be risky. And I'm sure Erskine has people watching Bagitelli's bank transactions."

Miranda sat back and folded her arms. She thought about their visit to the Sawyer sisters. "Do you remember what Dixie told us about Bagitelli?"

"She told us a number of things."

"I mean, you know. That he—what did she say? He talked to himself?"

Parker nodded thoughtfully.

"He sounded—I don't know."

"What?"

She raised her palms. "A little off?"

"Yes, I got that impression."

"That, the way he attacked Estavez in court, the switching of his plans and ditching the car to come to Atlanta when he knows the police are after him. This guy seems really—"

"Unbalanced?" Parker supplied.

"He sounds like a real nut job, Parker."

"Which makes him all the more dangerous."

"Yes, it does." Her spine began to tingle, despite how weary she felt.

She wanted to do more. She wanted to figure this out and find this crazy virtuoso tonight. But the cobwebs were forming in her head and she was losing her train of thought.

Besides, Parker looked even more exhausted than she felt.

She touched his shoulder. "Let's go to bed and pick this up in the morning."

"I agree. We'll follow up on finding someone our fugitive could tap for money. An excellent idea, by the way."

She felt herself melt at Parker's compliment, but was too tired to enjoy it fully.

They turned off the computer and made their way up the spiral staircase. They hit the showers, and then fell into bed with their arms around each other.

CHAPTER TWELVE

He sat in the cheap car he'd bought from a place in the city near the hotel. A seedy spot, very much in counterpoint to this one.

This was Mockingbird Hills.

A very nice area. More like the sort of places he used to be accustomed to. One he would think would be a little too dear for a defense attorney. But this was where the months of research he'd done in prison had led him.

He had confirmed this was where Antonio Estavez now lived with his wife. He could just see it at the top of the rise.

The Parker estate. Evidently his former lawyer was somehow connected to a prominent family in Atlanta.

Earlier he had seen the man in the car across the street guarding it. An undercover officer, he had decided. Somehow, the police had figured out where he was going. How, he had no idea.

He had been sitting here in his car since the late afternoon, watching, waiting, planning.

More than two hours ago, the attorney himself had rolled up the driveway in his Lexus and gotten out. Turning to the street, he had waved to another car. A Mazda.

The other car had paused for a moment, as if in acknowledgment, then moved on.

But when it was gone, the attorney had climbed back into his Lexus and driven toward the highway. He had followed him, and when they turned onto I-75, he realized they were heading to the downtown law firm.

Soon they reached the tall glass building. It was the right place. Chatham, Grayson, and McFee. The firm he had turned to over three years ago.

But there had been someone watching here, too. Another undercover car.

He couldn't make his move while he was being watched.

Grinding his teeth in frustration, he remembered driving past the entrance in shame.

You need to do something, Enrico.

"I know, Ludwig. I know. I will."

Just not yet.

He couldn't risk getting caught and being sent back to prison. He would rather die than go back there.

As he'd sat at a traffic light on Seventeenth, he vowed he never would. No matter what.

The light changed and he drove around the block.

As he neared the high-rise again, he spotted the lawyer accessing the tall glass revolving doors with his keycard. He could get to him now.

But there was that sedan parked alongside the building under a row of trees. It wasn't even a legal parking spot.

There was no way he could make his move now.

The panic coming on again, he made a sharp turn at the corner and headed back to the interstate.

And now here he sat in Mockingbird Hills, unable to think of what to do next.

His mind returned to the hours since his escape.

It had been after two in the morning when the bus had reached the depot in downtown Atlanta. He'd asked someone for the nearest budget hotel and made his way onto the street. Passing violent-looking drug dealers and thugs on the sidewalk, he wondered whether it would be his fate to die at their hands. But at last he had made it to the cheap hotel a mile or so away.

The man at the desk had been taking a nap when he entered the lobby. He didn't recognize him or question his use of cash. He'd paid for two nights, realizing he would have to be frugal with the rest of his funds.

The room smelled of disgusting odors, and he'd found a cockroach in the corner that had nearly given him a heart attack. He was about to call the concierge and complain when he remembered he could not risk anyone seeing him.

Besides, there was no concierge. Just the sleepy desk clerk.

His heart reeling between terror and hope, somehow he'd fallen asleep for a few hours before the sound of the maids woke him.

He slipped the Do Not Disturb sign on the door and got to work.

Dear Dixie. She had put a box of hair dye in the backpack, though he barely knew how to use it and found the instructions confusing. He had intended to make himself look older than he was with a bit of gray. Instead he'd been left with stringy locks of greenish blond scattered through his dark waves.

Disgusting.

He had been proud of his thick shiny hair once upon a time. It added more drama to his performances. But his hair had lost its luster after so many years of confinement.

So did it matter that he had ruined it and made himself more conspicuous in the process?

At any rate, he was glad Dixie had also tucked a ball cap into the bag.

He'd worn it to the cheap diner across the street from the hotel. No one had recognized him as he wolfed down bacon and eggs, and took the pills he had kept in his pocket since the nurse had given them to him at the prison the night before.

His mind had cleared then.

Enough for him to realize he needed a vehicle. And that he'd already asked someone outside where to get one.

Saying he had left his phone at home, he had risked asking one of the waitresses to call Uber. Graciously, she'd let him use the app on her phone. He wasn't very good with it, but he'd managed. The driver dropped him off at the used car lot, and he'd gotten the vehicle he was now inside after signing the name on his fake ID.

And here he sat.

Anxiety gnawed at him. It was too risky, coming here twice. Surely the police would spot this vehicle soon. He needed to get out of here.

He started the car, backed into a driveway, and headed out the other way. Out of the guard's sight.

He drove back to the hotel.

Back in his room, he paced for a while then got ready for bed. Sleep would help, but he had no more medicine.

He would have to act fast.

As he laid down, the longing for his old life hit him hard. The tours, the concerts, the adoring fans. The ladies. And his piano. Oh, how he wished he could play it again. And Rosalynd. Dear, dear Rosalynd. He loved her so much.

He had to see her once more if it was the last thing he did.

He had to get to Antonio Estavez.

He had to find a way. He would. He would come up with a plan. And as he drifted off to sleep, the pieces started to come together.

CHAPTER THIRTEEN

She strolled along the beach, the warm sand under her toes, the waves of the ocean in her ears.

She inhaled deeply, breathing in the salty air as she shielded her eyes against the bright sun and peered out over the blue, blue water.

Something was out there.

A boat? What kind? She couldn't tell, but as she watched it, a hard knot of dread began to form in her stomach. It was coming closer.

Something very bad was about to happen.

As she stared at it, a seagull swooped down from the sky and swatted her on the arm with its wing.

She batted it away.

It came at her again. She shooed it away again, her hand slapping at its feathers.

Again it tapped her.

"Oh no, you don't." This time, she grabbed it by the wing and held on tight.

"Miranda."

Miranda opened her eyes and saw the man beside the bed. She was holding his wrist in a death grip.

"Parker?"

She let go and stared up at him. He was fully dressed in his business suit, sans the coffee cup he usually had in his hand for her. Good thing. She would have spilled it all over the place.

His handsome face was lined with distress.

Putting a hand to her head, she let out a groan. "I'm okay. It was just a stupid dream." And not that bad of one. Except for that feeling of dread. She looked around. "What time is it?"

"A little after five. There's bad news."

She bolted up. "What?"

"Antonio called a few minutes ago. Coco's missing."

"What? How can she be missing? You had a bodyguard stationed at the house all night. Erskine had an extra patrol in the neighborhood." Dread stabbed at her—the real life version—reminding her of the sensation she'd had in the dream.

Parker reached for her hand. "We're about to find out. How soon can you be ready?"

Brushing the hair out of her face, she got to her feet. "Give me ten minutes."

###

The sun hadn't come up when they reached the Parker mansion, and the huge stolid place looked the same as they had left it last night.

The lamplights were still twinkling, and the branches of the white oaks were swaying in a warmish breeze, casting shadows across the manicured lawn and the porticos and Grecian columns of the structure.

Parker pulled up behind the Agency vehicle that was still alongside the curb.

That was funny, Miranda thought as she got out of the Mazda and followed Parker to the driver's side. Wasn't there supposed to have been a shift change?

But it was the same bodyguard. She recognized Bill Taylor's bushy red hair.

Parker tapped on the window with his knuckle and the man inside shot up and rubbed his mustache. Then he turned his head, and his jaw sank down to his chin.

Caught napping. Not good.

Quickly Taylor rolled down the window. "I'm so sorry, sir. I just couldn't keep my eyes open."

"Where's Granger?" Parker snapped.

Gordon Granger. Another one of the IITs Miranda had graduated with. On the flight back to Atlanta yesterday evening, Parker had called the Agency and arranged a fresh pair of bodyguards to take over for the two he'd put in place. Granger was supposed to be on duty here now.

"Granger called me and said he was sick, sir. Actually, I think he has an interview for another job."

Parker was fuming. "Why didn't you report in to me when Granger didn't show up?"

Taylor raised his palms. "There isn't anyone else, sir. Witherby's on that job in Austin, and Mr. Holloway let Tumbler, Fernsby, and Sallow go last week."

Now Parker looked like Mount Vesuvius bursting into hot lava.

Miranda was just as angry. Let them go? She thought Holloway's notes said he was planning that for next quarter. He must have jumped the gun. She didn't know those bodyguards, except for vaguely remembering their names on a payroll list, but they had to be good. Fernsby had been with the Agency a long while, as she recalled. Still it wasn't Taylor's fault they were so short handed.

Summoning his bottomless patience, Parker drew in a breath. "Can you stay awake until I can get you relief? We have a situation."

Taylor sat up straight. "Situation, sir?"

"The party you were watching is missing."

"But it was so quiet. No one went in or out all night."

Except he might have missed something if he was catnapping.

Parker's silence was deafening as Taylor's look went from shock to guilt. "Oh, no. Oh my God. I—I don't know what to say, sir."

"Just stay alert for another hour."

"Yessir. I'll do that."

Parker turned away and marched up the street to the mansion, his irritation rising with every step.

"What in the world?" Miranda muttered under her breath when she'd caught up with him.

"Do you remember Alex Witherby?"

Witherby. She recalled a big meaty linebacker type guy with sandy curls, gentle gray eyes, and a shy crooked smile.

"He got the lead on Sweetwater Park that broke that case." The case Audrey Wilson was involved in.

"Correct. I found him manning the reception desk yesterday while Sybil was on break."

"What?" He was too good to be a substitute receptionist.

"I sent him to Austin to keep an eye on Holloway. I have a good mind to—"

Instead of saying what he wanted to do to Holloway, Parker stopped talking and took out his phone.

Before they had reached the elaborate front door of the Parker estate, he had called all of the bodyguards Holloway had let go, rehired them, and doled out assignments. Tumbler was on his way over to relieve Taylor, and Fernsby and Sallow were on standby.

But what about Coco? "Should we call Erskine?"

"Let's assess the situation first."

"Right."

As they marched past the balustrades and up the front steps, Miranda noticed worry overtaking the anger on Parker's face.

"We'll find Coco," she told him. "We're going to get Bagitelli and send him back where he belongs. And this time, he'll be there longer."

With a nod, Parker pressed the bell.

They waited a minute, but no one answered.

Parker rang again.

Still no answer. No sound of movement or voices came from inside.

Miranda's stomach went tight. Had Bagitelli gotten to Estavez? Had the fugitive been hiding in one of the umpteen rooms in the place? Not like this would be the first time.

She reached for her Beretta, while Parker took something else out of his pocket and stuck it in the door.

She was stunned. "You still have a key?"

He nodded. "My father insisted on it."

Mr. P had always hoped they would get back together and live here again. She was glad the most important part of that had happened.

Parker reached for the handle.

"Bagitelli could be in there," Miranda whispered to him.

With another nod, he took out his Glock and opened the door.

CHAPTER FOURTEEN

They stepped into the huge palatial foyer and found it dark and silent.

The sparkling chandelier overhead quietly reflected moonlight from a third-story window high above. Along the walls, shadowy figures in the tall oil paintings sedately gazed down at the darkened grand mahogany staircase, the ornate furniture, and the marble tiles.

The air had the scent of the pricey fragrance the cleaning staff used.

As they made their way across the floor, past the sitting and drawing rooms, and through the halls that led to the back, Miranda didn't see any signs of a struggle. No broken Ming Dynasty vases on the floor. No antique tables turned over. No golden brick-a-brac out of place.

That didn't make sense, but this was a big house with tons of nooks and crannies.

At last, they reached the huge fancy kitchen at the back and found Estavez sitting in the breakfast nook, his head in his hands, an untouched cup of coffee on the table before him. The lights were on, and he was shaved and fully dressed in his business suit.

They must have startled him as they came in.

He looked up in shock, his face even more lined with despair and fatigue than yesterday. "Papa. Miranda. I didn't realize you were here." Then he eyed Parker's weapon.

"We let ourselves in." Parker holstered his gun and sat down while Miranda did the same. No Bagitelli here. But no Coco, either.

"Tell us what happened, son," Parker said gently.

Estavez looked lost. "I don't know what happened. I came home this morning and couldn't find Coco anywhere."

Huh? Miranda frowned at Parker. "What do you mean you came home this morning? We followed you here last night."

Estavez stared down at his coffee.

To give the lawyer time to put his thoughts together, Parker rose, went to the kitchen, and poured two fancy china cups of the expensive brand of coffee the Parkers drank. He brought them back to the table and set one down before Miranda. Then he sat down and added cream to his cup from a small, elegant matching pitcher.

He took a swallow. "What happened, son?" This time his voice was calm but firm enough to say he wanted a straight answer.

Estavez looked at him with his dark, swollen eyes. "I didn't come inside the house last night."

Miranda's back went stiff. "Why not?"

"I remembered I had night court."

"Night court that lasted until this morning?"

He turned to her as if he were arguing a case. "I slept at the office."

"Why?" Parker said, the calmness draining from his tone.

Estavez drew in a defeated breath. "Coco and I had a fight."

"A fight? When?" He'd spent most of yesterday with them.

"The night before last. It was bad."

Miranda knew about bad fights with your spouse. "How bad?"

Estavez didn't care for the question. "She's pregnant. She's touchy about everything. Everything I do is wrong." He squirmed in his chair like a guilty party on the witness stand.

That didn't sound like the docile Coco Miranda knew, but hormones could do a number on you.

Estavez raised his hands in a helpless gesture. "She thinks I work too much."

Not coming home all night when someone who wanted to kill you and your family was on the loose might give someone that impression. But this issue had started before the prison break.

"Didn't we talk about this, son?"

Parker had had a conversation with Estavez about spending more time with his wife when they'd come home from their ordeal on Santana's island.

Apparently, it didn't take.

He spread his hands. "I'm a lawyer. My job requires long hours. How am I supposed to support my wife and my child if I don't work?"

Miranda suspected there was more to it than that, but Coco and Estavez's marital issues weren't the problem right now.

They had to find Coco.

"Maybe Coco's asleep in one of the rooms on the third floor," she suggested.

Both she and Parker had done that a time or two when they hadn't been able to see eye-to-eye.

Estavez shook his head. "I checked every room in the house. Besides, her car is gone."

Miranda stared at Parker. She could see his thoughts were going in the same direction as hers.

Even being sleep-deprived, the people who worked for the Parker Agency were good. If Bagitelli had gotten Coco into her car and had driven away with her, Taylor would have seen it.

Wouldn't he?

She decided to say it out loud. "Coco might have left on her own. Before the bodyguard got here yesterday."

"A distinct possibility," Parker agreed. "When did you leave for work yesterday?"

"My usual time. Eight."

"Did Coco mention any plans for the day?"

"I don't remember that. As I said, we were still fighting. The last thing she said was that we were going to talk when I got home."

The dreaded talk. That was what Estavez was really avoiding. Miranda wondered if Coco had bolted. She'd done that with her ex and for good reason.

As much as she hated to say it, she had to ask. "You didn't—"

Estavez knew what she meant before she said it. "Raise a hand to her? Never. I know what she went through in her first marriage. I would never do that to her. Not ever. But when I'm angry, I can get loud."

She'd always thought of Estavez as a passionate Latin Lover type. A hot temper went with that. But she believed him. He wouldn't hurt Coco. No young man raised by Wade Parker would.

Parker changed the subject. "It was around one in the afternoon when you came to the office yesterday."

Miranda's mind went in a different direction. The worst case. She turned to Parker and spoke softly. "Bagitelli could have gotten to her then. Before you put the bodyguard in place."

"Ay. My poor Coco. My unborn child. I am a terrible husband." Estavez began to sob, once again tearing Miranda's heart out.

Parker reached across the table and touched his arm. "Blaming yourself won't help us find her, son."

Feeling bad for upsetting the lawyer, Miranda got up and strolled to the glass doors.

As she stared out at the dark porch and the big backyard, the tingly feeling she'd often experienced on cases began to whisper up the back of her neck, giving her chills.

On this one, the worse-case scenario was pretty bad.

Had Bagitelli come here and kidnapped Coco before they even knew he had escaped from prison? As Parker would say, it was a possibility.

Her mind went back to her first idea. The cheerier one. "Maybe Coco just went somewhere yesterday morning."

Parker frowned. "And stayed all night?"

"Depends on how mad she was."

"She was very mad," Estavez muttered half to himself. "Very, very mad."

"Well, there you go. Where do you think she might have gone?"

Estavez wiped his face and forced himself to think. "My first guess would be Joan's. Coco has been helping her a lot with her catering business lately."

Of course. Fanuzzi had been having a lot of trouble with her pregnancy. Gen had mentioned she was struggling with swelling now, and that Coco was helping out with the cooking.

"Let me call her." She dialed the number.

It rang and rang. At last a sleepy voice with the familiar Brooklyn accent answered. "What?"

Miranda glanced out the glass doors again. Uh oh. It was still dark out. Not even six yet. "It's me, Fanuzzi. Sorry to wake you. How are you feeling?"

Wrong question.

"I don't hear from you for weeks, and then you suddenly call in the middle of the night to check up on me?"

"Sorry," she said again. Might as well cut to the chase. "Actually, I need your help."

"I've been up most of the night with the runs. Call me later."

Eww. Fanuzzi never was one to mince words, still Miranda's heart went out to her friend. She hated she was having such a hard time with her pregnancy. "I'm really sorry to bother you, but—uh—have you heard from Coco lately?"

"Coco? Let me think." Fanuzzi let out a big yawn. "Ouch. Oh, my head's throbbing."

She heard groaning and wondered if Fanuzzi was about to barf. Fighting back a surge of guilt, Miranda was about to hang up when her friend came back on the line.

"Oh, right. Coco was here yesterday morning. I guess it was around eleven. We looked over the recipe for Canapés Lorenzo. She was supposed to help me practice apple fritters in the air fryer, but she wasn't feeling good, either."

"Oh?"

"Something was bothering her. She didn't want to talk about it, so I told her she could go home."

"And did she go home?"

"I thought she did."

Again, Miranda's stomach tensed. Was that when Bagitelli nabbed her?

"No, wait. She said she wanted some time to herself. She said she might go for a walk in the park."

"Which park?"

"I'm not sure. Why?"

Drawing in a breath, Miranda decided to tell her as little as possible. That was upsetting enough. "Coco didn't come home last night. We don't know where she is."

"What? Antonio must be beside himself."

"You could say that. Do you have any idea where she might be?"

"No, but I'm feeling kinda dizzy right now."

She'd bothered her best friend for nothing. "That's okay. Go back to bed. Sorry to bother you."

"Don't you brush me off like that, Murray. What's going on?"

Fanuzzi of all people knew that when someone wasn't where they should be, it could spell real trouble. Miranda couldn't keep it from her, or she'd never hear the end of it. "Did you see the news yesterday?"

"A little. A storm's brewing in Louisiana."

"Not that. There was a story about a guy who escaped from prison."

"Oh, yeah. Wasn't he a musician or something?"

"Yes. His name's Enrico Bagitelli."

"What's that got to do with Coco?"

"Estavez defended the guy when he went to trial. Bagitelli fired him, but then after he was convicted and sent to prison, he wrote Estavez a threatening letter."

"What do you mean by threatening?"

She just wasn't getting out of this one. Miranda took a deep breath and told her. "He said he was going to escape and come and kill Estavez and his family."

Fanuzzi let out a shriek. Not a mousy shriek. A mean, Brooklyn, don't-you-dare-screw-with-my-friend shriek. "Oh, dear Lord, Murray. You think this musician could have—Coco? Oh, dear Lord."

She shouldn't have told her. Now Fanuzzi was going to worry herself silly all day and there was nothing she could do to help.

"Do you need Dave?"

"Not yet. I'll call if we do. For now, just go back to bed and try to get some rest."

"Yeah, right. Okay." There was a pause. "Wait a minute."

"What is it?"

"Now I remember where Coco went yesterday."

Miranda's heart began to thump. "Where?"

"She said she was going to see Antonio's mother."

CHAPTER FIFTEEN

At this time of day, *Ay Chihuahua!*, the restaurant owned by Estavez's mother, was just an eighteen-minute trip down the interstate, even with the early morning commuters trying to beat the traffic.

The cheery little place off Peachtree in Midtown wasn't open yet, of course.

Estavez had insisted on taking separate cars, so they parked across the street and went in through a set of concrete steps at the back.

Inside, they were greeted by the sounds and smells of the kitchen staff in their white caps and aprons as they went about braising beef, mixing salsas, preparing guacamole, and chopping cilantro, onions, and those wonderful jalapeños.

Despite the situation, Miranda's mouth began to water.

She saw Estavez's two younger sisters working away at the sink. She didn't see Coco anywhere. But in the far corner she spotted the small, dark-haired woman with a round face and compact body sliding a big pan of delicious-looking meat into an oven.

Estavez's mama.

She looked up, caught sight of her son and gave him a stern look.

After closing the stove and wiping her hands on her apron, she made her way over to them.

Dulcea turned off the water, wiped her hands on her apron, and turned to see what was going on.

"Antonio," she cried. "Look, Belita. It's our brother."

Belita looked over at Estavez with gleaming dark eyes. "Have you come to help us wash dishes?"

Sternly Carlotta shook her head. "You girls go set the tables in the dining room while I speak to your brother."

Belita scowled. "But, Mama—"

"Go."

With sad faces the pair scampered away.

"Mama." Estavez gave his mother a big hug.

"I was wondering when you would get here." She nodded to her other visitors. "Miranda, Señor Parker."

"We're sorry to disturb you, Carlotta," Parker said.

"No problem."

Estavez couldn't wait for the formalities. "Mama, Coco is missing. Do you know where she is?"

The woman took a step back and shook her head at her son. "Why do you not wish to be with your wife, Antonio?"

Evidently, Coco had confided her problems to her mother-in-law.

Estavez ignored the question. "Is she here?"

Carlotta let Estavez stew another moment before she nodded. "She is upstairs."

Somewhere along the way, Miranda had learned that the family lived in an apartment above the restaurant, since they spent most of their time down here. Coco must have spent the night with them.

Estavez put a hand to his chest and raised his eyes. "*Gracias a Dios!* I must see her." He took a step forward.

Carlotta put out a hand to block him. "One moment, son. I will see if she wishes to see you."

Estavez looked stunned. Then he stared at his mother with pleading eyes. "Mama, I have to see her."

The woman was unmoved. "You will stay here, son."

As relieved as she was that they'd found Coco, Miranda didn't want to get in the middle of a family squabble.

She was about to tell Parker they should wait outside when he said, "Miranda, why don't you go with Carlotta?"

Say what? She blinked at him. "Me?"

"I think Coco needs the support of her friend right now."

And she was supposed to play marriage counselor?

No, that wasn't it. The penetrating look in his sexy gunmetal eyes told her Parker thought she was the best one to break the news to Coco about Bagitelli.

To keep the hysterics down to a minimum. "Okay."

"This way," Carlotta said.

CHAPTER SIXTEEN

She led Miranda around a tall aluminum shelving unit stacked with dishes to the rear of the kitchen and a door tucked away in the far corner. Behind the door was a wooden staircase that went up three stories.

They climbed to the top in silence, Carlotta unlocked the door to her apartment, and they stepped inside.

Miranda took in the open-style living and dining area which was filled with comfortable looking furniture. Here the festive decor of the main dining area downstairs was reflected in colorful folk art on the walls and matching patterns in bowls and plates in a crowded hutch.

Miranda followed Carlotta through the space to a T-shaped hall in the back leading to several rooms, all with their doors closed.

She felt awkward as they approached what must have been the spare bedroom.

Softly Carlotta knocked. "Coco? Are you up?"

Miranda glanced at the time on her phone. Just past six-thirty. Still pretty early.

She guessed this was her day to get peacefully sleeping pregnant women out of bed.

A gentle voice came from inside. "I'm awake."

"I have a visitor here to see you."

There was a shuffling noise and the door opened.

Coco stood in her blond loveliness dressed in a pale pink loose-fitting maternity blouse, light blue jeans, and a pair of open-toed straw sandals with a wedge heel. She looked very pregnant.

Her clothes were a bit wrinkled. She must have slept in them. Her hair was cut in long wispy layers and looked a little disheveled, as well. Her face and eyes were puffy, but came to life with an expression of shock.

"Miranda. What are you doing here? Did Antonio send you?"

Miranda had to tell the truth. "Estavez is downstairs. So's Parker."

Her pretty blue eyes opened wide with more shock. "What? Did he need a posse to come after me?"

"Actually—"

"You just don't know what I've been through, Miranda. Okay, maybe you do." She folded her arms and looked around the room as if at loss of what else to say.

"I need to get back downstairs," Carlotta said. "Why don't you two talk for a while?" She ushered Miranda inside the room and shut the door behind her.

No getting out of this one.

Miranda looked around the small girlish space. It was decorated in pastels and contained a shelf for stuffed animals. This must be Belita's room, not a spare.

Coco went over to the twin size bed and sat down on the white eyelet spread.

Steadying herself Miranda strolled to the nearby vanity, pulled out a stool and sat down. On the white surface sat a big pink bag. Makeup was spread out next to it. Had to be Coco's. She hadn't planned on staying overnight. This had been spur of the moment.

Coco let out a moan.

Miranda turned to look at her and saw she had her hands to her face. She was about to cry. "Oh, Miranda. I don't know what to do."

Miranda's heart went out to the poor girl. She'd felt protective of her since the first night they'd met.

But she couldn't think of anything to say except the obvious. "Do you think things aren't going to work out with you and Estavez?"

Coco blinked at her, stunned by her bluntness. Then she shrugged. "I don't know. We used to be close. Or I thought we were. We used to write songs together. You remember."

Of course, she did. They'd written the song Coco had sung at Miranda's wedding, such as that event had been. *Nuestro amor*.

"And then I got pregnant. I thought it was going to be so beautiful for us. But then I had to leave the Gecko Club, and Antonio started working all the time, and all we do is fight. I try so hard, but—" she sighed.

"But what?"

Her voice took on a worried tone. "He just doesn't want to stay at home. He's always away. He says he's at the firm or in court."

"He wants to make a good living for you and the baby."

"That's what he says."

"You don't think he means it?"

Coco gestured to her oversized girth. "Look at me. I'm all fat and puffy. Sometimes I'm as moody as Joan."

No one was as moody as Fanuzzi right now. "He understands."

"Does he?"

Miranda waited for the rest.

"There was a point in my marriage to Dexter when I knew he'd lost interest in me. That was when he got, well, you know. Violent."

"But Estavez would never—"

"No, he wouldn't. I'm not worried about that."

"What are you worried about?" Miranda already knew part of the answer.

Coco was gun-shy after her horrible marriage to Dexter. She of all people ought to know about that. She'd been the Queen of Gun-shy after her marriage to Leon. For years. But Coco had rushed into her relationship with Estavez without giving herself enough time to heal.

Coco waved her hands in the air. "It took him this long to figure out I was gone. Antonio didn't come home last night, did he?"

Miranda bit her lip, but she had to tell her the truth. "No, he didn't. He had night court."

She shook her head. "He's having an affair. I know it."

The words stunned her. That couldn't be true. It just couldn't be. But why had Estavez stayed at work all night?

Coco reached for a tissue from a box on the nightstand. "Oh, Miranda. I just don't think Antonio loves me anymore."

"Because you're pregnant?"

"Because he doesn't want to be with me." She began to cry.

Miranda wasn't the touchy-feely type, but she couldn't help getting up to sit beside her on the bed. She put her arms around her friend and tried to comfort her. Coco was breaking her heart, and she didn't know what to say.

She remembered the day Coco had sashayed down a courtroom aisle to come to Miranda's defense.

It was the first time the sexy Latin lawyer had seen her, and he'd been instantly moonstruck. He'd fallen head over heels for the gorgeous blond singer. Miranda could tell by the look on his face whenever they ran into her. As soon as Coco had divorced her wife-beating husband, she and Estavez had started secretly seeing each other.

Miranda remembered when Estavez had announced their engagement at a party at the Parker mansion. She'd thought they had moved too fast, and Parker hadn't approved.

She remembered when the pair ran off and got married. Parker had been livid. But then Miranda had found Mackenzie, and faced down Leon, and gotten shot. Months went by, and they started Parker and Steele Consulting, and over time, Parker had grown fond of the pretty young woman who was now his surrogate daughter-in-law.

She remembered when they announced Coco was pregnant. They'd been writing songs together. Everything had seemed rosy.

Maybe too rosy.

Had Miranda's first impression been right? Had the couple moved too fast? Was Estavez really tired of Coco? Was he cheating on her? What would that do to Parker?

No. Estavez would never do such a thing. Never. This was just a bumpy patch they were going through.

She grabbed Coco's hand and squeezed it. "Well, I think Antonio loves you," she said with all the conviction she could muster.

Coco sniffed. "How do you know that?"

Time to tell her the real message she'd come to deliver. She should have done that right away instead of getting into all this personal stuff. "Because of the way he's been so worried about you since yesterday."

Miranda let her words sink in and watched the lines form on Coco's forehead.

"What are you talking about?"

Miranda pulled her hand away and looked down at the floor. She really didn't want to upset her friend any more than she already was. It couldn't be good for the baby. But she had no choice.

"I take it you haven't been watching the news lately."

"No, I haven't."

"Well, there's this story in the headlines. A guy escaped from a prison near Macon."

"Oh, dear."

Miranda heard the "what does this have to do with me?" question in Coco's tone.

She went on. "He was convicted of attempted murder three years ago. Estavez defended him."

"He never told me about that."

"Well, the guy fired Estavez after the first court appearance."

"Oh?" She was even more confused now.

"There's a video of it. The guy got a little violent." No need to go into those details. "Anyway, after the guy went to prison, he wrote Estavez a letter."

"A letter? What—did it say?"

No backing out now. "It was a threat. The guy blamed his conviction on Estavez. He promised he would escape and—" she swallowed as the words caught in her throat.

"And what?"

"And kill Estavez and his family."

Coco blinked hard, taking it in, her breath going in and out. "But if he escaped from prison aren't the police going to catch him?"

"They can't find him. Parker and Estavez and I went to the Macon area yesterday to help search for him. We found out he took a bus to Atlanta."

Coco shot to her feet. "What?"

Miranda rose and took her friend's arm to steady her. "We've all been worried that he got to you. Especially Estavez. Parker has bodyguards at the mansion and at Chatham, Grayson, and McFee. If this guy shows up, they'll capture him."

Looking bewildered, Coco put a hand to her face. "Who is this man?"

"His name is Enrico Bagitelli." Miranda took out her phone and scrolled to a picture she'd snagged from a news story on the way over. Bagitelli's prison mugshot. "Here he is."

Coco stared at it in silence.

She needed something less disturbing. Miranda scrolled back to one of the photos they'd found last night. Bagitelli in a tux standing next to a grand piano in his former life.

"He's a musician?"

Miranda nodded. "A concert pianist. Parker says he's famous."

"Enrico Bagitelli." Coco mulled over the name. "Yes, I know him."

"You do?"

"Not personally. My mother and I used to listen to his CDs when I was learning to play the piano. I always thought his performances were inspiring."

They were inspiring, all right. "Apparently he was inspired to try to kill his sister-in-law. He ran her over with a sports car."

"With a sports car?"

"A Maserati Gran Turismo with a big V-8 engine. The victim's still in a coma. When she passes, the charge against Bagitelli will be upgraded to homicide."

Coco put her hands to her face, her big blue eyes filling with tears again. "Oh, my. Oh, dear. Oh, my. Antonio. I have to see Antonio. I have to speak to him, Miranda."

And with that, she spun around, snatched up her purse, and ran out of the door.

CHAPTER SEVENTEEN

Parker watched the young woman he now fondly thought of as his daughter-in-law burst through the rear door of the kitchen, hurry across the floor, and throw her arms around Antonio.

He was touched by the sight, despite how dire the situation still was. As well as much relieved to verify in person she was alive and well.

And that the baby inside her was, too.

"Oh, Antonio," she said in her sweet voice. "Are you all right?"

Antonio stroked her hair with tenderness. "I'm fine, *mi querida*. I am so relieved to have found you."

Carlotta turned to the couple. "Did she tell you, Coco? About the man who escaped from prison?"

"Miranda? Yes. Where is she?"

After coming down the stairs and entering the kitchen again, Miranda had heard the emotional reunion and had waited behind one of the aluminum shelving units until the embarrassing part was done.

She peeked around the corner and saw Parker smiling at the couple with their arms around each other, staring into each other's eyes as if they had just met and fallen instantly in love.

That was good.

She glanced over at Parker and locked eyes with him. His powerful gaze could always turn her insides to mush, reminding her of all the giddy emotions she felt for him, too. But just now there was more than love in his eyes.

There was worry.

Coco and Estavez and the baby were safe for now, but this case was far from over. Enrico Bagitelli was still out there.

They had to find him. And soon.

"I informed Carlotta about our fugitive while you were upstairs," Parker said to her.

Coco sucked in a breath. "Did she show you the picture?"

Carlotta shrugged a shoulder. "Yes, yes. He does not seem so frightening to me."

Parker didn't like that answer. "I assure you, Carlotta. An escaped criminal can be very dangerous. He's desperate."

She nodded solemnly. "I was wondering why Officers Scott and Nelson were paying me so many visits yesterday afternoon."

"Must be under Lieutenant Erskine's orders." Miranda was glad to hear that.

"Yes." Parker agreed. Then he changed the subject. "Since we're all here, perhaps we could have breakfast together, if it's not too much of an imposition."

Parker was going to make sure they wouldn't go hungry today.

But Coco put a hand to her mouth and shook her head. "Thank you, but I don't think I can eat anything. In fact, just the smell of food in here is making me a little ill."

Uh oh.

Estavez reached for her arm. "I should take you home."

Miranda tensed. They couldn't keep babysitting this pair. They had to keep hunting for Bagitelli.

She gave Parker a frown. "Did your new guy show up at the house?"

Parker nodded. "I checked on him just before Coco came downstairs."

"Oh, dear." Coco turned and rushed for the back door.

Estavez hurried after her.

Miranda followed and stepped outside just in time to see the poor girl hurl over the iron railing.

She turned her head away. "Sheesh." Coco was getting as bad as Fanuzzi.

Parker came up behind her with Carlotta and handed Coco a paper towel.

It wasn't until then that Miranda noticed a woman in a crisp cop uniform walking along the sidewalk. She came up to the bottom of the steps and surveyed the scene with bright hazel eyes.

She seemed young. Maybe mid twenties. Her copper-colored hair was pulled back in braids that hugged either side of her head, and she wore little makeup.

Looking a little green, she put a hand on Coco's shoulder. "Can I help you, ma'am?"

Her expression clearly said she hoped Coco would say no.

Which she did. "No, thank you, Officer. I'm okay now. I just need to go home. This is so embarrassing."

"Nothing to be embarrassed about, *mi querida*." Estavez gently touched his wife's cheek.

"You're a new one," Carlotta said to the officer to change the subject.

"Yes, ma'am." The cop nodded. "I'm Officer Campbell. Just checking in here to make sure everything's all right per Lieutenant Erskine's orders. You're Coco Estavez, aren't you?"

"Yes, I am."

Campbell turned to Estavez. "And you're the attorney whose family we're monitoring?"

"I'm the attorney who was threatened by the man who escaped from Bibb County Correctional yesterday."

"So Lieutenant Erskine explained." Campbell nodded toward the others. "And of course, everyone knows Miranda Steele and Wade Parker."

Miranda couldn't even muster a grimace at that remark, but she was glad they hadn't called Erskine in to find Coco. Talk about embarrassing.

"So how can I help?" Campbell asked.

Miranda's gaze went to the street. Two more manned squad cars sat behind the empty one that had to belong to Campbell. Probably Officers Scott and Nelson. "Do you think you could spare one of you to escort this couple home?"

"I think that would be an excellent idea," Parker said. "And that Hosea would approve."

"Certainly," Campbell said. "Just let me know when you're ready to leave."

CHAPTER EIGHTEEN

They got Coco and Estavez settled into the Lexus, and as the couple pulled away with Campbell's squad car close behind, Miranda returned with Parker to the restaurant's empty dining room.

Parker led her to the booth they always shared, while Carlotta brought out the breakfast she had insisted on making for them—two big plates of delicious huevos rancheros with refried black beans, warm tortillas, and an extra serving of Serrano chiles for her.

Just what she needed.

Along with the scrumptious food, Miranda wanted to indulge in the relief she felt now that Coco and Estavez were safe and sound. But one look at Parker's face told her she couldn't afford to.

She swallowed a bite of spicy scrambled eggs and reached for his hand. "They'll be okay."

He gave her a squeeze and picked up his coffee cup. "What did Coco tell you upstairs?"

No point in sugar coating it. "She thinks Estavez is having an affair."

Parker's brow rose in refined indignation. "That's impossible."

"I agree. But he hasn't been spending a lot of time with her, and it's making her suspicious."

He put down his cup with a clink. "I should have been firmer when I spoke to Antonio about working too many hours a few weeks ago."

It had been over a month since Coco had complained to Parker about Estavez working so much. "What else could you have said?"

Parker didn't answer.

Instead he began attacking his eggs. "Antonio shouldn't be upsetting her like this. She's carrying our grandchild."

Miranda had to smile that Parker thought of the baby that way. "Godchild, anyway."

The couple had asked them to be godparents, and with Gen's love life, this might be the closest Parker would ever come to a grandchild. Even though they were both too young to be grandparents.

Flush that thought.

They ate a while in silence, then Parker stopped, the lines in his face deepening. "When I brought Antonio into my home when he was sixteen, I hoped to instill a work ethic in him. I did not intend to create a workaholic."

This wasn't his fault. She swallowed another bite of the eggs. "He's just worried. Some people turn to work to relieve stress. A lot of stress, a lot of work." A tendency they both had in common with the lawyer.

Parker nodded grimly.

Instead of playing Pollyanna, Miranda decided to change the subject. "I'm thinking of getting Becker to do more research on Bagitelli while we do some legwork."

"Excellent thought. We can check out hotels near the bus station."

"Right. Bagitelli had to find a place to stay." She tapped her fork against her plate. "I wonder if he got wheels, too. Hard to get around this town without them."

"He would need money for that."

"Maybe he tapped into a bank account."

"Or found a friend he could borrow from."

She wasn't sure about that. "How could Bagitelli know he could trust him? Or her?"

Wondering about that, she finished her food. As she took her last bite, her cell rang.

It was Becker.

"Speak of the devil," she said to Parker as she answered it. "Hi, Becker. Sorry about earlier. Is Fanuzzi okay?"

"She's sleeping. Had a really rough night."

"So she told me. We found Coco at the restaurant, by the way."

"Did you? That's a relief."

"Yeah."

"Well, Joanie told me about the fugitive you're hunting, and I decided to do some research on him."

He was ahead of her. Good ole Becker. "What did you find? Wait a minute. Parker's right here. Let me put you on speaker." She laid the phone on the table and pressed the button.

"Good morning, Dave," Parker said in his boss tone.

"Good morning, sir." Becker's voice went up a notch. He was always self-conscious around Parker. He cleared his throat. "As I was saying, I was doing some research, and I talked to Steele's friend, Detective Chambers, at the APD."

"Good ole Chambers," Miranda muttered.

"He said the local police arrested a woman named Dixie Sawyer near Macon yesterday."

"Yes," Parker said. "We spoke to her then, as well."

"In fact, we gave Erskine the lead," Miranda chimed in.

"Chambers didn't mention that."

Of course he didn't. "Never mind. Go on."

"Anyway, Sawyer said she bought the fugitive a ticket to Tallahassee."

"Dixie told us that."

"She did?"

Miranda's shoulders sagged. Becker didn't have anything they could use. "Well, keep working on Bagitelli's background."

"Wait. I'm not done. Chambers said Sawyer gave the police the name of Bagitelli's friend in Tallahassee."

"She did?" Miranda knew that woman had been holding back on them yesterday.

"Eddison Stowe. He's actually the music director of the ASO. That's the—"

"Atlanta Symphony Orchestra. Yes, I know. So did you get Stowe's address in Tallahassee?"

"The police there have already checked it out. Stowe's not in Florida."

She sat up straight. "Do they think something happened to him?"

"No, he's at Symphony Hall downtown. Chambers said Erskine was going to talk to him this morning."

"Thanks, Becker. Good work. Keep digging."

"Sure will, Steele."

She hung up and stared at Parker. "Maybe that's really why Bagitelli came to Atlanta."

Parker was already getting to his feet. "Let's go pay Mr. Stowe a visit and find out."

She wiped her mouth and rose while Parker left a hefty bit of cash on the table for Carlotta. "At least we don't have to worry about Coco any more." For the time being, at least.

"That is a relief." He took her arm, and they hurried back through the kitchen.

CHAPTER NINETEEN

Coco sat quietly as Antonio pulled into the drive of the Parker estate.

Turning her head away, she took in the stones making up the massive facade and the elegant landscaping. It was such a grand place. Like living in a castle. And she'd felt like a princess ever since she'd moved in with Antonio. It was so generous of Mr. Parker's father to offer it to them. She couldn't believe it when he did. She had never even imagined living in a mansion like this.

But after a while, the house started to feel too big for just the two of them. And when Antonio was gone for days at a time, it was starting to feel like a big glorious prison. Maybe that would change now.

Something kicked at her, and she touched her stomach and let out a soft moan.

Concerned, Antonio turned to her. "Are you all right?"

She smiled at him, taking in the sleek black hair he always wore in a ponytail and his dark Latin features. He was so handsome. "I'm fine. Your child's getting active, though."

Antonio touched her protruding belly, and her heart melted. He wasn't just handsome. He was a beautiful person. She didn't understand why a famous concert pianist would come after him. He was the finest defense attorney in Atlanta. Why had Enrico Bagitelli fired him?

It didn't matter. All that mattered was that they were together.

She looked back and saw Officer Campbell had parked her police car alongside the curb. Another car up the road had to be the bodyguard from the Parker Agency. Another generous act.

"Are you hungry now?" Antonio said. "Would you like to have breakfast somewhere?"

She looked at the time on the dash. It was after eight, but she suddenly felt drained. "No, I think I'd like to go back to bed now."

"All right. Do you want me to walk you to the door?"

She frowned. "What do you mean, walk me to the door?"

"I have to go back to work."

Her cheeks flushed with the sudden rage. "You're leaving again?"

"I'm so sorry, *mi querida*. I have a very important meeting with a client this morning."

She couldn't believe her ears. No, this was how it was between them now. How could she have thought that would change?

"More important than being with your wife?" she snapped. "Even when an escaped killer is on the loose?"

Antonio bristled. "We have the Parker Agency people to protect us both." Whether it was guilt or annoyance in his voice, she couldn't tell.

But it only made her even more livid. "Oh, well that makes it just fine."

"I have to work, Coco. Someone has to bring in money."

How dare he. Wasn't it painful enough that she'd lost her job at the Gecko Club? "That was a low blow, Antonio."

"I didn't mean it that way."

She couldn't talk to him. "Never mind. Excuse me. I have work to do, too. I just remembered I need to learn how to make Canapés Lorenzo for Joan." She reached for the door handle and started to climb out of the car.

Antonio reached for her. "*Mi querida—*"

She pushed his hand away. "Don't you *mi querida* me. You should go back to your office now, or you'll be late for your *very important* meeting."

She grabbed her purse, got out, and slammed the door. Then she hurried inside the huge mansion.

CHAPTER TWENTY

Coco didn't slam the front door.

She didn't want to break the decorative glass. Besides, it was too heavy.

Instead, she closed and locked it, then dug a tissue out of her purse and began to bawl.

Her heart was breaking, and Antonio didn't even care. Why didn't he want to be with her? Why didn't he love her anymore? She must be a terrible person. Or maybe she was just boring. Maybe Antonio wasn't interested in her if she couldn't play piano at the Gecko Club.

She heard the engine of the Lexus start and peeked out just as he was backing out the driveway.

Officer Campbell hesitated a moment, then slowly drove past the Parker Agency car. She must have communicated to the driver with some sort of signal, because after a moment she sped up to follow Antonio.

Both of them must have seen her get out of the car and run inside.

How embarrassing.

As she wiped her nose, the baby kicked her again. Harder this time. Ouch. Poor little thing. What kind of a father was he or she going to have? One that was never home?

Maybe Antonio didn't want to be a father. But he'd been so excited when she told him they were having a baby.

She didn't understand.

And right now all she knew was that she had to go to the bathroom.

She used the guest facilities in the hall. After she washed her hands and face in the marble sink, she stared at herself in the mirror.

Her face was puffy, her eyes were red and swollen from all the crying she'd been doing. She looked awful.

No wonder Antonio didn't want to be around her.

Deciding she was a little hungry after all, she wandered down the hall to the kitchen. Even if she could go without eating, she should do it for the baby.

She put her purse on the table in the breakfast nook and started for the kitchen.

At the far end of the island, she stopped cold and let out a loud squeal.

There was a man standing near the sink, staring at her.

What in the world?

He was dressed in dark clothes, a rumpled shirt and jacket, baggy pants, and had a black ball cap on his head, with the bill pulled down to hide his features.

"How did you get in here?" she gasped, as soon as she could catch her breath.

He pointed over her shoulder. "Through the glass doors."

His low voice startled her. And he had a slight accent. Italian.

She peered hard into his dark eyes and recognized the man in the photos Miranda had shown her earlier, though he looked more worn and hardened than he had in the one from prison. And the hair sticking out from under that ball cap had strange greenish-blond streaks. It was true.

This was Enrico Bagitelli.

The famous classical pianist. Escaped convict. The man who had threatened to kill Antonio and his family. Dear Lord.

Her heart pounding, she shook her head. "Those doors were locked."

"You left a key under the mat."

Her mind raced. Had Antonio put it there? Had he told her about it? She couldn't remember. It didn't matter. Think. Say something.

"There's a guard out front," she blurted out.

"I know. I had to park two blocks away and go through the trees."

She peeked around the counter and saw the mud on his shoes and pant cuffs. "You went through the creek that runs back there?"

"It will be worth it."

His words made her shiver.

"Never mind about that. Where is your husband?"

Antonio. He wanted Antonio. No. If only she could get to her cell phone and call for help. But it was in her purse, back on the table.

"Where is he?" Enrico shouted.

She jumped. "At work."

"At work again? But he left you here alone last night to go to work."

He'd been watching the house. And he had probably followed Antonio to his office. He might have gotten to him then if it hadn't been for the Parker Agency bodyguard there.

"Why isn't he home now?" Bagitelli demanded.

"You'd have to ask him that." The anger she still felt from her fight with Antonio came through her tone.

Bagitelli frowned at her with what seemed like curiosity. Then he muttered something to himself. He sounded crazy.

It wasn't until then that she noticed he was standing near the block of knives on the counter. She'd just sharpened them for chopping the apples for the fritters. Joan said a good cook always had sharp knives.

As if Bagitelli had read her mind, he turned to the block, reached for a blade, and pulled it out. He'd selected the biggest one.

The butcher knife.

Feeling dizzy with fear, Coco leaned against the island and put a hand to her belly. "Please don't hurt me."

Bagitelli glared at her stomach in shock as if he'd just noticed it. "You are with child."

And he was going to kill both of them. She'd never get to see her baby.

The man muttered something again, then waved the knife at her. "You must come with me. Can you drive?"

She scowled. "Of course, I can. I'm not helpless just because I'm pregnant."

He blinked at her as if he didn't know what to make of that remark. Then he jabbed the knife in the air. "We need to go now."

"Wh—where are we going?"

"You'll see. I said now!"

Before the guard outside realized something wasn't right. She held up her hands. "Okay. My car's in the garage."

"No. We're going the way I came in."

"Through the woods?"

"Yes, through the woods."

"But I'm not sure I can—"

"You can and you will." He was getting louder and angrier. "Now turn around slowly and get going."

She didn't want to do it. She didn't want to go off somewhere with a man who was obviously disturbed, a man who had threatened to kill Antonio, a man who now had a butcher knife in his hand.

But she had no choice.

She did as he said and turned around.

Bagitelli stepped up behind her, grabbed her arm, and held the knife between her shoulder blades. "Slowly."

"Slowly. Sure." Her heart sinking with despair, she made her way to the table, picked up her purse.

Bagitelli stayed close behind her with that knife.

Hoping she could somehow send a signal for help, she stepped through the glass doors and onto the deck.

But as Bagitelli ushered her down the stairs and across the backyard, Coco feared no one would find her until it was too late.

CHAPTER TWENTY-ONE

The downtown arts center was a huge sprawling campus of white buildings that housed exhibition spaces, meeting rooms, and lots of stages, auditoriums, and performance halls.

After traversing what seemed like miles of honey-colored wooden floors, passing walls lined with modern art sculptures and strange paintings of geometric shapes depicting weird-looking people, Miranda and Parker found Eddison Stowe's office on the second floor.

As they approached the open door, Miranda heard a trumpet playing a series of notes impressively fast.

She peeked inside and saw a thin man at a sleek black desk holding a large computer screen. His wiry body was dressed in a black turtleneck and slacks, his hair was a closely cropped silver, and his narrow features were pinched together in concentration.

The look of a refined artist with impeccable taste in the middle of a creation.

Humming, he waved a skinny arm in the air, played another flourish on the trumpet, then reached for his mouse to make a note on the screen, which Miranda could see was filled with electronic sheet music.

Parker rapped on the door frame. "Mr. Stowe?"

The man shot up straight in his chair, reached for a pair of dark-rimmed glasses and peered at his visitors with a frown. "Yes?"

"So sorry to disturb you. We're wondering if we might have a moment of your time."

Stowe's frown deepened. "I was expecting our cellist. But yes, yes, come in," he said in an ultra cultured tone.

Miranda stepped into the roomy corner space.

It was bright, airy, and littered with musical things. A baby grand in the corner, clarinets on a shelf, festival awards and photos of performances on the walls. Next to the baby grand were chairs and stands with sheet music on them.

Stowe put down his trumpet and switched windows on his screen. "I don't see an appointment here. What news organization did you say you were from?"

"We didn't. I'm Wade Parker from the Parker Investigative Agency and this is my partner Miranda Steele."

Stowe's pencil thin gray brows shot up. "Private investigators?"

"We're looking into a police matter. We thought you might be able to give us some information."

Now Stowe's thin shoulders sagged. "This is about Enrico, isn't it?"

"Enrico Bagitelli, yes."

"The police came to see me at home last night. I told them everything. I don't know what else I can tell you."

Miranda glanced at Parker. Good ole Erskine was holding out on them. And so was good ole Chambers.

Parker put on his I'd-be-happy-to-make-a-generous-donation-to-the-orchestra smile. Though his family probably routinely did that, anyway. "We'd like to verify what we know."

"All right. Very well. Shall we sit?" He gestured to the corner opposite the piano where a sleek modern-style pale blue sofa and two matching chairs sat.

Miranda took the one nearest the door, while Parker sat in the other chair, leaving the sofa for the music director.

Stowe stepped to a small refrigerator behind his desk, removed three small water bottles and put them down on the marble coffee table between the couch and the chairs.

He sat down with a sigh. "What would you like to know?"

Parker gave her a nod.

Miranda smiled at the man and decided to start out easy. "You're a long time friend of Enrico Bagitelli, right Mr. Stowe?"

"That's correct, Ms—"

"Steele."

"Ms. Steele. We've known each other professionally for years. I met him in Vienna. I was visiting the city, hoping to steal the oboist away from the Philharmonic." He chuckled, then grew pensive. "Enrico was playing a concert down the street, so I went to listen."

He stopped talking.

"And?"

Stowe closed his eyes and pressed a hand to his chest. "And he was exquisite. I had seen many a pianist in my day, but I had never heard such power, such mastery of the instrument. His intonation, his cadence, his touch. It was all simply breathtaking."

Yeah, yeah, everybody thought he was great. That much they already knew.

"And?" Miranda said again.

Stowe looked at her as if she were a little dense. "Well, of course, I went backstage and introduced myself. We connected. I asked him if he would consider doing a concert here in Atlanta with the orchestra. His schedule was booked at the time, but a few months later, we managed it. After that, he performed here regularly over the years."

"You became friends."

"Yes. Of course, he was touring worldwide, and my schedule was always full, but we made time to chat now and then."

Old buddies. "I understand you have a house in Tallahassee?"

Stowe's back went stiff. The police had probably asked him the same question. "Yes, I do."

"Did you ever invite Bagitelli there?"

"Occasionally. We used to golf at the country club. He was a terrible golfer. Fiona would come with him. She always beat both of us."

Fiona. The wife and some time duet partner. "Would she? What about her sister?"

"Rosalynd? Yes, she would come, too. That poor girl. Such a tragedy."

So Rosalynd was Fiona's sister. "Wasn't that odd?"

"Odd?"

"To bring your sister-in-law on vacation?"

Stowe chuckled. "Enrico always brought people with him. Besides, a musician never takes a real vacation. There was always at least a few hours of practice every day."

"Rosalynd was part of the act?"

Stowe frowned as if he didn't like the way she put that. "Rosalynd was an accomplished pianist in her own right."

"There isn't much about her on the Internet."

Stowe thought about that a moment. "I believe Fiona had everything she could taken down, she was so grief stricken after the incident."

Understandable, but not the information they were looking for. Miranda reached for her bottle of water, twisted the cap off, and took a sip. "How often do you go there now, Mr. Stowe?"

"To Tallahassee?"

"To Tallahassee."

He shuffled uncomfortably in his seat. "Not very these days. In fact, I've been thinking of selling the place."

"But you were there recently, right?"

He inhaled through his narrow nostrils as if taking in rarified air from somewhere high above her. "No, I haven't been there for several months."

"So Bagitelli contacted you here in Atlanta?"

He coughed and stared at her. "The police asked me the same question. No, Ms. Steele, Enrico has not contacted me."

"Are you sure?"

"Of course, I'm sure. That's hardly something that would slip my mind."

She tapped her fingers on her knee and gave Stowe a hard glare. "How much money did you give him?"

Stowe's eyes flashed as his thin back went straight. "How could I give him money if I didn't see him, Ms. Steele?"

Clearing his throat, Parker put a hand on Miranda's arm as if pulling off an attack dog. "Mr. Stowe," he said gently. "We learned yesterday that Mr. Bagitelli was given a bus ticket to Tallahassee by the person who helped him escape from prison."

Stowe's eyes and mouth opened wide with what seemed like genuine shock.

"Once he got out, Mr. Bagitelli changed his mind and exchanged the ticket for one to Atlanta. Why would he do that?"

"I don't know, but he didn't come to see me." Stowe leaned forward, put his head in his hands, stroking his hair as if to soothe himself. "I've been busy preparing for our May concert and wasn't paying attention to the news. I didn't know anything about all this until an officer knocked on my door last night."

More was coming. Miranda waited for it.

Stowe began to shake his bowed head. "Poor Enrico. He made such a mess of his life. And now this. He had such a successful career. But nothing seemed to satisfy him."

"What do you mean?"

"That's not the right way to put it. I don't mean to give you the wrong impression. Enrico had a sensitive side. He could be so thoughtful and tender. He was generous, always looking to help new musicians improve their craft. But he could be temperamental and moody and impatient, as well. Especially when the music wasn't going just right. Over the last few years he seemed to be getting worse. I urged him to get help. I do think he was seeing a therapist."

That was news. "Do you know who that was?"

"No. He never told me. But I saw him taking medication, so I assumed."

And he probably hadn't taken any since leaving prison. Not good.

Stowe opened his water bottle and drank it all down in one swallow. Then he sat back and stared into space. After a moment, he began to speak. "That night. It was awful. Enrico had had a bad week."

"Bad week?" Miranda prompted, now trying to sound as gentle as Parker.

"We were rehearsing Tchaikovsky's *Piano Concerto No. 2*. Enrico thought the tempo was too slow, not forceful enough. He banged his fists down on the keyboard and began screaming at me and the entire orchestra. He called us imbeciles. He said we were all second-rate musicians and needed to go back to conservatory. The flautist threatened to quit. The first violinist wanted me to cancel the concert."

"And did you?"

He shook his head. "We worked things out with the orchestra, though Enrico was still angry with Rosalynd."

"She was playing?"

"She and Enrico were playing a duet of Beethoven's *Moonlight Sonata*. Nothing she could do pleased him. He was arguing with Fiona, too, as I recall."

"What about?"

"I think Fiona felt she wasn't getting enough recognition. I think she wanted to go out on tour on her own."

More news. "Oh?"

"That's just speculation on my part. But in the end the performance went off smoothly. And then—it was all over. The *Moonlight Sonata* was the last piece he played."

Suddenly, what he was saying clicked into place. "Are you talking about the night Rosalynd was—?"

He put up a hand, as if he couldn't bear to hear the words. "I was in the back, finishing up and going over my notes. I always jot things down after a performance. Fiona came rushing in through the back door, screaming. Ivan was there, too. He was Fiona's assistant. And some others. They said Enrico was on his knees in the parking lot and couldn't get up. That didn't make sense. And then they told me what had happened to Rosalynd. I ran outside, and then it was sheer chaos. There were sirens shrieking and ambulances and EMTs and police everywhere. It was dreadful. Absolutely dreadful. The last thing I remember was the vision of an officer putting Enrico into the back of a police car and driving him away." He dug his fingers into his forehead and grew silent.

Miranda sat staring at the man. So Eddison Stowe had conducted Bagitelli's last concert. The night of the "incident."

Silence hung in the air for a long moment, then she heard Parker draw in a slow breath. "Mr. Stowe, do you have any idea where Enrico might have gone?"

Coming back to the present, Stowe blinked and shook his head. "Not really. He owned several properties in New York. He liked Georgia. He and Fiona had a farm east of the city."

"East of Atlanta?"

"Yes."

"Do you have an address?"

He thought a moment. "No, I was never there. Fiona may have sold it. As I understand, she's retired to *Bellissima*."

Miranda frowned. "What's *Bellissima*?"

"It's a resort in Saint Simons that Enrico and Fiona owned together. Fiona owns it now. Rosalynd is in a private hospice near there."

"Do you have a phone number or an address?"

"No, I haven't heard from Fiona since the night of the incident."

They weren't getting anything more from this man, but Parker handed him a card anyway. "Thank you for your time, Mr. Stowe. If you think of anything else, please contact me."

"Yes, I will."

They got up to leave.

Looking a little lost, Stowe walked them to the door. "Mr. Parker?"

"Yes?"

"If you do find Enrico, please tell him I'm sorry."

CHAPTER TWENTY-TWO

Back in the car, Miranda pondered what Stowe had told them and how it would impact their next move.

"What does Stowe have to feel sorry for?"

Parker waited for a free spot, then pulled into traffic. "He feels responsible because he saw the signs of trouble and didn't do anything."

"Not much he could do. Bagitelli was a grown man." She held up a finger. "Before we leave—"

But Parker had already put on his blinker and was getting into the left lane. He gave her a sly grin. "We should take a look at the parking lot."

"Right."

He'd read her mind the way he'd done so many times before.

Despite the situation, it gave her a little thrill.

Parker pulled into a limited access road, rolled past a field where a huge white sculpture of what looked like a globe on steroids stood. He made a turn at the end of the long building on the opposite side.

And there they were.

The narrow stretch of parking lot lay before them, silent and ominous, even though it was broad daylight.

Parker stopped the car, and Miranda got out and strolled up the rising pavement to the curve.

She took in the wispy trees alongside the gray building with its horizontal concrete slabs. On the other side of the lot stood matching trees and the iron fencing that guarded the drop-off. The majestic Atlanta skyline jutted up in the distance.

Only a few cars were parked here now, spread out from each other, similar to the video. The typical white lines marked the spots for diagonal parking, a row on either side with a narrow lane down the middle.

"Let me have your phone."

Parker handed it to her.

She took it and brought up the video of the incident. She started it and watched the lone woman in black appear on the screen. Pausing the video, she took a few steps and held up the phone to match the scene. "Whoever filmed this was tall."

Crossing to the middle of the lot, carefully she moved over the asphalt until she was parallel to a big oak tree along the railing.

She pointed to the middle lane. "Rosalynd was walking right about here."

Stroking his chin, Parker studied her from a vacant space near the building. "And Bagitelli must have pulled out of one of these spots here." He gestured behind himself.

"Right." She pressed Play and studied the video again. Then she stopped it and took about five steps back. He was driving here, racing along in his Gran Turismo, and hit her hard. She moved back over to the spot where Rosalynd had been struck and considered the frozen image on the screen. "Hmm."

"What is it?"

She crossed back to Parker's side of the lot and held up the phone again. She turned her head one way, then the other.

Parker came up beside her and peered over her shoulder. "Ah, I see."

She was standing at the end of a parking space two over from the side of Bagitelli's vehicle. The image was smaller, of course, but the angle fit perfectly.

"Whoever took this video had to be standing right here."

"And he—or she— happened to capture Bagitelli's vehicle just as Ms. Rosalynd was hit."

"My guess is male from the height." Miranda felt irritated with the lack of information. "Was it someone getting into his own car? Why don't we have a name? And how did he capture what happened at just the right second?"

"Perhaps he heard the engine and wanted to prove someone was speeding in the parking lot."

"To turn him in?"

"It's a possible explanation."

They needed something definite. "Worried about safety a little too late."

With the phone still in position, she hit Play again, and let the gruesome scene play out once more.

Over her shoulder, Parker watched in silence, and they both tensed in disgust.

She thought of the things Stowe had told them about that night. "Bagitelli mows her down because she played some bad notes? There has to be more to it."

"More we need to discover." Parker sounded very determined.

She shook her head. "Why'd you do that, Enrico? Why'd you run over your own sister-in-law?" A thought came to her. "In that music video we saw last night, Bagitelli was playing *Moonlight Sonata* with Fiona, right?"

"Correct."

"We didn't find any duets with Bagitelli and Rosalynd."

"They may have been pulled down, as Stowe told us."

"Yeah. And maybe there was some jealousy among this trio. As in too many pianists spoil the tune?"

"Again, it's a possibility."

"A strong one, I'd say. If Bagitelli was fighting with both of the women in his life and career, and tempers were high, anything could have set him off. Especially if he wasn't taking his medication."

"Assuming he was on medication. Stowe was speculating about that."

Her shoulders slumped. Parker's devil's advocate had a point. They needed more information. And whether that information would help them find this sucker was anyone's guess.

She handed the phone back to Parker, dug out her own, and dialed Becker.

He answered on the first ring. "What do you need, Steele?"

"Can you get a transcript of the trial?"

"Already done. Had to do an end run around the process since the normal requests would have taken weeks."

She might have known. Her old work buddy never stopped impressing her. "Good work."

"Don't say that yet. It's over a thousand pages long."

She hated they were so shorthanded. Cursing Holloway's crush on his ex-wife under her breath, she straightened her shoulders and went into boss mode. "See if you can get Smith to help you." Though she had Smith training the IITs, along with her regular duties.

"Okay, but is there anything specific you're looking for?"

"See if you can find out who took the video of the incident."

"There was a video?"

She'd forgotten she hadn't told him about that. "Yeah. I'll send it to you. Find what you can about it in that transcript."

"I'll do my best."

"Oh, and we went to visit Eddison Stowe. We're at the arts center now."

"Are you? Does he have an idea where Bagitelli is?"

"No, but he told us Bagitelli owned several properties in Georgia with his wife, Fiona. A farm east of Atlanta, and a resort in Saint Simons. Not much to go on, but see if you can find those addresses."

"On it." He clicked off.

She thought about that poor injured woman lying in a hospice near Saint Simons for all these years. Her heart went out to her.

They had to find this guy.

"Where is Saint Simons, anyway?" she said to Parker.

"Along the coast. It's part of the Golden Isles, which includes Sea Island and Jekyll Island. It's more than eighty miles south of Savannah. It wouldn't do much good to head there."

No. A reclusive wife and a woman in a coma wouldn't tell them much. Besides, Bagitelli was still here, hunting for Estavez.

"Let's head to the bus station."

"Just what I was about to suggest."

###

They walked back to the car and were just climbing in when Miranda's cell went off again. Did Becker have something so soon?

Pulling it out of her pocket, she scowled at the display.

It was Gen.

Resisting the urge to roll her eyes, she answered. "Hi, Gen."

"Miranda, where in the world are you?" She sounded tired and even crankier than usual.

"Gen, I need to tell you about—"

"Do you really expect me to do all this planning for the baby shower all by myself? The *double* baby shower?"

"No, but there's something I—"

"Really, I didn't think you'd be this inconsiderate. Coco and Joan are supposed to be your friends, aren't they?"

"Put her on speaker," Parker said. Gen had been loud enough for him to hear everything she'd said.

Happily, Miranda pushed the button.

"Gen, this is your father."

Gen's tone turned sugary sweet. For her. "Daddy. Are you and Miranda together? I didn't mean to—"

"We're on a case. A personal one. Your brother's in trouble."

"Antonio? What kind of trouble?"

Briefly, Parker explained about the prison break, the threatening letter Bagitelli had written, and what they were doing to find the fugitive.

Sucking in a breath of shock, Gen turned into a feeling human being. "Oh, my. I can't believe it. Is Antonio all right?"

"He's fine. He's at home with Coco. Hopefully they're getting some rest."

Gen let out a worried moan. "This is terrible. Is there anything I can do?"

"Can you handle the preparations for the baby shower? I need Miranda's help right now."

Silence. After a moment, Gen spoke again, sounding uncharacteristically flustered. "I—er—well, all right. I suppose I can get Sybil to help me."

Parker didn't mince words with her. "Because of this situation, the shower may have to be postponed."

"Yes. I understand, Daddy. I'll make things tentative."

"I know you can handle it."

"Yes, Daddy. I'll handle it." She clicked off.

Gen sounded so dazed, Miranda felt a tinge of guilt. "I wish I were better at party planning."

Parker scoffed. "You and I both know Gen is extremely efficient at social gatherings. She'll figure things out."

Yeah, she would.

But as Parker turned onto Fifteenth Street and the sun hit her eyes, Miranda wondered whether they'd be having that double baby shower at all.

CHAPTER TWENTY-THREE

Coco stared at the treetops whizzing by above the interstate bridge and felt more helpless than she ever had in her life.

Even when she'd been married to Dexter.

The rumble of semis and box trucks and other cars around her made her want to burst into tears. But she couldn't do that.

She had to hold it together.

They had picked their way through the grassy backyards of the neighborhood, going through the trees and crossing the creek in a shallow spot. But she'd still gotten her open-toed designer sandals muddy, which made her mad.

Bagitelli's car had been parked along the curb between two houses whose owners she didn't know. It wasn't a nice car. It was an older model in a pea green with a front bench seat. He'd forced her into the passenger side, then made her scoot across to the wheel.

She had to drive so he could keep that knife on her. He held it low on the seat so nobody could see it.

They had gone through the neighborhoods passing the stately homes in the area. She'd peered out the window, hoping for someone jogging or walking a dog. She'd spotted a few people, but there was no way to signal for help.

Not with that knife beside her.

They headed toward Midtown, taking Peachtree and 13th Street and Memorial Drive. When they reached the on ramp to I-20 she knew there was no possibility of anyone helping her.

And now they had been driving for over an hour.

Where was he taking her? And why?

"Don't go too fast."

"Was I? Sorry." She really hadn't meant to. It was just nerves. Struggling to steady herself, she eased off the accelerator.

She dared to glance at him and saw he had her purse on his lap and was rummaging through it.

Was he stealing her identity? Her credit cards? "What are you looking for?"

"This." He pulled out her cell phone.

Oh, my. If only she could use it to call someone for help.

He held it up. "I heard someone in prison say you can track someone with one of these. Is that true?"

"I don't know. Maybe."

He pressed the button on the side and a jingle played as it went off.

He shook his head, muttering to himself. 'No, no. That wasn't enough. What else did he say?" He sat up. "That's right."

He toyed with her cell for several moments, and then pulled the bottom out of it. "The battery. You have to remove the battery."

She seemed to remember Miranda saying something about that. Or maybe it was Joan when she told her about what had happened to her and Dave in Paris.

Dave had been kidnapped. It had sounded so awful, and Coco knew Joan hadn't even told her all the details. But she knew that was how Dave had lost the tip of his little finger.

She shuddered.

And then she remembered that Miranda and Wade were still looking for Bagitelli. They were the best detectives in the world. If they could find Dave in Paris, surely they could find her.

They would, she told herself. They had to.

But as another eighteen wheeler roared past her window and she glanced down at the knife on the seat, she only hoped they would do it in time.

CHAPTER TWENTY-FOUR

Miranda stood at the ticket counter of the downtown Atlanta bus station and stared into the eyes of a surly looking dark-haired woman in a navy form-fitting suit.

"For the third time, ma'am, I don't know anything."

"Are you sure you didn't see this man?" Miranda held up her phone with Bagitelli's picture. "He would have arrived on the one a.m. bus from Macon Thursday morning."

"I'm on the day shift, ma'am."

So the woman kept telling her. "Surely you have video of passengers entering and exiting the station." She'd already spotted the cameras.

The woman thinned her lips. "You'd have to talk to the manager about that."

"All right."

"All right?"

"All right, let me see the manager."

With a murderous look, the woman straightened her shoulders. "I believe he's in a meeting until noon."

Miranda lowered her voice to a growl. "I'd like to remind you this is a police matter."

She was unimpressed. "The police were here earlier. They already talked to the manager."

"Did the manager give them the video?"

"Do I look like someone he would consult? Excuse me. I have work to do." She gestured for Miranda to step aside.

Parker gave the woman his best to-die-for smile and handed her his card as he eyed her name tag. "If you do learn any information that might help us, Ms. Sweeney, please feel free to give me a call."

Without returning his smile, the woman took the card and again gestured for both of them to move aside.

Even Parker's charms hadn't worked on that one.

Suppressing a growl, Miranda stepped away and took in the station. The linoleum floor that needed mopping. The bored people sitting around in uncomfortable looking wire benches waiting for their buses to board. A man on a cell phone, his luggage assembled around him on the floor. A woman complaining to her companion about her boyfriend's snoring.

They knew Bagitelli had been here. They knew what time he was here. They just didn't know where he went from here.

She noticed a heavy-set security guard eyeing them. Maybe he could get them that video.

She trotted over to him. "Excuse me, sir. We're with the Parker Agency and—"

"Yes, ma'am. I heard you over there. You were very loud."

Annoyed by the comment, Miranda twisted her lips. "Well, then. Can you help us get that video?"

The guard rocked back on his heels. "I'm not authorized to do that ma'am. But if you want to know what went on here last night, you should ask George over there."

"George?"

"We just call him that. Don't know his real name. He's a regular. Always here, sitting by the door, waiting for who knows what. Homeless guy." The guard nodded toward the row of vending machines along the wall.

Miranda scanned the noisy screens and spotted a gangly man stretched out on the floor between the exit and the last machine.

She glanced back at Parker.

He seemed resigned to the choice. Only one they had at the moment.

"Thank you, sir," she said to the guard and headed for the dude.

George—or whoever he was—had a scraggly beard on a receding chin, long matted hair, and was clad in a pair of faded work pants and a shirt that had seen better days. His shoes looked in good shape, though. Air Jordans.

As she approached, she got a whiff of him. He smelled pretty gamey.

Ignoring the odor, she cleared her throat. "Excuse me, sir."

He didn't answer. It wasn't until then that she saw the earbuds under all that hair. He had his eyes closed and was humming to some tune on his cell phone, which was plugged into an outlet on the wall. The reason he'd chosen this location to nest in, she surmised.

"Excuse me," she said louder, but the man seemed to be in a trance. Might have had a buzz on. How could this dude have seen Bagitelli?

Parker reached over and tapped him on the shoulder.

Instead of startling. George—or whatever his name was—opened one eye and grinned. It was kind of a creepy grin.

He pulled out his earbuds. "Ah, the detectives. I was wondering when you'd get around to me."

"Oh, you were, were you?" Parker's BS sensors were up.

George waved toward the desk. "I heard you talking to Sweeney over there. She's a hard one."

"Then you know who we're looking for," Miranda said.

"Sure do. That escaped convict."

This guy was more alert than he looked. "Did you see him last night?"

"Sure did. He came through here just before three in the morning. Didn't know he was wanted then. I saw the story this morning on the TV." He pointed to a flat screen running the news in the corner of the ceiling.

"Do you have any idea of where he went from here?" The answer would be no. Miranda was sure this was another dead end.

But George said, "Sure do. I talked to him."

Miranda blinked at him in surprise. "You did?"

"Sure did. He was looking for a place to stay."

"What did you tell him?" Parker said.

"I told him he should try Spire Gardens on Pollard, near what used to be Turner Field. Cheapest place I know. If you don't mind crawly critters."

Miranda wondered how George knew about the place. Maybe he'd stayed there before his funds ran out. Maybe Bagitelli's would, too, and he'd join him on the streets.

"MARTA don't run at that hour," George continued. "I s'ppose he took a cab to the hotel. Or he might have walked. It's just a little more than a mile. But it's a dicey stroll at that hour."

Miranda was stunned. This was it. The lead they so desperately needed. They might find Bagitelli in his room.

Parker held out a bill to the man. "Thank you, sir. You've been very helpful."

George waved it off. "Keep it."

"You've provided an important service to the authorities."

"Just doing my civic duty. Oh, and if you think I'm homeless, you're wrong. I'm a minimalist."

Miranda wrinkled her nose. "A what?"

"An extreme minimalist. In fact, I'm on a pilgrimage. I'm trying to see how many days I can survive on just twenty dollars. This is day forty-two."

This dude was either crazy or filled with wisdom. Either way, all Miranda felt toward him was gratitude.

"We wish you the best," Parker told him.

George saluted him before he replaced his earbuds. "Same to both of you."

CHAPTER TWENTY-FIVE

They were past Madison now.

Coco's heart sank as she saw the sign for the next county. "Where are you taking me?" she dared to ask.

"Patience," Bagitelli said in his Italian accent, as if he were scolding a child. "It isn't much farther."

They had left the interstate a while ago.

As they'd rolled along, the trees had grown denser, the fields wider, and the homes sparser. They passed cows and horses grazing in fenced in meadows.

This was farmland.

Acres of farmland dotted by dense pine forests. You could bury a body under those trees and no one would find it for years.

Coco spotted a black colt grazing near its mother along a white fence near the roadside. She wished she could climb onto her back and gallop away.

"No, Papa. I will not." Bagitelli was muttering to himself again. He'd done that a lot since they'd left.

"I must play again. I must. You know they would not let me play there."

His words suddenly made sense to her. "You mean in prison?"

He turned to her, surprise in his dark sunken eyes. "Yes, of course, in prison. They would not let me play piano in prison."

She felt a wave of compassion for him. "That's terrible."

He shuddered visibly. "It was like a death."

"Oh, I know. Isn't it awful?"

He glared at her. "What do you know about it?"

The anger she still felt at her former boss made the words spill out. "I used to play at a club on the Strip."

"You play the piano?"

"Yes. And I sing. Pop songs. Not the classical pieces you do."

"You know my work?"

"Yes. I used to listen to you when I was learning to play. I always thought you were magnificent." Actually, she'd sort of had a crush on him.

He stared at her in disbelief.

"Anyway, I used to play at this place on the Strip. An upscale place. The Gecko Club. Three weeks ago, the manager fired me."

Bagitelli frowned. "Why did he do that?"

"He said I was too fat."

"Didn't he know you are pregnant?"

"Yes, he did. But that part was even worse. He said a pregnant lady wasn't the right image for the club."

"How rude."

"Wasn't it? I was so mad, I went home and cried for days."

Bagitelli shook his head. "Why do women cry when they are angry? Tears are for sadness."

"I don't know, but we do."

He was silent for a long moment, and just when Coco thought he was going to start talking to himself again, he sat up and pointed out the window.

"This is it. Turn in here."

They were here? Oh, dear. What did that mean?

But she did as he said. Slowing the car, she turned onto a narrow paved drive and followed it. Lazily it wove around a clump of willow trees. Dense oaks stood on the other side. She knew it.

This was where he was going to kill her.

But after she steered the car through several more curves, the woods opened up to a huge yard and a sprawling house as big as the Parker mansion.

Stunned, Coco took in the elegant cobblestone siding, the majestic white columns, the tall half-circle arched windows.

"What is this place?"

"*La Mia Terra.*"

The Spanish she'd learned from Antonio told her the Italian words meant something like, "My Land." Bagitelli owned this place? But not anymore.

"Turn off the car."

His words made her shiver, but she did as he said. He snatched the keys out of the ignition, picked up the knife, and pointed at her. "Now open the door and get out."

"Okay." The driver's side door squeaked as she opened it.

She slid out and stood, feeling stiff and uncomfortable from the long drive. She wanted to stretch, but didn't dare.

Bagitelli climbed out after her, holding both the knife and her purse. "Come."

They headed across the yard and up the steps. When they reached the front door, Bagitelli put his hand under one of the stones and pulled out a key.

He was good at finding hidden keys, wasn't he?

He put the key in the front door, and it opened.

Then gesturing with the knife, he ushered her inside.

CHAPTER TWENTY-SIX

Coco's footsteps echoed against a real hickory floor as she moved through a foyer and into a high-ceilinged sitting room with a huge stone chimney and leather furniture in masculine browns and tans.

"This way."

Bagitelli led her to a more formal living room, past a cozy looking sofa done in a neutral paisley, antique-looking side tables and lamps, and into a spacious dining room with a large polished table, old-world style chairs, and a candelabra chandelier.

It reminded her of the dining room in the Parker mansion.

They moved under another archway and reached an open area with more sofas, a Persian carpet, and a built-in bookcase. A huge kitchen sat off to the side. It had richly carved cream-colored cabinetry, brushed bronze pulls, and a huge island with an ivory granite top.

Bagitelli went to the far end of the island and put down her purse and the knife.

She should have tried to make a run for it.

But the room beyond the kitchen had Coco sucking in her breath. She stepped to the edge of a large semicircular space filled with dazzling light from the tall windows. Outside lay a lush green field.

And inside, taking up most of the floor, were two shimmering ebony grand pianos.

"Oh, my," she sighed. "They're gorgeous."

Clasping her hands together, she moved to the nearest keyboard and stared down at it reverently.

Bagitelli's dark Italian voice came over her shoulder. "Would you like to try it?"

She turned to him. "Do you mean play it?"

"I don't know whether Fiona has had them tuned recently, but she seems to have kept up the rest of the place."

That much was true. She hadn't seen a speck of dust anywhere.

Wait. Fiona? Was that his housekeeper? No. Now she remembered. Fiona was Enrico Bagitelli's wife. They used to play duets together. They must have practiced on these very instruments.

"Go ahead," Bagitelli urged.

Cocoa hesitated. "I haven't played in three weeks."

He smirked. "I haven't played in over three years."

Once again, her heart broke for him. She couldn't imagine not being able to play for so long.

She'd try. She pulled out the bench, sat down, and ran her fingers over the keys in an arpeggio. The rich overtones resonated through the room, sending chills through her.

"You were right. It is in tune. And its sound is incredible."

"It's a Bechstein. They both are."

She'd seen the logo on its side, and knew it was the very top of the line. Made in Germany and costing hundreds of thousands of dollars. She'd never dreamed she'd play one.

"Well?" Bagitelli said.

Taking a deep breath, she mentally ran through her repertoire, played the opening bars, and broke into *Stormy Weather*.

One of her favorites.

The lyrics were hard to get through. She'd forgotten how sad they were, but pushing thoughts of Antonio out of her mind, she sang through all the verses and ended strong with "keeps raining all of the time" on a dramatic glissando.

As the notes hung in the air, she turned her head and saw there were tears in Bagitelli's eyes.

"That was lovely."

"Thank you."

"You have such intensity of feeling."

A compliment like that from the world famous musician was more than she had ever dreamed of. There was such longing on his face. She knew he wanted to play, too.

Straightening her shoulders she looked him in the eye. "Your turn."

"Me? It has been too long."

"It comes back. Like riding a bicycle."

He scowled and shook his head. "What if I have lost what I had?"

"What if you haven't?"

He stared at her as if she'd almost convinced him.

"Let's play something together. I know. Didn't you used to play this with Fiona?"

Turning back to the keyboard, she played the familiar staccato introductory notes, alternating hands.

Bagitelli came alive. He rushed to the other keyboard, sat down and played the whimsical notes of the *Waltz of the Sugarplum Fairy*.

Coco continued the bass line, keeping the rhythm to his melody. And sneaking a peek under the piano lids, she saw a smile on his face.

As soon as they finished, she started another one of the duets he was famous for. And another and another. They played through the first movement of Beethoven's *Fifth*, a tricky Mozart Sonata, Schubert's *Marche Militaire*.

She wasn't afraid anymore. How could someone with so much music in his soul be dangerous?

And in a strange sort of way, Coco thought that neither of them had ever been happier.

CHAPTER TWENTY-SEVEN

Letting out a breath of frustration that was almost a groan, Miranda took in the plain single room on the third floor of Spire Gardens.

It was a generic hotel room. Chair by the window. Dresser. TV. The bed was unmade. The Do Not Disturb sign on the door had given her some hope, but there was no other sign of life here.

No clothes in the drawers or the closet. No backpack.

It looked like Bagitelli had checked out without letting anyone know.

A grimace came from the woman they had found at the desk and talked into letting them see this room. "I'm so sorry, Mr. Parker, Ms. Steele. It seems the man you're looking for isn't here."

She'd told them that man had registered under the name John E. Smith, and had a drivers license to that effect.

Now Dixie Sawyer could add identity theft to her list of offenses.

The ID information wouldn't do them much good, either. Dixie had been smart enough to use two of the most common names in the US.

Miranda strolled over to the overstuffed trash can and saw empty soda cans and food wrappers. The smell of some of it told her it was a day old. He hadn't wanted the maids in here cleaning up and noticing anything suspicious.

"There's something here."

Miranda turned and watched Parker disappear into the bathroom.

She hurried over and peeked inside. Used towels were piled in a corner on the floor. The complimentary soaps had been used, and the sink needed cleaning.

But Parker was focused on the trash can in there.

He pulled on a rubber glove he retrieved from his pocket, bent over the receptacle, and lifted a box with a lovely model on the front.

Miranda's brows rose. "Hair dye."

"Blonde and Beautiful." Parker's voice was filled with disgust.

She tiptoed over and saw the remains of the dye job paraphernalia in the bottom of the can.

So now the description the police had out for Bagitelli would have to be changed.

She let out a huff. "Doesn't tell us where he went from here."

"No, it doesn't." Parker put the box back and took off his glove.

Just then, the door opened, and a short, round-faced woman entered. She stared at the woman from the desk in obvious confusion. "I am so sorry, Ms. Patel. Is there something wrong here? The Do Not Disturb sign was on the door for two days. We could not clean."

"There's nothing wrong, Mia," the woman sighed. "But it seems we've been harboring a fugitive."

Mia's mouth opened in horror. "A fugitive? How?"

Parker stepped to the door and addressed the maid. "Did you happen to see the man who was occupying this room, ma'am?"

"No, sir. I don't think so. Wait. Yesterday morning. He stopped me at the end of the hall near the elevator and asked me where he could get breakfast."

"What did you tell him?"

"I told him most everyone goes to the diner next door."

Had they just found a real lead?

"Thank you. That's very helpful."

"You are welcome. Oh. But it wasn't breakfast time. It was almost time for lunch. After eleven."

"Thank you again." Her pulse rushing with excitement, Miranda started for the door.

As she reached it, Ms. Patel said, "Is there anything else we can do?"

Parker turned back to answer. "Call the police. And don't clean this room until they get here."

CHAPTER TWENTY-EIGHT

They hurried down the creaky elevator, out the front door of the lobby, and across the parking lot.

"There it is." Parker nodded to a box-shaped place beyond a deserted fenced-in pool.

As fast as she could go, Miranda hurried across the rough pavement to the entrance under a bright yellow sign reading "Grits & Gravy."

But when she saw the sparse crowd inside through the window, her heart sank. "It's after ten, Parker. Do you really think anyone's going to remember a customer from almost twenty-four hours ago?"

"We're about to find out."

He opened the door for her, and she stepped inside to the smell of coffee, bacon, and waffles. They moved to the counter.

A family sat at a booth in the corner. Mother, father, two kids. The youngest was a little boy indulging in pancakes with whipped cream, which he'd managed to get in his hair. His mother scowled and began wiping him with a napkin.

At the other end of the counter a large man was sipping on coffee.

At the grill stood a young man in a brown apron, blue shirt, and matching cap making loud scraping noises with his spatula.

Two waitresses in similar uniforms were chatting near a refrigerator case of pies. One was shorter and older looking. The other was young and thin.

"And so he was like, 'did she really mean that?' And I was like, 'she sure did. Cross my heart.'"

"And did he go for it?" asked the thin one.

"Sure did. Said he was breaking up with her tonight. And then he asked for my number. Do you think I should text him?"

Parker cleared his throat loudly, and the younger waitress spun around, wide-eyed.

The older one tapped her arm. "Looks like you've got a customer, Amanda."

Amanda put on a big I-want-a-nice-tip smile, took out her order pad and pen, and approached. "What can I get for you?"

"Information, we hope."

"What sort of information?" Amanda seemed even younger close up. She wore little makeup and had a tiny nose ring in one nostril. That and a few wisps of dark hair escaping from under her cap gave her a naive look.

Matching her graciousness, Parker smiled back as he handed her his card. "My name is Wade Parker of the Parker Investigative Agency and this is my partner, Miranda Steele. We're looking for a person of interest."

Her eyes went wide. "Person of interest?"

"A man. He stayed at Spire Gardens. We think he had breakfast here yesterday morning."

She looked perplexed. "We get a lot of people from Spire Gardens. What time was he here?"

"We understand it was late morning. Between eleven and noon."

She scratched under her cap with her pen. "Yeah, I was here then, but that's our busiest time. Can you give me a description?"

"We'll do better than that." Miranda pulled out her phone, flipped to Bagitelli's prison picture, and held it up.

Amanda squinted at the image, her nose wrinkling. But she recognized him. "His hair was a different color."

"Let me guess. Blonde?"

"Sort of. More like streaks of pale green. Like he'd gone to a bad hairdresser."

"Okay." That had to be him. A classical pianist wouldn't be in the habit of dying his own hair. Very likely he would have botched it.

"And he had a ballcap on. Kinda like he didn't want anybody to see his face. But I saw it when he ordered. I remember those eyes." Amanda pointed at the screen.

There was more.

"What else do you remember?" Parker said gently.

Amanda bit her lip. "Well…"

"What?"

She shifted her weight as if she had an itch somewhere. "Is this guy in trouble?"

Miranda glanced at Parker and knew it was time for the big guns. "He escaped from prison before dawn on Thursday," she said. "He was convicted of attempted murder."

Amanda's hand went to her heart. She began to shake her head. "Oh, no. That can't be."

"Why do you say that?"

"Well—" She squirmed some more.

Miranda leaned over the counter. "Well what?"

"He—he said he needed a ride. I let him use the Uber app on my phone to get one."

"You let a stranger use your phone?"

"He seemed harmless enough. I was right here watching him."

Miranda wanted to give this girl a lecture on security.

Parker picked up the questioning. "Do you know where he went?"

"No. He didn't say."

"May we see your phone?"

"What for?"

Now she wanted to be cautious?

Parker smiled patiently. "We'd like to check your ride history."

"Okay, sure." She reached into her pocket.

A shrill voice came from the back. "Amanda!"

"That's the manager. Hold on a minute." She hurried over to the open door. "What is it?"

She disappeared into the opening, and the voices became muffled.

Miranda ground her teeth and muttered under her breath. "This is a waste of time."

Instead of telling her to be patient, Parker remained silent. His look was hard and angry.

Miranda was about to ask someone to go get Amanda when the heavyset man at the end of the counter finished his coffee, slid off his stool, and waddled up to the cash register.

He was dressed in overalls and a T-shirt, and had short gray hair under a ball cap, which he tipped at them and nodded. "Couldn't help overhearing your conversation. I think I know where the man you're talking about went."

Miranda put a hand on her hip. "Oh yeah?" Or was he just looking for gossip?

He chuckled at her skepticism. "Yes, ma'am. I'm a regular here. Yesterday I was standing outside having a smoke. The man asked me if I knew where he could get a good used car cheap."

"What did you tell him?"

"I told him Wheel Deals was probably his best bet."

"Wheel Deals. That's a dealership?"

"Yes, ma'am."

"And you think that's where the Uber driver took him?"

"That's what it looked like to me. I saw the man using Amanda's phone when I went back inside. She's a trusting sort. I didn't know he was a criminal, or I would have stopped her and called the cops."

Parker was already searching on his phone. "This Wheel Deals. It's on Metropolitan Parkway?"

"That's it. Just a couple miles south of here."

"Thank you for your help, sir."

"No problem. I hope you catch that guy. There was something about him that seemed a little off. Hope he don't hurt nobody."

Parker stiffened as they turned to go. "That's exactly what we're hoping to prevent."

CHAPTER TWENTY-NINE

It had seemed like a good idea to walk to the hotel from the bus station instead of fighting traffic and hunting another parking space. But now they had to hoof it all the way from Spire Gardens back to the car, passing the same sleazy-looking crew as they had an hour or so ago.

The overly-tattooed men hanging around cyclone fences and in the recesses of old, abandoned buildings reminded Miranda of the dudes who'd worked for a client of hers when she'd been on her own.

The extreme minimalist pilgrim, George, hadn't mentioned the walk was a dicey stroll at any hour.

But at last they reached the Mazda and found it hadn't been broken into.

Glad she hadn't had to waste time using her martial arts skills to teach some scumbag a lesson, Miranda slid into the passenger seat and buckled up as she locked the door.

Quickly Parker put the car in gear and pulled off, but when they reached I-85, they hit late morning traffic.

It was mostly trucks and work vehicles on their way to unload deliveries, repair plumbing, or cut grass—and taking their sweet time to get there, but it still slowed them down.

Miranda let out the groan she'd been suppressing since the hotel. "Bagitelli's three steps ahead of us, Parker. And if he's got wheels now—"

"All we can do is follow the leads we have." He sounded calmer than he was.

Still, he was right. They had to follow the leads and put one foot in front of the other. Even if they had to go at a snail's pace.

She was about to cuss at the traffic when her cell rang. It was Becker.

Hoping for a miracle, she answered, putting her phone on speaker. "What do you have for us?"

His reply was a big yawn. "Sorry. Rough night."

Once more guilt stabbed at her for disturbing her friends earlier. "Is Fanuzzi asleep?"

"Finally. I'm trying to keep as quiet as I can. Pretty easy reading this transcript. Lots of boring legal procedural stuff." He yawned again. "Smith's going to work on it later. Right now, she's at the firing range with the IITs."

Miranda's heart sank. "You haven't gotten anything out of the transcript?"

"So far, mostly that Bagitelli's second defense attorney didn't do a very good job. Looks like he didn't even try to prove the pianist was innocent. He just kept saying 'my client didn't mean to hurt the victim.' And he said Bagitelli insisted he didn't remember driving the car that night."

Hard to paint him as innocent with that video. But that didn't tell them where Bagitelli was now. "You didn't call to tell me that."

"No. I've got information on those properties Bagitelli used to own."

She sat up straight. "Shoot."

"The farm east of the city is actually a horse farm. Or it was. Sole ownership was transferred to Fiona after Bagitelli's conviction."

"Does she still own it?"

"She owned it jointly with Bagitelli, so it passed to her. Bagitelli was her legal name, though she went by Fiona Delacroix."

Miranda recalled that from her research with Parker. "Her stage name, right?"

"She used it that way. Fiona claimed to be a descendant of the French Romantic artist of the same name, but Delacroix was actually her mother's maiden name. Seems her mother divorced Fiona's father when she was ten."

"Oh." Sounded like Fiona hadn't had an easy life, even if she was loaded.

"Anyway, the farm is about forty miles southeast of Madison. They named it *La Mia Terra*. That means 'my land' in Italian."

How original. "What else?"

"*Bellissima* is a popular beach front resort on the southern coast of Saint Simons Island. It's pricey, but it's got everything. Beachfront villas, resort residences, hot tubs, tennis courts, oceanfront five-star dining, a golf course. Even has a music hall where Bagitelli used to give concerts. He also owned a private home nearby. They called it the Villa. Fiona secluded herself there after the conviction, but the past year she's started to give occasional concerts there with Ivan Bruzek."

Stowe had mentioned Ivan. "I thought he was her assistant."

"Sounds like he's her duet partner now. They're putting on a concert tonight at nine, in fact."

Hmm. "Anything else?"

"The sister-in-law is in Island Oasis Hospice Care. It's in Brunswick, about thirty minutes from *Bellissima*."

Close but not too close. Miranda didn't know what to make of that. "Is that it?"

"For now."

"Okay, thanks. Send all that over to me in an email."

"Will do."

"Oh, and good work. Keep at that transcript."

"On it. Right after I get more coffee." Yawning again, Becker hung up.

She appreciated his dedication. He was pretty amazing. But she wasn't sure what good the information he'd dug up would do them right now.

With a sigh, she stuffed her phone back in her pocket and saw Parker had turned off the interstate. They were approaching a small lot south of Metropolitan that was wedged between a red brick warehouse and a construction site.

"Lots of chain link fencing around here." Each property's barricade was about eight feet tall.

"Not unusual for this area," Parker said without commenting on Becker's call.

"I'll bet Dobermans roam the premises at night."

"I'd wager you're correct."

She looked up at the big sign on the pole and read it aloud. "'Wheel Deals. If you need wheels, we've got a deal for you.'" Three red exclamation marks ended the statement, followed by a yellow happy face. "Creative."

"Let's see how happy they were to deal with our fugitive." Parker turned into the lot and cruised down a row of used cars with various prices scrawled across their windshields.

The numbers seemed a tad inflated to Miranda. "They definitely want to make a profit."

"Hmm." Parker pulled into an empty spot.

Miranda scanned the inventory. It seemed to consist of four double rows of cars with about a dozen vehicles along each. A trailer sat near the back of the lot. She didn't see any customers anywhere. "What approach should we take?"

"Let's look around for a bit. If they think we're potential buyers, we'll see an eager salesman in short order."

"Sounds good to me."

They got out and began looking over the vehicles on display.

There was a ten-year-old Ford Fusion. A dark blue Accord. A white Volvo.

Most were in the range of several thousand dollars. Too much for the cash Bagitelli had.

Miranda was peeking through the window of a red Corolla that had seen better days when a high-pitched male voice came over her shoulder.

"Well, hello there, little lady. What can I do you for?"

Raising a brow, Miranda straightened and caught sight of a short skinny man coming out of the trailer. He hurried toward her with quick strides.

He looked to be in his early thirties, and he had on khaki slacks, a bright blue jacket, a matching bow tie, and a smile as big as Kentucky.

When he was a few yards away, he pointed an accusatory finger at her. "I see you have your eye on that Corolla. It's a real beauty. Cloth seats. Keyless entry. Powerful A/C. Just the thing to cool down a hot number like yourself."

Miranda was thinking about showing this guy a kick in the good spot that could raise his voice another octave when Parker stepped forward and cleared his throat. "Good day, sir."

"Oh, hello—uh, sir. I didn't see you there."

"Obviously."

He fumbled with his blue bowtie. "My apologies. I was just excited imagining you and your lovely lady behind the wheel of this beauty." He pointed a finger at the Corolla, then extended a hand to Parker. "Manny Dandy. At your service."

Raising a dignified brow, Parker shook hands. "We're sorry to disappoint you, Mr. Dandy. But we're not in the market for a vehicle today."

"You're not?" Dandy's face turned from overjoyed to an expression that clearly said, "Then what are you doing here wasting my time?"

It was Miranda's turn to do the honors. She dug into her pocket, pulled out a business card, and handed it to the dude. "I'm Miranda Steele, and this is Wade Parker. We're from the Parker Investigative Agency."

"You're private investigators? Our company is completely above board. All our inventory is obtained legally and registered properly. We have the CARFAX on—"

Parker held up a hand. "We're not here about your vehicles, Mr. Dandy."

"You're not?" Dandy squeaked.

"Except for the one you might have sold to this guy." Once again Miranda took out her phone, scrolled to Bagitelli's picture and showed it to Dandy.

Dandy stared at it with bulging eyes and a drooping jaw.

"Have you seen this man lately?"

Dandy's jaw went up and down a few times before the words came out. "He was here yesterday."

"Around noon?"

"Yes. How did you know?"

Parker gestured to the phone. "This is Enrico Bagitelli. He escaped from prison in Macon around one a.m. Thursday."

Dandy shook his head. "No, that can't be right. That wasn't his name."

Parker narrowed his eyes at the man. "Did you sell him a vehicle, Mr. Dandy?"

"No. That wasn't him. It might look like him, but he had to be somebody else. He had greenish-blonde streaks in his hair."

Miranda stuck the phone in Dandy's face. "Are you sure this wasn't your customer?"

"Okay. I sold somebody who looked like that a car yesterday."

"What did you sell him?"

"Oh, it was a real sweet number. A Crown Vic. Lovely green sedan. New paint job. Eight cylinders, four point six liter engine. A real beauty. And a real steal."

Miranda put her phone away. "How did he pay for it?"

"Pay for it?" Dandy raised his shoulders. "I don't remember. I'd have to check the paperwork."

"Let's do that now." Parker's tone was dark and threatening.

"We're awfully busy in the office."

Right.

"Now," Parker repeated.

Clearly Dandy wished they would leave, but he was probably smart enough to see that would get him in a lot of trouble.

He raised his hands in surrender. "Okay, okay. Follow me."

They followed him through the cars and up the aluminum steps of the trailer. Inside, the air was stuffy and the decor sparse. Dandy hurried over to a cube in the corner.

Inside the cube was a desk made of a simple slab of fake wood. Behind the desk sat a man in a light suit with thick curly dark hair and thick dark-rimmed glasses.

The man stood up, smiling, ready to shake hands. "Did you get us another customer, Manny?"

"Not exactly. This is Roger Arrowhead, our Finance Manager. Roger, these folks are private investigators asking about the guy we sold the Crown Vic to yesterday."

Roger sank back into his chair without shaking hands. "Say what?"

Dandy consulted the card Miranda had given him. "Miranda Steele and Wade Parker." He set the card gingerly on the desk.

"Do you have the paperwork from that sale?" Parker asked.

"What do you need that for?"

"They say it's not legit," Dandy told him.

"Of course, it is. I have it right here." Looking insulted, Arrowhead turned to a filing cabinet behind him and opened a drawer. After a minute, he pulled out a manilla folder. "Here it is." He opened the folder on his desk. "John E. Smith. Have a copy of his driver's license right here."

Miranda snatched the paper out of his hand and peered at it. It was Bagitelli, all right. Looked almost the same as his prison photo. Dixie Sawyer had a few skills, didn't she? The information on it was fake, but it was worth having.

She held up the paper. "Can we have a copy of this?"

"Why?"

Dandy pointed his thumb at their guests. "They say he's an escaped criminal."

Arrowhead scowled. "That's not possible. We checked him out. Everything came out fine."

"Are you sure?" Miranda said.

"Well, we only did the preliminary credit check. But it was fine."

Miranda glanced at Parker. It was identity theft, all right. "How much did he pay for the vehicle?"

Roger looked at Dandy. "You gave him the special deal."

Dandy scratched his head. "Yeah, I guess I did."

"What's the special deal?"

Dandy shrugged. "Zero percent down."

"So he paid you nothing yesterday?"

Arrowhead tapped a finger on the paperwork. "We arranged financing. Low payments of fifty-six twenty-five a month."

Probably for the rest of his life.

Parker drew in a breath. "The vehicle has a Temporary Operating Permit, as required by law, doesn't it?"

"A TOP?" Arrowhead bobbed his head. "Of course, it does. All our vehicles do."

"Can you look that up?"

"Uh—"

Miranda leaned over the desk. "Did we mention we're working with the police on this matter?"

Arrowhead ran a finger under his collar. "I'd be happy to look it up for you, Ms. Steele. But our system's down right now. I've got a call out to our technician. He should be here in about an hour."

Oh, brother. That was all they needed.

"We'll wait," Parker growled and stomped out of the room.

CHAPTER THIRTY

Miranda followed Parker to the part of the trailer that served as a lobby. It was a small area with a couple rows of metal chairs, a vending machine, and a fake potted palm in the corner.

He sat down and reached for his phone, while she paced.

She hadn't seen him this angry in a while. This case was getting to him.

"It's going to be okay," she told him. "Once we get that TOP number, it will give us what we need to find that vehicle."

He nodded. "I'm texting the information to Hosea, as well as the other details about the Crown Victoria."

"Good idea."

Once he finished, he called his bodyguards and told them what to be on the lookout for.

"Neither of them has seen a vehicle matching the description we have," he told her after he'd hung up. "No sign of activity at either station."

Miranda sat down next to him and stared out the window at the road beyond the cars for sale and the chain link fence. Not much traffic out there. No sign of a computer repair guy heading this way.

Twenty minutes went by and nothing changed.

She was thinking about calling in Becker when Parker's phone went off.

"It's Antonio." He put it on speaker, but turned the sound down a bit so that only she could hear. "What is it, son? Is everything all right?"

"I'm not sure, Papa."

Miranda felt Parker tense.

"What's wrong?"

"I've been trying to call Coco, but I can't get a hold of her."

Miranda frowned. "Aren't you at the Parker estate with her?"

"No. I dropped her off at home this morning and went back to work. I had a meeting with a client."

He hadn't been home much in the past twenty-four hours. She had to ask. "Did you have another fight?"

His defeated exhale came through the phone. "She didn't understand why I had to go back to work."

Miranda didn't understand that, either.

Parker was having trouble with it, too. With a disgusted look, he handed the phone to her and got to his feet. He strolled to the end of the chairs and stared out the window.

"And now she won't answer my calls," Estavez moaned.

"Maybe she's asleep," Miranda told him.

"She's a light sleeper. She always answers her phone."

"Maybe she went back to your mother's?"

"No. I just called there."

"Fanuzzi's?"

"Not there, either."

Miranda decided to mention the obvious. "Maybe she just doesn't want to talk to you."

"Maybe, but I have a bad feeling."

She'd been having bad feelings since all this started. They weren't getting any better. She inhaled. "Well, we have bad news and good news."

"What's the bad news?"

"Bagitelli has wheels. We're at the lot where he bought a car yesterday."

"So he could be anywhere." Estavez sounded far away.

"Anywhere he can get on a full tank of gas."

Estavez cursed under his breath. "What's the good news?"

"We know the make and model." She gave him the details. "Neither of the bodyguards has seen a vehicle matching that description. We just gave the information to Erskine."

Estavez was silent, digesting the news. Finally he spoke. "I'm going home to talk to Coco. I think she's blocking my calls."

At that, Parker came back to where Miranda sat. "Why do you think that, son?"

"It only rings twice and then goes to voicemail."

Her stomach growing tight, Miranda stared up at Parker. That could mean she blocked him. Or something worse. They needed to find out which.

Fast.

"We'll meet you at the house," Parker told Estavez. "We should get there around the same time you do."

Miranda handed the phone back to Parker and stomped back over to the Finance Manager's office.

"Arrowhead," she growled.

Startled, he sat straight up in his chair. "What is it, Ms. Steele?"

She pointed at her business card on his desk. "We have to leave. As soon as you get that TOP number, call us."

"Yes, ma'am."

Then she turned and hurried out the door with Parker.

CHAPTER THIRTY-ONE

They played for hours.
Piece after piece from the master's famous repertoire. More classical tunes than Coco realized she knew. *The Sorcerer's Apprentice*. Brahms' *Hungarian Dance*. *The Waltz of the Flowers*. *Clair de Lune*. She even tried to follow him on *Chopin's Prelude No. 24*.
When they got to Sinding's *Rustle of Spring*, she had to stop.
She couldn't keep up with the intricate finger movements. The rapid, right hand arpeggio that always sounded like a waterfall to her, was gorgeous, but too fast. And when he reached the powerful D-flat major climax, all she could do was lean her chin in her hand and listen in awe. The emotion was so raw, so overwhelming.
Prison hadn't diminished this man's ability at all.
Now the sonorous notes of the *Moonlight Sonata* were reverberating up to the high ceiling.
He played it with tremendous feeling. And as she peeked around the instruments, she saw his face was covered with tears.
He played the final chord, raised his head to the ceiling, and cried out. "Rosalynd. Oh, my beloved Rosalynd. What have I done to you?"
Rosalynd? Who was that? The woman he had killed? Or tried to.
Coco was about to ask when Bagitelli rose from the piano bench with an anguished cry. He hurried to the kitchen and began opening cabinets, slamming them shut again. "Where is it? I know it's here. Fiona always kept some here."
He began opening and closing drawers. He was scaring her again.
But she got up and went to the end of the island. "What are you looking for?"
"Never mind," he growled, making her jump.

Coco eyed her purse and the butcher knife still on the far end of the island. She wanted to grab them, but Bagitelli was at the cabinets there now, slamming away.

"Where is it?" he cried.

"What are you looking for?" she dared to ask again.

"Medicine."

"What kind of medicine? I have aspirin in my purse." If only he'd let her get to it.

He ignored her and pressed both hands to the sides of his head as if he had a ferocious headache. "No, Papa. I played it correctly. I played it with love."

Papa? There was no one there.

He pointed toward a blender on a far counter. "Ludwig. You know it's true. You know it." He spun around and faced the stainless steel refrigerator. "No, Papa. I cannot do that. I will not do that." He started to cry again. "Rosalynd. My poor, poor Rosalynd."

"Is that your sister-in-law?"

Bagitelli spun around and glared at her with his large bloodshot eyes, as if he'd just remembered she was here. "They said I tried to kill her. They are liars. I would never hurt her. I loved her. I still love her. I am innocent."

Coco's heart was in her throat. "Would you like to talk about it?"

Bagitelli's wild eyes rolled around the room. "Yes. Ludwig. You are right. That's exactly what I must do."

Suddenly he grabbed her purse and spilled its contents out on the granite slab. Fumbling through hair brushes and makeup, he found her phone again and its battery. He put them together, picked up the butcher knife, and came toward her, waving it.

Coco screamed and backed away. "Please don't hurt me. Don't hurt my baby."

Bagitelli caught up to her and held out the phone. "Call your husband."

"What?"

"You heard me. Call your husband."

CHAPTER THIRTY-TWO

When they passed the bodyguard's vehicle in front of the Parker estate, Miranda's whole body tensed.

It was empty.

"What's going on, Parker?"

"We're going to find out." Parker pulled up behind Estavez's Lexus, which was already in the driveway.

They got out and rushed to the front door. This time they found it open.

Not a good sign.

Hands on their weapons, they hurried through the halls, and back to the kitchen again.

They found Estavez standing under the archway staring at the floor. His hands were balled into two tight fists.

When he saw them come in, he pointed downward. "Look," he said, tears in his voice. "Just look."

Miranda made her way around the table and looked down at the floor. Her heart nearly stopped. "Shoe prints."

"Muddy ones," Parker stepped past them and bent down to examine the marks on the polished tile.

But Miranda had already seen what they were. "A man's shoes."

"Looks like an athletic pair."

No doubt the pair Dixie Sawyer had stuffed in that backpack she left in her car.

And then Parker rose and followed the prints out to the breakfast nook and all the way to the sliding glass door.

With one finger, he slid back the door, revealing the deck and more prints. "It's open," He said grimly.

"*Dios mio!*"

Estavez's anguished cry tore Miranda's heart out. Parker's face was harder than the granite countertops.

"Oh, no. Oh, no."

At the sound of a man's voice, Miranda hurried to the open door and saw Bill Taylor, the Agency's bodyguard, climbing up the stairs from the lawn.

"I'm so sorry, sir," he said to Parker.

Parker stepped onto the deck. "What happened here, Taylor?"

Looking distressed, Taylor came to a halt on the second step. "When you called earlier, I decided to risk a ride around the neighborhood. Two blocks away I found a woman walking her dog. She said she'd been out this morning and saw an old green Crown Vic parked near the sidewalk. Pea green, she said it was."

"No." Miranda couldn't breathe.

"She said a man and a pregnant woman were getting into it. I found a trail of muddy shoe prints and followed it here."

Miranda put a hand to her head. "They must have gone through the creek."

"Did you see any blood?" Parker asked.

"No."

"There's none in here, either."

That gave them a little hope.

"Her purse is gone," Estavez said. "She always leaves it on the table."

They all stared at the empty spot without any idea of how to find her.

A phone rang.

Miranda jumped as she watched Estavez pull his cell out of his pocket.

"It's Coco."

"Put it on speaker," Parker said. "No one else say a word."

Nodding, Estavez laid the phone on the table and pressed the buttons. "Coco?"

"Oh, Antonio." She was crying.

"*Mi querida*. Are you all right? Where are you?"

"I'm okay. I'm—at a farm."

She didn't sound okay. She sounded terrified.

"He—he wants you to come."

"Who does?"

There was shuffling, and a dark voice with a slight Italian accent came through the phone. "Antonio Estavez."

"Yes, this is he."

"This is Enrico Bagitelli. If you want to see your wife again, you will come here to speak to me. Alone."

Miranda could almost see Estavez's heart pounding through his shirt. He looked at Parker.

Parker nodded.

Estavez spoke into the phone again. "Yes, I will come. Tell me where you are."

"*La Mia Terra.*" He reeled off the address, but Miranda already had it in the email Becker had sent. "Turn into the lane between the willows and the oaks."

"I'll be there as fast as I can."

"Remember. Come alone. No police."

He hung up.

"I'm going to that farm." Snatching up his phone, Estavez started toward the front of the house.

Parker grabbed him by the arm.

"Let me go, Papa. I have to save my wife."

"You're not going to that farm, son. We are."

"You heard what Bagitelli said. Come alone."

"They always say that," Miranda told him. "We know how to handle a situation like this. You don't."

"I must save her." With a wild look of adrenaline-reinforced terror, he pulled out of Parker's grasp and ran down the hall.

Miranda shot after him.

Parker turned to Taylor. "Gather all the evidence you can here and lock up. Don't call the police until I tell you to."

"Yes, sir."

CHAPTER THIRTY-THREE

Miranda ran through the halls of the mansion after the desperate lawyer, glad she knew the layout. When she pushed through the front door, she spotted Estavez already climbing into his Lexus. But he wasn't going to get very far.

Parker's Mazda was blocking him in.

She hurried over to the Lexus and yanked open the driver's door before Estavez could lock it.

"Move over. I'm driving."

They might not be able to stop him from going to that farm, but she wasn't going to let him behind the wheel.

Parker raced past her and got into the Mazda. "Follow me there."

They were on the same wavelength.

"You're too upset to drive," she told Estavez.

With a sullen scowl, leaving the engine running, he got out and hurried around to the passenger side just as Parker squealed out of the driveway and down the street.

Miranda buckled up, waited for Estavez to get in, and followed Parker, with the tires of the Lexus protesting just as loudly.

They sped through the neighborhoods to West Paces Ferry, and Miranda took the curves and hills of the familiar lanes as if she were in a slalom race.

Parker was still way ahead of her, but she kept up.

And yet, as they headed for the interstate, the sound of Bagitelli's agitated voice on the phone came back to her. He was definitely crazy. There was no telling what he might do. And that farm was a long way away.

Even with their speed, she feared they might not get there in time.

CHAPTER THIRTY-FOUR

They zoomed down I-75, zigzagging around a Chevy Spark, an eighteen wheeler hauling groceries, and several SUVs.

After taking the curvy ramp to I-20 like it was a carnival ride, there was more skirting around drivers, most of whom enjoyed laying on the horn.

Miranda wanted to return the sentiment, but instead she concentrated on the Mazda's rear end. She liked to drive fast, but Parker was faster, and she was struggling to keep up with him.

She only hoped no cops ran them down.

Half an hour later, on the straight stretch of highway that ran all across the state to the Savannah River, they were roaring past Decatur where tall trees peeked over the interstate's sound walls. Businesses and towns began to grow sparse as they flew past signs for restaurants and gas stations and their corresponding exits.

After another forty minutes, they hit Rockdale County.

Even though Parker was leading the way, when she'd pulled out of the driveway, Miranda had handed Estavez her phone and told him to punch the address for *La Mia Terra* into the GPS to give him something to do.

Now she watched the towns passing on the screen.

Conyers, Covington, Oxford. They reminded her of the trek to that house where they'd caught up to Adam Tannenburg months ago. He had been a musician, too.

A very sick one.

Nerves prickling her insides, she glanced at Estavez and saw him rubbing his temples and moaning.

"She's going to be okay," she told him, sounding more confident than she felt. "Coco's a strong woman. She'll keep her head."

He nodded, but she could tell he knew she was just trying to keep him from panicking.

Shaking his head, he stared out the window. "I am such a bad husband."

"No, you're not."

"Yes, I am. Look what I've done to my wife."

"This isn't your fault. It's going to be okay. We're going to get Coco away from Bagitelli and send him back to prison. Then everything will be back to normal." She hoped.

"And what is that?"

A good question. "You know. Marriage. Work. Life." They were about to have a baby, for Pete's sake.

Estavez growled at himself. "I can handle clients. I can handle any case in the courtroom. But marriage? Most of the time I don't know what I'm doing."

An odd statement, coming from a man raised by Parker. Parker always oozed confidence, especially around women. She always thought Estavez did, too.

But then marriage was a different game.

She wasn't the one to give out marital advice, but since she'd met Parker, she'd learned a thing or two about commitment. And forgiveness.

"None of us knows what we're doing when we get married," she told him. "Everybody makes mistakes."

Estavez shook his head. "All I do is make mistakes. Coco is right. I work too much."

Miranda was surprised to hear him admit that. Glancing over at his handsome youthful face, the pain on it told her he wanted to say more.

She let him.

"I never should have left Coco alone today. I thought I was protecting her. I thought if Bagitelli wanted me, he would come to my office, or catch me going to my car."

Was that what he'd been thinking? "The Agency bodyguard must have scared him away."

"He must have seen the one at the house, too."

Which was why Bagitelli had found a back way in. Miranda wished the Agency had had more manpower to put in the neighborhood, but it was too late for that now. "We have to stay focused." She nodded toward the GPS. "We're getting there as fast as we can. This will all be over soon."

Estavez's face went hard with determination. "If we capture this madman, if we save Coco, the best thing I can do for her is to let her go."

Say what? "What are you talking about, Estavez?"

"I'm no good for her, Miranda."

Coco had told her Estavez didn't want to stay at home with her. "Is that why you've been working so much?"

"I work because it's all I know how to do. I look at my beautiful wife, I watch her belly growing bigger, and I can't bear it. I have to get away."

Miranda thought of the fears Coco had confessed to her. If she was going to do amateur marriage counseling, might as well go all the way. "Do you still love her?"

It was a question Mr. P had asked her once.

He turned to her in shock at the question. "Of course, I do. I love her more than my life."

"Then why do you want to leave her?"

He slumped in his seat again. "I don't know how to explain it."

"Try me."

He took a moment to gather his thoughts. "I have two younger sisters."

"Yes, I know. Dulcea and Belita." She'd seen them at the restaurant this morning. Dulcea was in high school. Belita was about nine, as she recalled.

"Dulcea and I have the same father. He was killed when my mother was carrying her."

"I didn't know that." Parker had never told her much about his surrogate son's past.

"Years later, my mother remarried the man who was Belita's father. He was in the army and was killed in battle overseas when she was two."

"That's awful. Your mother's been through a lot."

"Yes, she has."

Miranda didn't know where Estavez was going with this, but she let him talk.

"My father was a very bad man. He was a drug dealer who was in and out of prison the whole time my mother was married to him."

"Oh." Something else she didn't know, though she'd imagined something like that scenario.

Estavez let out a bitter smirk. "If he made any money selling drugs, he didn't spend it on his family. We were destitute. My mother struggled for years until she could scrape together enough money to buy the restaurant. I was sixteen when my father was killed in a gunfight. My mother was carrying Dulcea. I was so angry when I heard the news. The questions haunted me. Why did he let himself get killed? Why didn't he take care of us? Why didn't he love us?"

As they passed the exit to Madison, Estavez took several deep breaths.

"That was when I took to the streets. I joined a gang and started robbing convenience stores. I didn't do that long. That was when Señor Parker found me."

That part she knew about. "You cut him with a knife."

She was very familiar with the scars on Parker's abdomen.

"He should have sent me to prison. Instead, he took me to his house and raised me as his own son."

With Carlotta's permission. "And you grew up to be a successful defense attorney, and now you have a beautiful wife. You're about to become a father. Happy ending, right?"

He shook his head and his voice dropped to a low whisper. "What if I turn out to be like him?"

"Like your real father?"

He nodded.

"But Parker raised you."

"But my father's blood is in my veins. The first time Coco and I had a fight, I could feel him coming out in me. I was so angry, I couldn't think straight. All I knew was that I had to get away from her."

This reminded her of a conversation she'd had with Mackenzie once. Nature over nurture. Or vice versa.

"From that moment, I knew all I could do is to make sure Coco and the baby are provided for. I swore to myself I would not leave her destitute like my father did. That is why I work so much. I have to take care of her while I can."

"You're a good man, Antonio. I know that. Parker knows that. And Coco especially knows that."

"What if I hurt her the way my father did?"

"You've already hurt her."

"What do you mean?"

Miranda hesitated only a second, then let it out. "She thinks you're having an affair."

"No, no, no. I could never do that to her. I couldn't live with myself."

That was a relief to hear, but there was no way she could fix this mess. The couple would have to do that for themselves.

She took a deep breath and once again donned the marriage counselor's hat. "Right now, we have to concentrate on getting to Coco and getting Bagitelli back in prison. But as soon as we do, I think you need to have a long talk with her and tell her everything you just told me."

He blinked at her as if that was something he'd never thought about.

Slowly he nodded. "You are right, Miranda."

She was glad to hear him say that. Now if they could just get to that scenario.

Somewhere in Morgan County they turned off the interstate and headed deep into the country.

Miranda watched the dot on the GPS map inch near its destination. And then, there it was, just as Bagitelli had described it. The narrow lane lined with willows and oaks.

Parker's taillights glowed as he turned into it.

Here we go, she thought, and followed him.

CHAPTER THIRTY-FIVE

Halfway down the shady lane, Parker pulled the Mazda over as close as he could get to the trees.

While Miranda followed suit behind him, he turned off the car, got out, and came over to her window.

She lowered it. "What's the plan?"

"We'll go the rest of the way on foot and get an idea of the layout."

She nodded. "Sounds good."

He pointed at Estavez. "Meanwhile you stay in the car."

"But Papa—"

"That's an order, Antonio. Once we leave, wait forty minutes. If we don't contact you by then, call Hosea, apprise him of the situation, and tell him to call the local authorities."

Estavez stared at Parker with glassy dark eyes, his face turning pale at the words, but he didn't argue.

Miranda got out of the Lexus.

Parker turned to her. "Are you ready?"

There was so much at stake here. If anything happened to Coco or the baby, she'd never forgive herself. She couldn't bear to think what it would do to Parker or to Estavez.

They had to get this one right.

She drew in a breath. "More than I've ever been."

"Forty minutes," he repeated to Estavez, and they took off.

###

It would have been a nice walk under different circumstances.

The landscape was beautiful, there was a gentle breeze, and the temperature was just right. There was even a scent of flowers in the air. Probably magnolias.

The road was paved all the way, but the twisty path it took, curving in and out of the trees, set Miranda's nerves on edge, even though the design was probably for aesthetics. She was glad when they reached the end of it, and the grounds opened up to a wide grassy lawn.

There in the middle of the yard sat a magnificent structure, as fancy as any grand mansion in Buckhead. The facade was an expensive looking gray-and-sand colored cobblestone accented by tall white columns, giving the place a half English cottage, half Southern mansion flare.

There were a lot of windows. Tall ones.

"Bagitelli has good taste," Parker said under his breath.

"And big bucks." Or he used to.

Surely there was some cash stashed somewhere in that house. That wasn't his focus right now, but she'd bet he'd use it for a getaway once he finished whatever he planned to do with Estavez and Coco.

The thought made her stomach tense.

She scanned the yard. "I don't see a car."

"There's a three-car garage near the back."

She stepped to Parker's other side and it came into view. She looked at the side of the house. "No one at the windows that I can see."

The bushes and a stone retaining wall made a nice perimeter around the residence.

"There's enough cover for one of us to get to the back. Has to be a rear entrance somewhere," she whispered.

Parker nodded. "While the other goes in through the front. Assuming we can gain access."

Meaning the door could be locked and bolted.

"Won't know until we try."

Once more Parker examined the entire structure with his gaze. "I'll take the back."

"Okay."

He studied her intently for a moment. "Be careful, Miranda. Don't take any unnecessary risks."

They'd both taken too many risks ever since they'd been together. And here they were, doing it again, despite their best intentions to retire. "I won't if you won't."

He almost smiled. "Agreed. Ready?"

She gave his hand a squeeze and he took off, crouching behind the shrubs.

Make it quick, she thought.

Bending down, she made a dash for the house and scrunched herself under the first window in a row of arched panes. Duck walking, she made her way under the rest of the windows, dodging shrubs all the way to the front door.

She stared up at it.

The fancy entrance was carved mahogany with a decorative glass inlay. But the glass was frosted, and Miranda hoped no one saw her through it as she scooted to the other side. She straightened and reached for the handle.

The door opened easily.

Intentional, she thought. A trap.

She'd been in situations like this before. Drawing her weapon, she took a deep breath and stepped inside.

CHAPTER THIRTY-SIX

She found herself in a hallway at the foot of a staircase.
To the right stood a tall white archway opening to a large sitting room with a high ceiling and lots of crushed leather furniture.
Cautiously, she stepped into it.
Stone fireplace. Elaborate antique brass ceiling lights. Fake plants in pretty ceramic pots here and there. Garden scenes in fancy frames on the walls.
The rustic chic look.
Suddenly she heard piano music.
It sounded like one of the pieces they'd heard Bagitelli playing on the Internet. If the fugitive was engrossed in making music, it might be easy to nab him.
But where was the sound coming from?
Moving slowly with her back to the wall, she followed the notes past another seating arrangement of sofas and side tables, a dining room, and finally to another tall white archway.
Peeking around the edge, she could see a huge kitchen off to the side that opened to a space with nothing but high cream-colored walls, hardwood flooring, and two grand pianos near a row of windows.
Coco sat at the nearest one bathed in light, looking ethereal. She was playing away.
Bagitelli had to be nearby, but he wasn't at the other piano.
Miranda peeked around the arch again. Coco was concentrating on the music. It was pretty. Delicate and sad, like all the songs she played.
Then, as if she sensed a presence, Coco stopped playing and looked in Miranda's direction.
She spotted her right away.
Her big blue eyes went round with shock. "Miranda."

Miranda put a finger to her lips to hush her. Then she mouthed the words. "Where's Bagitelli?"

Coco frowned and cocked her head.

"Where's Bagitelli?" she said again silently.

Before she got an answer, a shadow appeared along the wall, and a man stepped around the corner.

It was Parker—with his Glock drawn.

He hurried over to Coco and reached for her.

She jumped off the piano bench to evade his grasp. "Wade. What are you and Miranda doing here? Where's Antonio?"

"Where's Bagitelli?" Miranda groaned. Might as well say it out loud now that Coco had announced their presence.

Coco scowled at Miranda, then at Parker. "Enrico's gone."

"Gone?"

She raised her palms. "He left about an hour ago."

Miranda didn't get it. "But he made you call Estavez and demand he come here alone."

"I know. That's why it was so strange when he ran out the door. He took my cell phone with him, or I would have called back." She sank down on the end of the piano bench. "Antonio didn't come, did he?"

Parker holstered his weapon. "Antonio's outside. Where did Bagitelli go?"

"I have no idea. He just got agitated and left. He's got some kind of mental condition, doesn't he?"

Miranda glanced at Parker, wondering what Bagitelli had put Coco through. "We think so. Did he hurt you?"

"No, but he kept talking to people who weren't there. His father, I think. He called him 'Papa.' And someone named Ludwig."

"That would be his mentor at Juilliard," Parker said.

The one who'd died years ago.

Coco rose and went over to the open kitchen. She gestured to the cabinets. "He started looking in there for medicine. And then after he made me make that phone call, he rushed all over the house trying to find it. He was convinced his wife, Fiona, had left some here."

"Did she?"

Coco shook her head. "He couldn't find any. He was getting more and more agitated. And he kept talking about Rosalynd. Is that the woman he tried to kill?"

"Yes. She's Fiona's sister."

Coco's brow creased. "He kept saying he was innocent. He said he loved her. Funny thing is—"

"What?"

"I—I think I believe him. He let me play one of his pianos. We played together. It was such a beautiful experience. He was so...himself. Like he used to be when he was performing. How could anyone so talented be a killer?"

Coco was too much of a softie. "Did he say anything at all about where he was going?"

"He said he had to find Rosalynd. He had to see her again before the end."

Miranda tensed. "The end of what?"

"I don't know."

In the distance, they heard the front door open. It was followed by the sound of heavy footsteps rushing across the wooden floor in the far rooms.

Miranda spun toward the archway and raised her Beretta, ready for Bagitelli to materialize under the arch.

Instead Estavez appeared.

He was holding a thick stick he must have found under the trees. He intended to use it as a weapon, she supposed. In his dark business suit and starched white shirt and tie, with his long jet black hair tied in a ponytail, he made a good imitation of a Highland warrior. Or maybe a lawyer-warrior.

But that branch wouldn't have done him much good.

She lowered her arm, glad she hadn't shot him. "You were supposed to stay in the car."

Ignoring her, he stared at Coco, emotion flooding his face. "Are you all right?"

"Oh, Antonio." Coco stared back, her voice quivering. "You came to save me."

Estavez dropped the stick, rushed over to her, and threw his arms around her. "*Mi querida.* My darling Coco." He kissed her and ran his hands over her face as if trying to convince himself she was real. "Are you sure you're all right, my love? Did he hurt you?"

"I'm fine. He threatened me with a knife, but he didn't use it. He left it over there on the island next to my purse." She pointed toward the kitchen as she turned to Miranda. "I didn't touch it. I thought you might need it for evidence."

Parker stepped toward the island and peered across the surface. "The police will," he said darkly.

Estavez turned to him. "I've already called Lieutenant Erskine. I couldn't wait forty minutes, Papa."

"It's all right, son."

Holstering her weapon, Miranda moved to Parker's side and lowered her voice. "We have to find Bagitelli before he gets to his sister-in-law."

He nodded.

"Becker said Rosalynd is in hospice care near *Bellissima*. Do you think Bagitelli went there?"

Coco heard her. Eyes glowing, she gasped aloud. "Yes. That was the name Enrico said. *Bellissima.* He said he had to go there. He said he had to see Rosalynd."

Miranda felt a chill go through her whole being. "That must be where he's heading."

Parker turned to Estavez. "We need to go after him. Can you take Coco back home, son?"

"Yes, Papa."

Miranda didn't like the idea of the couple going back to Atlanta alone. But before they could leave, there was a loud rap. Estavez hadn't locked the door, and after a moment they heard it open.

"Greene County Sheriff's office," called a deep voice with a South Georgian accent. "Anyone in there?"

"We're back here." Parker stepped forward to greet their visitors.

After a lot of noisy clomping across the floor, three strong-looking men appeared under the arch. They were wearing badges, short-sleeved tan shirts, black slacks and ties—and fully loaded duty belts.

The one with the widest girth and the shortest hair moved toward them, his thumbs in his belt, eyeing them with suspicion. "I'm Officer Howard. We got a call from a Lieutenant Erskine in Atlanta about the fugitive who escaped from Bibb County Correctional."

Telling him said fugitive was supposed to be here.

"We'll have to update that report." Parker said, and he explained who they were, how he knew Erskine, and what had happened here.

While he was talking, one of the officers began taking notes, while the third went to the kitchen and snapped a photo of the butcher knife and Coco's purse. Then he bagged the knife and gave the purse back to Coco.

"He took my phone," Coco told him. "Maybe you could track it or something?"

Miranda blinked at Coco in surprise, wondering if she was rubbing off on the girl. It was a good idea, though Bagitelli had probably turned the phone off.

"We'll do that." The officer taking notes wrote down her number.

Officer Howard turned to them. "I think we've got enough for now. You're all free to go."

"Thank you, sir," Estavez said, and he took Coco's hand and headed out of the house with her.

Parker moved closer to Officer Howard. "We believe Mr. Bagitelli is on his way to Saint Simons. Ms. Steele and I are headed there now."

Howard returned an unemotional stare. "We'll get this evidence to the station. I'll call Lieutenant Erskine and the authorities in Saint Simons. We'll find Bagitelli."

That was no reason for them to quit hunting him.

"Can you spare someone to accompany Mr. Estavez and his wife back to Atlanta?" Parker asked.

Howard frowned. "You just said Bagitelli is heading for Saint Simons."

"I believe that's where he's going. But one can never be too careful."

And Parker's protective nature extended to all of his family.

After considering the idea, Howard pointed to one of the officers. "Garcia, you're on escort duty."

"Yessir." The man hustled past them.

"Excellent. Now if you'll excuse us." Parker reached for Miranda's hand, and without further conversation, they hurried to the front of the house.

Outside they discovered three sheriff's cars parked on the lawn. Officer Garcia was in the one nearest the paved lane, already starting the engine.

They rushed past the vehicles and down the pathway. They found Estavez and Coco at the Lexus, arms around each other.

As she neared the couple, Miranda overheard the lawyer speaking in his low Hispanic accent. "There is so much I want to say to you, Coco, so much I need to tell you. I promise until this ordeal is over, I will not leave your side again."

His words made her smile. Her pep talk must have worked. She was happy for them, but she and Parker were in a hurry.

"Do that at home," she called to them. "We've got to go."

Estavez glanced up and flushed as he saw her and Parker rushing toward the Mazda. Without another word, he and Coco bundled into the Lexus.

As Miranda climbed inside the car next to Parker, she couldn't help feeling a sense of satisfaction. "They're going to be okay," she told him.

Parker waited for Estavez to move out of the way, then did a nifty three-point turn, and zoomed over the path to the two-lane.

Wheels squealing, he turned onto the road and they were off.

"If we can find Bagitelli before he kills his sister-in-law," he told her with the resolve of a gladiator, "everything will be right again."

CHAPTER THIRTY-SEVEN

Miranda punched at the buttons on the GPS. "How far is it to the hospice?"

"About four hours."

Long way. As the map materialized on the screen confirming Parker's statement, she couldn't hold back a groan. "Wish we had the Cessna."

"Not practical at this point."

Right. Going back to Atlanta to get it wasn't an option. "If the Crown Vic Bagitelli bought was a police car, it can do over a hundred miles an hour."

"The real police will catch him if he tries to drive that fast."

No, they were going to catch him first. She was sure of it. Especially when Parker shifted the Mazda into turbo mode.

So here they were again, racing down the rural two-lane roads through South Georgia, possibly breaking the sound barrier and definitely all the speed limits, hoping they could somehow catch up to this guy. She was glad the sun was behind them and not in their eyes.

And that the Green County officers had alerted the locals.

As they passed towns and road stops, instead of pulling them over for speeding, squad cars flashed their lights and blew their sirens, urging them on. When they reached the outskirts of Milledgeville, two police cars pulled out and escorted them through the town to the city limits.

Good thing. The speed limit around here was twenty-five.

Miranda was also relieved the traffic was almost non-existent. Except for the occasional slow-moving pickup truck or even slower-moving farm tractor. But Parker whizzed around them like they weren't even there, making her heartbeat kick up a notch or two.

She watched the dot on the GPS move. Were they gaining on Bagitelli?

They had to be, but there was no sight of a pea green Crown Vic on the roads.

Thirty minutes later, Officer Howard from Green County called and said, as promised, he had put a trace on Coco's phone. They'd found it on the side of GA-44 near Eatonton, about forty miles back.

"Bagitelli must have tossed it out the window once he realized he still had it," Miranda muttered after Parker had hung up. She blew out a frustrated breath. "We can't lose him, Parker."

"We won't. We have a good idea of where he's going, and Officer Howard has already asked the locals in Brunswick to set up a guard at Rosalynd Allen's room at the hospice."

She rubbed her arms. It was the best they could do. But they had to be right this time. They just had to be.

When they got to Dublin, Becker called.

"Sorry I haven't checked in. I just picked up the kids from school and got them settled doing their homework."

Was it that late already? "Is Fanuzzi still asleep?"

"She's resting. She was able to get down a little chicken soup earlier. Boy, she's crabby. She's not even sure she can make it to the baby shower tomorrow."

"Sorry to hear that." Miranda twisted in her leather seat. She'd forgotten all about that party. If they didn't catch Bagitelli soon, she might not make it, either. "What have you got for us?"

"Right. Well, I didn't get all the way through the transcript of Bagitelli's trial yet."

"Okay."

"The defense put everyone who was there that night on the witness stand. One reason why the document's so long. Funny thing, though, nobody seems to have seen exactly what happened to Rosalynd Allen. It was the video that proved the defendant's guilt. But anyway, among all that, I found the testimony of Bagitelli's psychiatrist."

"Oh." That was new.

"Dr. Francis Viotto," Becker said. "Great credentials. Some years ago she had a highly rated practice in New York and was a consultant to Columbia University Medical Center. On the witness stand, she said Bagitelli first came to her office in New York, shortly after his mentor, Ludwig Kraus passed away. She treated him, but refused to talk about his condition. Said it fell under client-patient privilege. The judge agreed."

So Bagitelli did have a mental issue. "Was he on medication?"

"Seems to have been, but again the doctor didn't give details. Anyway, after a few years, Dr. Viotto began treating Bagitelli regularly. Six years ago, she retired to Saint Simons Island, where the Bagitellis spent most of their time when not on tour. They even bought her a house. Bagitelli was her only client there."

Wow, "She treated him up until his arrest?"

"That's what she said. And she also insisted he was innocent. Oh. I managed to find her current address."

Her brows shot up in surprise. "You're a genius, Becker."

"I'm sending it to you in an email along with something else."

"What?"

"I was finally able to dig up a video on the sister-in-law."

Miranda couldn't help grinning. "I'm telling Parker to give you a big bonus."

"Just doing my job. Gotta run. The spaghetti sauce needs stirring." He hung up.

Excited, she turned to Parker. "Did you hear that?"

His look was intense. "I did. Go ahead and have a look at that video." He'd watch it later. Right now he had to keep his eyes on the road they were flying over.

Her email pinged, she opened the message from Becker, and clicked the link.

The video was a little slow to download, but after a minute, the now familiar image of two grand pianos appeared on the screen.

Bagitelli was at one, his eyes closed in the rhapsody of the music. At the other keyboard sat a woman with long honey blond curls dressed in a sparkling midnight blue gown.

She was very pretty. Her delicate frame gave her a fragile air, but she played with the same intensity as her partner.

They were playing the *Moonlight Sonata*.

Miranda was surprised she recognized it.

She waited for the song to end, and when the last bit of music evaporated, the audience broke into frenzied applause, complete with whistles and shouts.

"They really like her."

Parker's face was pensive. "I have to say she played that piece better than Fiona."

"Yeah, she did."

While the crowd was still going wild, Miranda watched the pair rise from their benches and meet in the middle of the stage between the pianos. Bagitelli took Rosalynd's hand and they both did a deep bow.

When they came up, he gestured to her, letting her take a bow alone. As Bagitelli watched the delicate woman modestly relish the adulation, his face beamed with obvious joy, and his eyes glowed with unmistakable emotion.

Stunned, Miranda stopped the video. "Why didn't we see it before?"

"See what?" They were approaching another pickup truck, and Parker couldn't look at the image.

"The way Bagitelli is looking at Rosalynd. It's clear as day. He was in love with her."

Parker zoomed around the puttering vehicle, but remained silent, considering her words. After a quarter mile, he risked a glance at the image frozen on the screen. "That's a very interesting observation."

"Yeah." Her mind began to race. "So maybe Bagitelli tells Rosalynd how he feels, says he's in love with her and he's willing to divorce Fiona for her. But Rosalynd doesn't want to betray her sister."

"Or she didn't return his affections."

"Right. And so he gets angry, and in a fit of rage, runs her over. It fits."

"It's a theory."

"A good one."

"Agreed."

"And now all he can think of is revenge. First it focused on Estavez, and now he's turned it on Rosalynd."

She had an image of the pianist sneaking into Rosalynd's room at the hospice, putting a pillow over her face, and smothering the poor frail woman, sealing her fate. Miranda's whole body tensed, her breathing became deep, and the old determination, the need to right wrongs, the need to protect the innocent burned inside her like a wildfire.

"We have to stop this guy before he gets to his sister-in-law."

Parker inhaled along with her, and she could feel the same blaze inside him. "We will."

CHAPTER THIRTY-EIGHT

It was just before five-thirty when they pulled into the parking lot of Island Oasis Hospice Care.

A large facility hidden among a cluster of oak trees, the hospice was made up of several connecting buildings, each with a matching creamy white stucco exterior. A red clay scalloped roof sat over the entrance like arms outstretched in welcome.

Friendly place.

As they got out and hurried to the front entrance, Miranda was glad to see a police car nearby.

Parker held the door, and she stepped into the cool silence of a large empty waiting room.

She took in the space. Comfortable couches in muted colors, serene paintings of birds on the wall, a large blue tank where fish swam lazily back and forth. Soft music came from somewhere. The decor was obviously intended to create a comforting, soothing atmosphere, but none of it could erase the somber tone of the place, or the odor typical of hospital-like settings.

A middle-aged woman with short brown hair who was dressed in pink scrubs was working away behind a pale blue Corian reception desk.

Parker strolled up to her with an authoritative air.

She looked up and gave him a smile filled with kindness. "May I help you, sir?"

Parker glanced at her nametag. "I hope so, Ms. Whitlock. I'm Wade Parker and this is Miranda Steele—"

Her look turned to surprise. "Oh. Of the Parker Agency in Atlanta."

How did she know that?

After scanning the room as if there were people in it, Ms. Whitlock leaned over the counter and spoke in a whisper. "Sergeant Cruz said you would be coming. I understand you're looking for a fugitive?"

"Yes, ma'am. Unfortunately, we think he might have unpleasant designs on one of your residents."

Parker's flair for understatement didn't faze the woman at all. She nodded in agreement. "Yes. Rosalynd Rose Allen. She's been with us for over three years now. It was terrible what happened to her."

Apparently Whitlock had been here long enough to know the whole story.

Getting impatient, Miranda took out her phone and scrolled to the photo of said fugitive with the unpleasant designs. "This is Enrico Bagitelli. We have reason to believe he was heading to this hospice. He should have arrived by now."

Ms. Whitlock took her phone, frowned at the photo, then handed it back. "Yes, that's the picture Sergeant Cruz showed me. That man hasn't been here. At least, he didn't come through the front door."

He could have slipped in through a side entry.

"What room is Ms. Allen in?" Parker said.

"Three-Fourteen. Officer Beam is watching her now. No one's seen anything unusual."

Miranda looked at Parker. That couldn't be right.

"May we speak to Officer Beam?"

"Yes, of course. The elevator is just down that hall."

"Thank you, Ms. Whitlock."

They hurried over the polished floor past empty rooms that held beds and supplies and medical equipment. Turning a corner, they found a short hall with two elevators.

They rode the first one to the third floor and found the room. It wasn't hard. It was the only door with a police officer standing in front of it.

"Officer Beam?" Parker called out before they had reached him.

The man in the tan police shirt and dark slacks turned to them, eyes wide. He seemed young. Early twenties at most. Probably fresh out of the academy.

"Can I help you?" he said in a less-than-manly voice.

Miranda noticed his elbow bend. Getting ready to reach for his sidearm. At least he was staying alert.

Parker did the same introductions he had downstairs and got the same reaction.

"I'm sorry, Mr. Parker, Ms. Steele. I haven't seen anyone except the staff on this floor."

Once again, Miranda scrolled to Bagitelli's picture and held it up. "You didn't see this man? Maybe dressed in scrubs?"

"You mean like a disguise?"

"Exactly. His hair would have had some greenish blond streaks from a botched dye job."

Beam frowned. "No, ma'am. I have the same photo on my phone. Sergeant Cruz mentioned the hair. I haven't seen anyone who looks like that."

Again Miranda looked at Parker in disbelief.

He blew out a frustrated breath. "We'd like to see Ms. Allen, if we may."

"Uh, I'm not sure I can give you that permission. Visitors are family only for her, though I understand she rarely gets any."

Fiona didn't come to see her sister? Probably still too traumatic for her.

Parker was about to go find a nurse when a man in a white coat and stethoscope came around the corner.

Looking up from his digital tablet, he scowled at them. "Can I help you?"

Officer Beam answered for them. "These are the detectives Sergeant Cruz said would be coming here. They'd like to see Ms. Allen."

Considering the request, the doctor studied Parker, then Miranda.

He was tall and slender, and seemed to be in his late forties. His thin coppery brown hair was parted at the side, and he wore gold wire-rimmed glasses, a dark tie, and a blue dress shirt under his coat.

His name badge read "Benjamin Hart MD, Neurologist."

Dr. Hart let out a sigh that was half annoyance, half resignation. "I suppose that would be all right, but keep your voices down. Come in." He opened the door and Miranda followed him inside the room with Parker just behind her.

The lights were low and the air cool, but it was the smell of antiseptic that hit her first. And then it was the sight of the woman in the hospital bed that had Miranda hugging herself tightly.

With the help of a breathing tube, Rosalynd Rose Allen inhaled and exhaled under the blankets, looking even more frail than she had in that video Becker had sent her.

Her honey blond hair was tangled and caught up in a band atop her head. There was an IV in her arm, a feeding tube in her mouth, and a multitude of wires and sensors leading to a monitor that beeped steadily away.

The doctor went to the screen in the corner and began pushing buttons and making notes on his tablet as various numbers flashed.

"I'm afraid there isn't much to see here," he said softly. "This patient suffered severe head trauma due to her accident nearly four years ago. She also had internal bleeding and several fractures and lacerations, which, of course, have healed. Her spinal cord is intact, though."

Miranda watched the woman breathe and thought of her visit to Leon's hospital room almost two years ago. She'd wanted to loosen a connector on one of the ventilator tubes to do him in. Had Bagitelli already snuck in here and done something like that?

But alarms would go off, wouldn't they? The machines would beep and tell the staff something was wrong.

Wouldn't hurt to make sure.

"Can you check her equipment to make sure it hasn't been tampered with, Doctor?"

As if insulted, Dr. Hart narrowed his eyes at her, but then he began checking the tubes and wires. "Everything seems intact," he said when he was finished.

"Nothing in the IV?"

Frowning, the doctor squeezed the clear bag suspended from a pole. "I don't see anything, but I can have a nurse change it."

"Can you check for any medications in her bloodstream?"

Dr. Hart's chest expanded as he inhaled. "I can have some blood work done as a precaution, but if you're thinking the fugitive came in here and tampered with anything, I think that's highly unlikely."

He was right. She was grasping at straws.

"On a brighter note, Ms. Allen has been having some unusual neural activity lately."

She glanced at Parker, who was frowning. "Unusual in what way, Doctor?"

"Her latest EEG detected impulses in her reticular activating system that we haven't seen before."

Miranda wished doctors would speak English. "Does that mean she might wake up?"

"I can't say. It could just be an anomaly. But there's always hope." He smiled briefly and took more notes on his tablet.

With a grim face, Parker turned to the doctor. "We don't know where Enrico Bagitelli is right now, Dr. Hart, but a witness told us he was determined to see Ms. Allen."

The doctor nodded. "We'll keep a close watch on her until he's captured, then."

"Thank you."

It was all they could ask for.

CHAPTER THIRTY-NINE

Back out on the sidewalk, Miranda scanned the parking lot and saw no sign of a green Crown Vic.

"Where is he, Parker?"

"Somewhere else. From what Coco told us, Bagitelli was behaving irrationally."

"Which means he could have changed his mind about seeing Rosalynd."

Parker's lips thinned as his gaze narrowed. "Perhaps he decided to wait until dark to make his move."

Made sense. She thought of the patient she'd seen in that room. "That poor woman. She was so frail, so helpless. How could anyone do that to another human being?"

Parker murmured his agreement. But they both knew there were plenty of people vicious enough to hurt others in all sorts of ways. They'd met too many of them personally along the way.

She blinked. "Wait. Coco said Bagitelli was frantically hunting in the cabinets for medicine."

"If the prison was dispensing a prescription to him, he wouldn't have had a dose since his escape."

A chill went down her spine. "Which means his mental condition is out of control. Maybe he went to see his shrink to get more."

"He wouldn't have gone to a drug store."

"No." She pulled her phone out of her pocket and found the email Becker had sent. "Looks like Dr. Viotto lives near the resort."

"Let's go pay her a visit."

But Miranda was already starting for the car.

###

Twenty minutes later, after crossing four legs of the marshy Mackay River, they followed a road lined with thick live oaks and cypress trees, their gnarled branches heavy with Spanish moss and drooping over the road as if in mourning.

It led them to a private drive which ended at a circular driveway.

The Mazda's tires crunched on the gravel as they pulled up to the front of a magnificent white house designed with an old Southern flair.

Miranda eyed the carefully crafted symmetrical lines, the fancy roof, the wide cathedral window in the middle of the second floor. "What do you think this place is worth?"

"My guess would be about two million."

"The Bagitellis were generous."

She got out of the car and felt the humidity against her skin as she took in the palm trees and huge ferns artfully arranged around matching twin staircases that led to a wide wraparound porch.

As the leaves of the foliage waved gently in the warm sea breeze, she climbed the stairs with Parker to a huge wooden door.

There was a bell. She rang it and waited.

Another big fern, this one potted, sat in a corner of the porch. Nearby hung an old-fashioned swing. Miranda suddenly wished she could be swinging on something like that with Parker somewhere. Maybe after they found Bagitelli.

No one came to the door.

Parker drew in a breath and knocked. It was his I'm-tired-of-waiting knock. He was getting impatient.

Still no answer.

"Maybe the doctor doesn't live here anymore." Miranda said. "Becker might have gotten hold of an old record."

Parker tried the handle. It was locked. Giving up on the door, he started toward the far corner of the porch, his footsteps a rhythmical series of sharp raps on the white wooden boards.

Studying the house, Miranda followed him. "A lot of windows." Like Bagitelli's place had had.

There was a whole row of tall, full-length panes along the front and another set along the side, but either curtains or blinds hid the interior from view.

They continued around to the back of the porch. Here there were more windows, but one was a trio arrangement, and the middle pane turned out to be a back door. Miranda hurried over to it and tried the handle.

Also locked.

Still, there were no curtains here.

She cupped her face against the glass and peered inside.

There was a cozy white couch with soft cushions and a matching ottoman. Two matching recliners sat off to the side. A comfy place to treat clients? But the doctor was retired.

A white cabinet stood against the wall. Couldn't tell what was in it. Against another wall stood a wrought iron shelving unit filled with ceramic whatnots.

She didn't see a soul anywhere.

Turning around, she gazed out at the green expanse that was the backyard. "No car. I don't see a garage anywhere."

"Which indicates Dr. Viotto is out."

Miranda strolled over to the white wooden steps leading to the yard. A manicured path bordered by thick palmetto ferns wound around palm trees and disappeared into the dense trees beyond.

"Bagitelli could be hiding somewhere in there."

"He could be. But his car would be nearby."

And someone would spot it sooner or later. She folded her arms. "If he came here and couldn't contact the doctor, where would he go next?"

Gazing out at the expanse of greenery, Parker thought a moment. "Fiona?"

"His wife? Doesn't she hate him for what he did to her sister?"

"That's what we've assumed. But actually we know very little about Bagitelli's personal life."

That was true. Even Allen Stowe at the arts center in Atlanta hadn't seemed to know of any feelings Bagitelli had had for Rosalynd.

But Fiona would. "Let's go see her. It's worth a try."

"I agree."

As they made their way back around the front of the house, Parker took out a business card and a pen from his coat pocket. Leaning on the exterior wall, he wrote, "Call me. Re: Enrico Bagitelli."

He slipped the card under the front door, and they headed back to the car.

CHAPTER FORTY

They drove through the rest of the moneyed neighborhood with the A/C on full blast. Even with the shady tree cover, it was in the mid-eighties here, maybe fifteen degrees warmer than Atlanta, and the humidity was making Miranda uncomfortable and fidgety.

After a mile or so, they reached a section with shops and middle class housing.

Miranda tapped her foot on the Mazda's floor mat. They were getting close to the shore now, and she was growing edgier.

After another ten minutes, they followed a curve, and at the end of an adjoining road, the ocean came into view.

She sucked in a quick breath at the sight of it.

Not because of its beauty. Though, of course, it was gorgeous with its vast misty blue waves stretching to the horizon. It was because the last time she'd seen the Atlantic, she'd been in it.

Or rather under it.

The thought of thrashing about in the cold water, fighting for her life and nearly losing it, made her throat go tight. She'd thought she was as good as dead. And would have been. If it weren't for Parker.

She felt his hand reach for hers and give it a tender squeeze.

"Bad memories?"

"Yeah."

He must be having them, too. But they were just memories, she told herself sternly. That was all. Jay Charles York was the one who was dead and gone.

Besides, he had nothing to do with who they were after now.

Shaking off the feeling, she concentrated on the road. They cruised through another neighborhood, turned a corner, came to a stop at an intersection.

And there they were. A sandstone sign etched with elegant cursive writing told them so.

Bellissima.

As Parker eased through the stop sign, Miranda took in a large five-story structure of ivory stucco with soft grey trim and a red clay roof. Lots of separate compartments.

Hotel suites. Each with a roomy arched balcony overlooking the ocean.

As they drove on, similar structures came into view. Some were villas, some held more hotel rooms that seemed to be lower priced. One extravagant building looked like a fancy restaurant.

"Fiona owns this place?"

"I'm sure she employs a manager to run the business."

Must be nice to have the income from tourists rolling in while you were in seclusion.

Miranda thought about Fiona Bagitelli, hold up in a big house along the ocean all these years while her sister lay dying in a hospice and her husband rotted away in prison. She felt sorry for the woman.

She twisted in her seat. "I'm not so sure about this, after all, Parker."

"About visiting Fiona?"

"About finding Bagitelli there. If he's already shown up at her place, she would have called the police. And they would have let us know."

"Unless he's holding her at knife point."

"She's got to have better security than that. And she has to know he's on the loose."

Parker considered that a moment. "You're probably right, but she can still give us insight into where Bagitelli might be."

She hoped so.

Parker stopped at the end of the road, and something else caught her eye. "Turn down there."

"Are you sure?"

They were getting close to the ocean again.

"Yeah."

He pulled into the parking lot she had indicated and drove across to a bit of pavement between two of the buildings.

Then he stopped.

She sat up and stared out the windshield. The view didn't bother her now. "Look at that."

Sitting on a stretch of beach was an outdoor stage in the shape of a huge golden seashell.

It was situated close enough to the resort so that the water wouldn't reach it at high tide. Cream-colored concrete steps curved up both its sides, and there were seats for what looked like several hundred people.

A golden seashell with wings.

Another sign in cursive writing stood nearby. Miranda read it. "'Fiona and Ivan in concert tonight at nine.' Just like Becker said."

"Indeed."

She tensed as a thought struck her. "Coco said Bagitelli couldn't resist playing the piano with her. If he knows about that concert, I'll bet he'll be there."

Parker scanned the venue and nodded. "I think you're right."

"We should go. If we don't find him before then."

"I'll see if I can get tickets."

###

The address for Fiona that Becker had texted her took them another mile or two north of the resort proper.

The curvy lane was lined with thick bushes, lots of palm trees, and quaint seaside cottages that must have been worth beaucoup bucks just because of the ocean view. They had to be getting close.

As the road rose gently, Miranda sat up.

Hidden beside a cluster of palm trees stood a four-story red brick structure. The state of the brick and the narrow, old style, white framed windows told her the building was old. Really old. Might have been there since Revolutionary War days.

Had it been a lighthouse?

That couldn't be Fiona's place. Miranda wondered if anybody lived here. At the end of a large sandy yard a long wooden structure stretched all the way to the water. Was it a pier?

She squinted hard, trying to find the street number. It was so overgrown with palmetto, she almost didn't see it. Finally she spotted some digits on a post and read them out loud.

Then she groaned. "Wrong address."

Parker glanced out the window. "We're close."

He drove on, and her frustration melted as around another curve the correct number came into view.

There it was.

Bagitelli's villa sat on a rise, set off from the road and lined by two rows of tall palm trees. The building was done in the same style as the resort, and had the same ivory stucco exterior. But this three-story construction sported symmetrical twin towers on either side. Each had a capped roof and double arched windows on each floor that gave it an Italian Renaissance look.

Villa. It was twice as big as Dr. Viotto's place. And it looked like a castle.

But then, as she'd already learned, Bagitelli was loaded.

Parker pulled over to the side of the road and they got out, gazing up at the huge structure.

The front yard was beautifully landscaped with the typical shrubs and greenery they'd seen in the area. Behind a row of plants with long sharp tongues, wide stone steps led to three cathedral-like doors that made up the front entry.

But before heading that way, something else caught Miranda's eye. She tapped Parker's arm, but he was already looking at it.

A smaller detached structure stood off the side of the house.

A garage.

She leaned toward him. "Let's check that out."

He nodded.

The road was squishy underfoot as they made their way along a row of thick shrubs to the driveway. As they rounded the last bush, Miranda's heart sank.

No pea green Crown Vic sitting on the concrete.

Then she saw something else. "Wait a minute."

The garage was a huge three-car deal, done in the same classic style as the house. The door for the car on the far right was open.

Heart pounding, she hurried over to it, and peered inside.

And then she stood frozen, unable to believe her eyes. "Is that what I think it is?"

Backed into the third slot sat a candy apple red Maserati.

Parker came up beside her. "The Gran Turismo."

Miranda eyed the shark tooth grill with the distinctive logo. "But is it the same car? It's in pristine condition."

Parker stepped closer to the vehicle and studied the hood. "It's been repaired."

"What's it doing here?"

"Let's go find out."

They hurried back around to the front and rang the bell.

CHAPTER FORTY-ONE

As they waited, Miranda was struck by the fact that the odd three-door formation making up the entrance to the house was similar to the garage. Consistent designer.

But if he were here, would Bagitelli have come through one of these front doors? Probably not.

She was beginning to think he was inside holding everyone hostage when finally someone opened the middle door.

It was a young woman in her mid-twenties with her dark hair pulled back in a ponytail. She was wearing light colored slacks and a pale blue blouse.

"Can I help you?" she said, sounding annoyed and not at all like a hostage.

Must be the new assistant, since Ivan had been promoted.

"We need to see Fiona Bagitelli," Miranda told her in a police-like voice.

Blinking at her, the woman straightened her thin shoulders. "She goes by the name Fiona Delacroix, and she's not taking visitors. I'm sorry." She started to close the door, but Parker wedged himself against the frame before she could.

He handed her a business card and gave her one of his drool-worthy smiles. "Good afternoon, Miss. I'm Wade Parker and this is Miranda Steele of the Parker Investigative Agency in Atlanta. We need to see Ms. Delacroix on an urgent matter."

She ignored Parker's charm, and her lips thinned as she studied the card. "I'm sorry, Mr. Parker. Ms. Fiona gave me strict instructions she's not to be disturbed."

"It's regarding her husband," Miranda said.

The woman frowned at her. "If you mean Enrico Bagitelli, he's in jail. She reminds us of that nearly every day." She rolled her eyes.

Interesting tidbit. "Enrico Bagitelli escaped from jail early Thursday morning. We believe he's in the area and may try to attack her."

The woman stared at her open-mouthed as if she were trying to decide whether or not this was a story made up by some autograph seeker.

"Your boss may be in danger." Parker's low tone was ominous.

But the woman still hesitated. Finally she opted to err on the side of caution and opened the door, rolling her eyes again in resignation. "All right. Come in."

With Parker close by her side, Miranda entered a narrow high-ceilinged room, stepping onto a pale gray tile floor. White shiplap walls hung with seafaring bric-a-brac gave the visitor the impression of entering a boat.

The young woman stepped over to a blue marble table in the corner and picked up a tray with two glasses filled with what looked like pink lemonade. "Follow me."

She led them down a long corridor painted in another shade of pale gray and decorated with various landscapes and music paraphernalia. Then she took them up a tall staircase, and toward a door near the back of the house.

As they neared it, Miranda heard piano music.

The woman opened the door. "Wait here."

As she stepped inside, the music stopped and a low throaty voice with a lot of condescension floated into the hallway. "No, Ivan. You missed the G-flat again."

Miranda pushed the door open and took in a large great room filled with cozy ivory sofas, armchairs, soft blue accent cushions, and a matching tufted cotton area rug. The walls were white and accented by pale wooden beams along the high ceiling. Beyond the furniture a whole wall of windows opened to the ocean, giving the impression you were floating on a cloud.

And before the windows stood two large white grand pianos.

Miranda recognized Fiona seated at the one on the left, though she was wearing pale blue slacks and a lightweight blouse printed with blue sailboats rather than a black sequined gown. Her dark hair was in a messy braided bun at the back of her swan-like neck.

A large man sat at the other piano dressed in khaki shorts, flip flops and a peach print Hawaiian shirt.

Fiona turned her head and stared at Miranda in utter shock. "Lauren, I said no interruptions."

The young woman set her tray down on a glass coffee table in front of one of the sofas. "I'm sorry, Ms. Fiona. These people say they're investigators and that Mr. Bagitelli has escaped from prison."

Fiona shot up from her bench, clutching her throat in alarm. "What?"

She hadn't heard.

Parker stepped into the room, dominating it. "My apologies for barging in like this, but I assure you, it's urgent."

He made his way across the floor and extended a hand to Fiona as once again, he introduced himself and Miranda.

Weakly Fiona shook his hand, looking lost. "You say Enrico escaped from prison?"

Miranda crossed the room to Parker's side. "Early Thursday morning. Has he tried to contact you?"

"No. Why should he?" As if looking for aid, Fiona turned to the man who was rising from the keyboard.

"This is Ivan Bruzek, my duet partner."

The man took a few steps forward, then stood beside his piano staring at them in silence.

He was taller than Fiona, maybe six-two, and bulky. His frame was more like a prize fighter's than a classical musician's. His peach print shirt contrasted with his tan skin. He had a large square-shaped face with a wide nose that looked like it might have been broken once or twice. His dark gray hair was piled in curls atop his head and cut short on the sides. His brows were curly like his hair, and his eyes were deep and ferocious looking.

"Why are you trying to upset her? She has a performance tonight." Ivan's voice was low and threatening. And had a bit of an accent.

Russian, Miranda decided, folding her arms. "Obviously, you two haven't been watching the news."

Fiona blinked as if coming out of a trance. "We've been so busy with rehearsals." She gestured toward the sofas. "Let's sit down and talk."

"Very well," Parker said.

Fiona turned to the young woman who was waiting for instructions at the door. "Lauren, go get them something to drink."

"Nothing for me, thank you," Parker told her.

"I'm good," Miranda said, taking a seat in an armchair near the couch.

"All right. Go and practice your scales, then."

The young woman nodded and left the room as the pair settled onto the sofa close to each other.

Fiona took a few deep breaths to steady herself. "I don't understand why Enrico would be coming to me. I haven't seen him since he went to prison. I divorced him officially last year, though we're keeping that news private. Ivan and I are going to be married in the summer." She took Ivan's hand and smiled at him tenderly.

He returned an awkward grin.

Miranda risked a glance at Parker, who had taken a seat in the smaller sofa across from her. She could tell by his expression, he was skeptical.

"Ms. Delacroix," he said.

"Please, call me Fiona."

"Fiona, then. We have reason to believe Mr. Bagitelli wanted to visit his sister-in-law, but we could find no trace of him at the hospice in Brunswick."

Fiona glared at him, startled. "You've been to Brunswick?"

"We were there earlier. There's a police guard stationed at Ms. Allen's door. The staff is on alert."

Fiona's long fingers stroked her throat nervously. "That man tried to kill my sister. I suppose you know all about that."

"Yes, we do."

"Poor, poor, Rosalynd." Fiona wiped her face with the back of her hand, as if she were about to cry.

Miranda leaned toward her. "The receptionist at Island Oasis Hospice Care said you haven't been there in quite a while."

Fiona stared at her as if she'd asked what underwear size she wore. "I don't want to disturb my sister. The doctors said it's important for Rosalynd to have complete quiet. Besides," her voice broke a little. "I just can't bear to see her that way. It takes me days to recover after a visit." She turned to Ivan and pressed her forehead against his arm.

"There, there, my dear." Ivan patted her shoulder with a large hand that could probably reach several octaves on the keyboard.

Miranda couldn't help feeling sorry for the woman. She wasn't over the trauma of the experience. "We think Bagitelli is looking for medication," she said.

Fiona swiped a finger under her eye and frowned. "Medication?"

"For his—psychiatric issues." She couldn't put it any more nicely.

"Oh." Fiona drew in a breath. She got what Miranda was talking about. "I don't really know much about my ex-husband's condition. That was between him and his physician."

"Dr. Viotto," Parker said.

"Yes." She looked surprised he knew the name.

"So you don't have any of his medication here?"

"No. I got rid of all of Enrico's things. I never expected to see him again."

Keeping his gaze fixed on Fiona, Parker shifted his weight. "Can you tell us about your relationship with Mr. Bagitelli?"

She blinked at him. "What has that got to do with anything? As I said, we're divorced."

Miranda wondered if that relationship had been stormy. "We're just trying to figure out what he's thinking and where he might go next."

Fiona smoothed her slacks. "Well, we met while I was at Juilliard. Enrico was my tutor there. I was a freshman and he took an interest in my playing."

"I thought you studied at the Paris Conservatory, as well."

Fiona let out a sad little laugh. "Oh, we told the reporters that for publicity. I never went abroad until I met Enrico."

Okay.

"Enrico graduated and went on tour. I graduated later and also went on tour. We met occasionally on the road, and after a while we decided to appear at each other's concerts and play a duet or two. It was popular, so we finally joined forces and began touring together." She looked down at her hands. "We fell in love and were married. It was all very wonderful. A dream come true for me, really. And then Ludwig Kraus died."

"Bagitelli's mentor."

"Yes. Enrico loved him so very much. He was devastated. That was when everything changed."

"How?"

"Enrico became restless and anxious. He started talking to himself. He became more and more demanding. Controlling." She drew in a tight breath. "That was when my sister contacted me and wanted to play a concert with us. I didn't want her near Enrico. I was afraid he'd hurt her."

And he did. But none of this told them where Bagitelli was now. This visit had turned out to be another dead end. They'd disturbed this poor woman for nothing.

Miranda started to get up.

Before she could, Parker cleared his throat. "By the way, Fiona, we noticed a Maserati in your garage. Bagitelli was driving a Grand Turismo the night your sister was injured, wasn't he?"

Fiona's face went stone cold. "Yes, he was."

"Is that the same vehicle?"

Smoothing back her hair, the woman made a sound of sheer disgust. "After the police in Atlanta were done with it, they contacted me. They said it was legally mine. I didn't know what to do with it. Enrico never let me drive it, he was so possessive of it. But I had it delivered here and had it repaired. I suppose I should have sold the thing, but I couldn't bring myself to even think about that. I told Ivan we should take it somewhere and burn it." She put a hand to her lips.

Why burn it? Before Miranda could ask, Ivan held up a large hand. "Please don't upset her anymore. She has to perform tonight."

Fiona turned to the bulky man at her side. "Oh, Ivan. Maybe we should cancel."

He took her hands in his. "But the tickets. We would have to refund them."

"We can reschedule."

Ivan's expression was doubtful. "Those who are tourists might not come back."

Fiona studied the condensation on the untouched lemonade glasses as she considered that conundrum.

Finally, she lifted her head and got to her feet. "No, you're right, Ivan. I will play. I won't let my ex-husband intimidate me out of rebuilding my career."

That settled that.

As everyone rose, Fiona turned to Miranda and took her hand, suddenly turning into a gracious hostess. "You and Mr. Parker must come to the concert tonight."

Parker smiled graciously. "We were thinking of getting tickets." He didn't say why.

"I'll leave some at the box office for you. Please come. Attire is semi-formal."

Miranda had been thinking about that plan. "Uh, I'm going to need some clothes," she said to Parker.

"There's a wonderful dress shop in town," Fiona said. "It's in Shops by the Sea. They're open late."

Miranda forced a grin. "We'd better get going then."

"Again, we're sorry for disturbing you. But if you do hear from your ex-husband, please give me a call." Parker handed her a business card.

Fiona took it and smiled thoughtfully at the embossed lettering. "I'll certainly do that. Thank you for your concern, Mr. Parker."

CHAPTER FORTY-TWO

And then they were back in the Mazda, heading down the shady lane and past the old house with the pier—with no clue how to find Enrico Bagitelli.

Before they'd left the villa, Fiona had also given them a complimentary room at the resort.

Miranda thought about her anxious smile as she reached for her phone to make the arrangements. "Fiona was laying it on a bit thick, don't you think?"

Parker slowed for a stop sign. "Do you mean her overt affection for her new duet partner?"

Miranda smirked. "That, too. But why give us tickets to the concert and a room at the resort?"

"She may simply be trying to acquire more fans."

She narrowed an eye at him. "Or she was currying favor. But why?"

"Insecurity?" Parker suggested.

"Maybe. It sure shook her up when you asked about the Maserati."

"We had to know."

They did. And even though Miranda wasn't going to bring it up, she was glad Parker had. "She said she wanted to burn the car. Pretty intense reaction."

"Fiona went through a pretty intense experience with the vehicle." Parker's tone was compassionate.

She had, and Miranda could sympathize. But something felt off about that whole visit. She could tell Parker felt it, too, even though he wasn't admitting it. "Maybe we should have told her we think Bagitelli will show up at the concert."

Parker shook his head. "It would only upset her more."

And there would be security. Plus, she and Parker would make sure Bagitelli didn't get to her.

So there was nothing to do but get ready for tonight.

Miranda leaned back against the headrest, hoping they were right. "One thing that visit told us. Fiona's resentment toward Bagitelli is real."

"Yes, I sensed that."

She scanned the road ahead. "And I don't see a pea green Crown Victoria anywhere."

Parker let out a breath of frustration, echoing hers.

Feeling drained, she rubbed her forehead. "I feel like I'm losing it, Parker."

"You're hungry. Once again, I've neglected my duties."

It had been a long time since those huevos rancheros at Carlotta's.

To lighten the mood, she gave Parker a playful bat on the shoulder with her hand. "You really are getting slack."

Parker smiled. "To make up for it. I promise to put fifteen pounds on you when this case is closed."

Her brows rose. "Oh, yeah? Well, I just might let you."

Chuckling, Parker made a turn, and they drove a few miles west to their destination.

###

Shops by the Sea was an outdoor mall made up of several blocks of pretty white stores with cheery green awnings and homey dormer windows.

Everything to make tourists cozy enough to part with some cash.

As they cruised through the parking lot, Miranda noticed several posters advertising Fiona and Ivan's concert tonight. She wondered how big the crowd would be and whether Bagitelli would really risk showing up.

The mall was crowded, and a couple of cop cars were circling the lot, as well. The Green County officers must have alerted the whole area, right to the shore.

The dress shop was on a corner, but there wasn't a free parking place to be had. Not nearby anyway.

"Let me drop you off." Parker said. "Perhaps you'll find something appropriate before I locate a space."

"Yeah, right." But she got out of the car and headed for the store while Parker squealed off.

As the Mazda's tail lights disappeared around the corner, Miranda started toward the sidewalk. Two young women scurried past her, almost running into her.

Both of them were carrying books.

"Hurry, Jasmine," said the one on the right without even acknowledging Miranda. "I don't want to miss her."

"No chance of that. Look at that line."

Miranda turned her head and saw a long queue of people waiting to get inside the shop in the middle of the row.

It was a bookstore.

For a moment she stared at it. Was that what she thought it was? She headed for the line, where people of all ages, mostly women, were chatting excitedly.

"I just love the way she writes."

"This book is just heart-stopping, isn't it?"

"Did you read the chapter about the bank shooting?" Someone said. "I could hardly sleep after I did."

Miranda squinted at the cover of the book under the woman's arm.

Sure enough. *My Ordeal* by Audrey Wilson.

Holloway had said Austin was the first stop on the tour. She guessed Saint Simons was the second one.

A sudden burst of irritation made her head straight for the door.

"Hey, you can't cut in line," a heavy-set dark-haired woman snarled at her as Miranda tried to get inside. "Wait your turn to see Audrey like the rest of us."

Miranda had seen all she wanted of Audrey Wilson. "I'm getting a book on cooking fish," she snapped, and pushed through the entrance.

Inside, the atmosphere was electric with excitement.

Breathing in the smell of new books, coffee, and the fragrances the women were wearing, Miranda scanned the display at the very front. It was loaded with coffee table books about local history and attractions, but no one was paying them any attention.

Everyone was in the line that led to a table where all the commotion was.

Miranda stepped to the far corner of the display and managed to get a clear view.

In a strappy red summer top with a chunky chain necklace around her neck, Audrey Wilson sat smiling and signing and generally drinking in the adulation from her adoring fans as she spoke to each person in line, as if she were the most famous celebrity in the world.

Piles of *My Ordeal* lay stacked beside her, but most of her fans had already purchased their copies. Her highlighted ash blond hair was longer now, falling a few inches past her shoulders. But it still gave her that innocent girl-next-door look.

Miranda knew better.

She'd never forget what that woman had done to Parker's Lamborghini. Okay, there had been mind control involved. Miranda had experienced it herself and so had Parker.

But still, a Lambo was a Lambo.

Above the heads of the crowd, she could see lanky Holloway in his usual walnut brown suit and tie, hovering over her. He looked like he was about to drool.

It wouldn't be good if either of them saw her.

She made a beeline for one of the aisles and ended up in the Cookbook section. Consistent with what she'd told the woman outside. Sort of.

No one else was in this aisle, so she hurried past the volumes on Italian, Szechuan, and Low Country cooking to the opposite end and peeked out.

She could see the pair from the back now, but Holloway still looked like he had his tongue hanging out while Audrey sucked up the limelight.

A man in a uniform stood near another bookcase, just behind Holloway. The prison guard assigned to watch her.

Where was Witherby? Parker had sent him to keep an eye on this pair.

She scanned the aisles across from her, and there in the Comics and Graphic Novels stood the tall meaty bodyguard with the babyface and the light sandy curls.

Hidden by the books, Witherby pretended to browse the latest chronicle on Darth Vader. But every so often he peeked out to keep an eye on his targets. Professional. Just what he was sent here to do. He began scanning the rest of the shelves.

Miranda grabbed a book on Keto cooking and hid her face in it.

It would be embarrassing for all parties if Witherby knew she was spying on him.

But then Witherby did something she didn't expect. He turned his head and peered at someone in the shelves behind them. A strange expression came over his face. If she didn't know better, she would have called it goo-goo eyed.

What in the world was he looking at?

Miranda turned her head as well and peered into an aisle down the way, which sat perpendicular to the ones she and the bodyguard were standing in.

And she nearly dropped the book she was holding.

It was Gen.

Dressed in her stark black suit with a white tailored shirt, Parker's daughter looked skinnier than usual. Her short white-blond hair was neatly combed, but she stood hugging herself, looking pale.

Her dark eyes were boring into the back of Holloway.

How did she get to Saint Simons? She must have looked up Audrey's tour schedule and hopped a plane. And who was planning the baby shower? Miranda had a feeling that wasn't coming off.

Miranda looked back at Witherby.

He was still staring at Gen, his expression as dreamy-eyed as Holloway's.

No. It couldn't be. But there it was, right in front of her. Witherby had the hots for Gen.

And here she'd thought he had better judgment.

She looked at Gen again and saw her dark eyes were glistening with tears. Now she was staring at Holloway with a look that nearly broke Miranda's heart.

No, girl, she thought. You can do better than that.

She looked back at the signing table and saw Audrey crook a finger at Holloway.

Holloway bent over to listen.

Audrey attempted to whisper, but it didn't come out that way. Somehow, the acoustics in the room carried Audrey's voice straight to Miranda's ears.

"It's lonely in the hotel, Curt. Why don't you stop by my room later on?"

Holloway's face turned beet red. He mumbled something Miranda couldn't hear, then straightened and fumbled with his tie.

Miranda growled under her breath. She knew that woman was playing him. She'd have him running all over the country with her for weeks, when his head should be back at his job at the Agency.

She and Parker might never get to retire.

And then she heard a tiny squeal from behind her. She looked behind her again and saw Gen holding a handkerchief to her face, her shoulders bobbing.

Miranda wanted to rush over to her and give her a shake. She wanted to hurry over to Holloway, give him a kick in the rear, and tell him to get back to the Agency and get to work.

But Parker had promised him a week. And there was no getting through to Gen.

She should get out of here. She took a final glance at Witherby.

He was gone.

"Ms. Steele," someone whispered behind her.

She spun around.

Speak of the devil. The baby-faced bodyguard was right behind her. He'd spotted her and must have snuck around the bookstore's perimeter to get to where she was hiding.

"What are you doing here?" he hissed. "Is Mr. Parker with you?"

She shook her head and whispered back. "He's outside. We're on a case."

"Oh."

"There's a fugitive from Bibb County Correctional on the loose. We think he's in the area."

"Yes. I heard something about that. Baggy something."

"Bagitelli. Enrico Bagitelli. He was a famous classical pianist."

"Oh," Witherby said again, folding his arms over his linebacker pecs.

Miranda took out her phone and scrolled to the too-familiar photo. "This is his prison mug shot. He tried to dye his hair blond, but it came out in light green streaks. Have you seen anybody who looks like this?"

He studied the picture, then shook his head. "No, I haven't."

"He's driving a pea green Crown Vic."

Witherby thought a moment, then shrugged. "I'm sorry, Ms. Steele. I've been concentrating on my assignment."

And on Gen.

"I'll let you get back to that, then." She hesitated a moment. "Witherby, let's make a deal."

"What kind of a deal?"

"You don't tell Parker I was here in this bookstore, and I won't tell him you're smitten with his daughter."

His gentle gray eyes went wide. He didn't know what to say for a moment, but at last he nodded. "Deal."

"Good. Now get back to work. Your real work."

"Yes, ma'am." He scurried to the end of the aisle and disappeared.

Presuming he was going back to his post, and not to Gen, Miranda left the store as fast as she could and hurried to the dress shop.

If Parker was waiting for her there, wondering where she'd been, she'd have to come up with as good a story as Audrey's bestseller.

CHAPTER FORTY-THREE

She made it to the shop about thirty seconds before Parker came through the door.

She felt him come up behind her and turned to the rack, which happened to be one-piece suits.

"Not exactly what Fiona specified," he murmured in her ear.

She turned around and gave him her sweetest grin. "You know me and clothes."

He returned a penetrating look that said he knew exactly where she had been. He must have seen the line. But she didn't think he'd seen Gen or he'd be more upset.

Then his expression melted into a tender smile. "Let's look over here."

"Okay."

She tried on several numbers Parker selected. Most were itchy and didn't feel right. She was in no mood to pick out clothes, but they managed to find a nice knee-length dress in a breezy fabric with a handkerchief hem. It had a sunny, teal palm tree print over a pure white background.

Miranda stretched out her arms and spun around in front of the mirror. "Perfect for a concert on the beach."

Parker grinned at her tenderly, no doubt recalling the first time he took her clothes shopping. "I agree. And the color makes your eyes so blue."

His gaze made a thrill go up her spine. "Glad you think so. Let's get it and go. I'm starving."

###

After stopping to snag a few more accessories, they decided to try the restaurant at the resort.

They checked into the room—which was nice, but not as fancy as the suites Parker usually booked for them—stuffed their packages in the closet, and made their way downstairs.

A hostess seated them on the patio under a table shaded by a pretty blue umbrella and overlooking the ocean. Because they were starving, they ordered appetizers right away, indulging in smoked oyster and artichoke dip and blackened grouper tacos with Southern chow chow.

For the main dish, Miranda had a scallop paella with Bomba rice and spicy andouille sausage that was flavored with cilantro, paprika, and saffron, while Parker opted for grilled Atlantic Salmon with a roasted sweet potato and green beans almondine. Their beverage was sweet tea.

It wasn't quite dark, but a full moon was climbing the sky over the azure water. Enjoying the warm sea air against her face, Miranda tried to pretend the sound of the waves was soothing instead of a reminder of almost drowning.

As she stuffed herself, she eyed the other diners. Nearby sat a table of parents and kids, laughing and joking. Farther away, a group of ladies enjoyed drinks and secrets together. At another spot, a couple ignored their food as they drank in each other's eyes looking very much in love.

Normal life. Like the one they were supposed to be having.

She sat back and sighed.

Parker reached for her hand. "I feel the same way."

She narrowed an eye at him. "How do you know how I feel?"

"The same way you know how I feel."

She usually did get that right. And just now, she felt worn out and frustrated with the elusive pianist. She could tell by the lines in Parker's face he did feel the same.

"The local cops have got the area pretty much under patrol, don't they?"

Parker nodded. "While I was hunting for a parking spot, the Green County sheriff texted me and told me he'd conveyed all the data to the Saint Simon police."

"They've got to find Bagitelli sooner or later."

"I expect so. I also received a text from Antonio. He and Coco are back home, having a quiet dinner and spending the evening together talking."

"That's good to hear."

"It is, indeed."

She let out another sigh. "Maybe we should let them."

"Let them?"

"I mean let the police handle finding Bagitelli. Now that Estavez and Coco are safe, it isn't really our case anymore. And didn't Erskine tell us to stay out of it?"

Instead of frowning, Parker grew pensive.

It was tempting, after all. Go back home to Parker's penthouse, jump into the sunken tub with him, eat strawberries, drink champagne, and make love all night.

Delicious. What they were supposed to be doing. Being retired.

Parker's low voice pulled her out of her thoughts. "What about the concert?"

Drawing in a breath, she let her gaze wander to the bandshell on the beach in the far distance. There was light there, and tiny figures were setting up equipment on the stage.

She knew in her innermost being Bagitelli would be there tonight. Could she really walk away from that?

Before she could think of how to answer, Parker's phone rang.

"Wade Parker." He listened for a moment, then put a hand over the speaker. "It's Dr. Viotto," he whispered to Miranda.

Miranda sat up straight.

He listened for another moment. "Yes, I understand."

He listened some more.

"Yes, Doctor. Thank you for calling. We'll be right over."

He hung up and turned to Miranda. "She wants to talk."

Suddenly all thoughts of sunken tubs and champagne dissolved into vapor. Was Bagitelli sitting in his former shrink's living room right now?

Feeling the familiar rush of excitement, Miranda tossed down her napkin and shot to her feet. "Let's go."

CHAPTER FORTY-FOUR

Dusk was falling, and all the windows in the big white house nestled among the mossy cypress trees were ablaze with light when Parker's Mazda crunched up the circular drive for the second time that day.

To Miranda's surprise, she spotted a tall, long-legged woman sitting on the swing on the wrap-around porch.

As soon as she and Parker got out of the car, the woman rose.

"Mr. Parker?" she called in a strong determined voice.

Parker headed for the curving steps. "Yes. And you're Dr. Viotto?"

"I am."

Parker stepped aside so Miranda could scamper up to the porch first. "This is my partner, Miranda Steele."

"Ms. Steele." The doctor shook hands with both of them.

She was a statuesque woman with an oval face and a receding chin. Her dark hair had a lot of gray in it and was cut in a short breezy bob. In defiance of her age, Miranda suspected. Her oversized glasses were framed in a classy blue tortoise shell that matched the casual blouse she wore over a pair of white jeans. White sandals completed the leisurely look.

Miranda put the doctor in her early seventies, but she looked fit and hardy.

"I'm also sorry I wasn't here earlier when you stopped by. I was out jogging. I didn't see your card until I was checking the locks for the night. What's this about Enrico Bagitelli?"

"May we talk inside?" Parker asked.

"Yes of course. Come in." With a concerned frown, she opened the front door and led them down a short hall and into a sitting room with a deep red Persian carpet and brown leopard print wingback chairs facing a huge walnut bookcase. A matching antique table stood between the chairs.

The doctor switched on the old fashioned lamp on the table. "Please sit down. Would either of you like anything to drink?"

"No thank you," Parker told her, waiting for the ladies to be seated.

Miranda shook her head as she took one of the chairs and scanned the volumes on mental illnesses on the shelves.

"Help yourself to the mints. Some patients find them soothing." The doctor waved to a candy dish on the table as she moved to the window and pulled the floor-to-ceiling curtains that matched the chairs shut.

She was acting awfully casual. Either she was giving Bagitelli time to get away, or he wasn't here.

"We were under the impression you were retired." Miranda eyed the round white candies and popped one in her mouth.

The woman settled into a high-backed chair near the window. "I'm semi-retired. I still see a few clients here and there."

Parker took the chair on the other side of the table. "Dr. Viotto, we understand you used to treat Enrico Bagitelli exclusively. Is that correct?"

"Yes, I did. Until he was arrested and sent to prison."

"I regret to inform you that Enrico Bagitelli escaped from prison Thursday morning and is suspected to be in the area."

"I know that."

Miranda swallowed the mint she'd been chewing. "How did you know?" Had Bagitelli been here?

The doctor blinked at her as if the answer was obvious. "It's my habit to jog in the nearby leisure park in the early evenings. Tonight Officer Briggs saw me and flagged me down. He's a patrol officer with the Saint Simon police department, and I often see him around town. We chat, and he keeps me informed about what's going on in the area. This evening he told me Enrico had escaped from prison and was thought to be here in Saint Simons. He said I should be careful. I told him I had my pepper spray with me, but I doubted Enrico would hurt me."

Miranda shot Parker a glance. "People around here know you treated Bagitelli?"

"Some of them do, though of course, Enrico was concerned about his reputation during the time." She grew quiet, probably due to doctor-patient confidentiality.

But Miranda could see there were memories going through her head. Sad ones.

Parker fixed the woman with a stern gaze. "Dr. Viotto. Has Mr. Bagitelli been here to see you?"

She looked surprised at the question. "No, he hasn't."

"Are you sure?" Miranda asked.

She looked around the room as if at a loss for words. "I don't know whether he stopped by while I was out, but I haven't seen him."

"We think he's looking for medication."

"Oh, dear." Her fingers traced her neckline as she thought about the possibility. "That's right. He wouldn't be able to get any since Thursday. That's disturbing."

Miranda leaned forward. "In what way? Do you think he's more violent without his meds?"

The doctor drew in a slow breath. "I can't tell you everything, but I need to explain Enrico's condition to you."

Miranda tensed. "What exactly is his condition?"

Dr. Viotto's dark brown eyes bore into her with solemn intensity. "Enrico Bagitelli has schizophrenia."

She'd suspected something like that from the beginning. So had Parker. Still, it stunned her to hear the psychiatrist who'd treated Bagitelli say it out loud. "That doesn't mean multiple personalities any more. Right?"

"That's correct, Ms. Steele."

"It means he has difficulty determining what's real and what isn't," Parker said.

"Exactly. In Enrico's case, he hears voices. And when he's off his medication, he sees people from his past."

Parker's brow rose. "He has hallucinations."

"Yes." The doctor leaned forward in her chair and clasped her hands together. "Few people know Enrico had a troubled childhood."

Miranda recalled reading Bagitelli was born and raised in Naples. There had been nothing about a troubled childhood, but something like that had probably never been public knowledge. "We understand he began playing piano at three."

Dr. Viotto smiled sadly. "Yes, and he loved it. His father taught him, but Giovanni Bagitelli could be a stern taskmaster."

"Oh?" Miranda could relate to growing up with an overbearing parent.

"He would tolerate no mistakes from the boy. If Enrico missed a note or two, he would be sent to bed without supper."

Parker's face grew hard. "Harsh."

"Yes. As far as I could tell, Giovanni meant well. He saw Enrico's rare talent and was trying to develop it. It wasn't until Enrico was an adult that he learned his father had the same malady."

Miranda blinked at the doctor. "Schizophrenia?"

"Yes. In his case, it's hereditary."

Like father like son. Sad.

"To continue, Enrico showed no symptoms growing up. He told me he had felt disoriented when his father died and his mother and he moved to New York. It was a natural reaction, but Enrico didn't feel settled until he began working under Ludwig Kraus."

"His mentor at Juilliard."

"Yes. Ludwig Kraus was a real father figure to him. He was a gentle teacher and allowed Enrico the freedom to develop his own artistic style. Enrico didn't believe he would have become such a success without him. He met Fiona, and tutored her for a while, then they went their separate ways. But they met again while touring and eventually joined forces, so to speak."

"Ms. Delacroix told us about that," Parker said.

"Oh. You've seen Fiona?"

"Earlier today."

Dr. Viotto stared down at the floor. "And then Ludwig Kraus suffered a sudden heart attack and passed away. Enrico was beside himself. It was as if he'd lost his guiding light. That was when the hallucinations started. And when Enrico came to see me."

"He and Fiona stopped touring then," Miranda recalled.

"Yes, I advised that. It took some time to diagnose Enrico's condition. And it took a long while to find the right combination of medication that worked for him, but we eventually landed on two antipsychotics that blocked the abnormal dopamine signals and kept the hallucinations in check. He and Fiona went back on the road."

Miranda shifted in her chair. "And after that is when Rosalynd Allen came along."

The doctor frowned. "As I recall she came along just after I moved here to Saint Simons to be near the family. They had decided to settle here."

A little later than Fiona had said.

"She moved in with them at *Bellissima*."

So she was accessible. That added weight to Miranda's theory about the love triangle. "Did Mr. Bagitelli ever confess any feelings he had for Rosalynd?"

"She was young and beautiful and very talented. He was excited to work with her, but no, he never said he was falling in love with her or anything like it. As far as I knew, it was a purely professional relationship."

Miranda watched the doctor closely. She was completely sure of her reply, but Bagitelli might have been holding something back from her. You didn't run someone over with a Gran Turismo for purely professional reasons.

Parker picked up the conversation. "We understand at the trial you testified Mr. Bagitelli was innocent of what happened to Rosalynd."

"Yes, I did."

"Why?"

"Enrico insisted he was innocent. I believed him."

"You mean when he insisted he was innocent in court?"

"No. When I was allowed to see him in jail."

"You visited him after his arrest?"

"Just once." She drew a hand across her face. "Enrico said he couldn't remember what happened the night Rosalynd was injured. When I asked him how he knew he was innocent if he didn't recall anything, he got upset with me and told me to leave. I discovered he had fired his lawyer, who had an excellent reputation, and had hired someone from a firm he'd seen advertised on television. The new lawyer was fresh out of law school and in over his head."

"There was a video of that night."

"Yes, I know. It was proof of his guilt, but I still doubt it. Videos can be altered."

Miranda had wondered about that, but the video clearly showed Bagitelli getting out of the Maserati that night.

Dr. Viotto continued. "When Enrico attacked his first attorney I knew something was wrong. I contacted the doctor at the facility where he was being held and learned they had his dosage incorrect."

Miranda stared at Parker.

She could tell he was stunned by that news. Bagitelli had attacked Estavez because his meds were off? Had they been off when he wrote that letter threatening to kill Estavez and his family? He'd had an opportunity, but Bagitelli hadn't actually done that, had he?

"Do you still believe Mr. Bagitelli is innocent, Doctor?" Parker said.

She raised her palms in surrender. "I have no idea. Ours isn't an exact science, as you know. And sometimes Enrico didn't take his medications."

Miranda thought about how temperamental Eddison Stowe said Bagitelli had been that last week of rehearsals. "And you think he might have forgotten to take them the night Rosalynd was run over?"

"He might have, but that's why Fiona was in charge of dispensing his doses at the proper times."

Miranda sat up straight. "Fiona? When we visited her earlier, she told us she knew very little about Mr. Bagitelli's condition or what he was taking for it."

The doctor frowned with confusion. "I don't know why she would say that. I had Enrico's permission to tell her everything we discovered in therapy. He wanted her to know, and he wanted her help with his medications. He knew he was forgetful, too absorbed in his music and absent-minded to take them on time."

A chill went down Miranda's spine. "Did you ever treat Fiona?"

"No, I didn't."

"Not even after the trauma of what happened?"

"I offered, but she refused. She's a strong woman."

Parker's look turned even harder. "Dr. Viotto, you said you still treat patients here?"

"Yes. Here in my home. I have an office in the back."

"Do you keep medications here?"

Her body went stiff. "As a matter of fact, I have some samples. A former client in New York recommended me to her niece. I started her on the same combination of medication I prescribed for Enrico. But—"

Instead of continuing, Dr. Viotto shot to her feet and left the room.

As if they were being pulled by the same string, Miranda rose along with Parker, and they followed the doctor through the door, under a wide paneled archway, down a spacious hallway hung with medieval looking sconces, past a staircase, and finally into the room Miranda had seen from the back porch earlier.

Nothing looked like it had been disturbed.

She scanned the comfy-looking white couch with its overstuffed ottoman and the matching recliners. What she hadn't seen from the glass door was the black baby grand in the far corner.

She moved over to it and studied the keys. "Did you have this here for Bagitelli?"

Dr. Viotto nodded. "It helped him relax during our sessions. He was such a talent."

Miranda noticed the bench was a little askew.

Parker saw it, too, and moved over to the glass door. He tried it and it open. "Did you unlock this door when you came home, Doctor?"

"No. I'm sure it was locked when I went for my jog."

It had been. Miranda had tried it when they were here earlier.

Looking shaken, Dr. Viotto moved to the white painted cabinet against the wall. She opened one of the panels. "I always keep this locked, too."

But it wasn't locked now.

The shelves inside were filled with boxes of meds, several prescription bottles, and some tubes.

"Two boxes of samples are missing," the doctor announced, hugging herself to suppress her alarm.

Miranda put her hands on her hips. "Let me guess. The same antipsychotics you prescribed for Enrico Bagitelli? The ones you were going to try on the new patient?"

"Yes," she breathed, and she sank down onto the ottoman and put her head in her hands.

Miranda's mind raced. "Did Bagitelli know your schedule? When you go out?"

She nodded. "It hasn't changed since I moved here. I'm a creature of habit, I'm afraid."

Parker studied the door. "How did he get in without breaking the glass?"

"There's a hidden compartment in the railing of the porch. I keep a key in there."

Miranda raised a brow at Parker. "And Bagitelli knew about it?"

"Yes. I wanted him to feel comfortable to stop by if he ever needed me in an emergency. I keep the key to the cabinet there." She waved at a row of small drawers under the panels.

Parker walked over to the cabinet and pulled out one of the drawers. After only an instant, he lifted out a small key.

The doctor gestured at it. "That's the one."

"Bagitelli saw you take it out and use it."

"Yes, yes. I trusted him. I feel so foolish now."

Parker turned to Miranda. "This confirms Bagitelli is in the area."

Yeah, it did. But it didn't tell them where he was.

Miranda strolled over to the ottoman. "Doctor, Fiona and Ivan are giving a concert at the bandshell on the beach tonight."

"Yes, I know. They started playing together recently. I was happy to hear Fiona was getting on with her life."

"We have a theory Bagitelli will show up there tonight."

Dr. Viotto blinked, considered that a moment, then slowly nodded. "I think that's a distinct possibility."

Parker looked at his phone, then at Miranda. "If we want to make it to the concert, we'll have to leave now."

Right. Miranda pointed at a nearby arch. "Is this the way out?"

"I'll show you." The doctor rose and led them around to the front door where she stood rubbing her arms. "I'm so sorry about all this. I feel I should have known. I should have done something."

"You did what you thought best." Parker's voice wasn't as comforting as before. But he extended a hand to the doctor and they all shook again.

Dr. Viotto squeezed Miranda's hand, pleading with her intense dark eyes. "If you find him, Ms. Steele, please let me know. I want to help if I can."

"We'll do that."

And as she hurried down the steps to the Mazda with Parker, Miranda was more determined than ever to capture this guy.

CHAPTER FORTY-FIVE

They sped back to the resort, stopped by the concierge for hair and toothbrushes, combs and toothpaste, then rushed up to their room and jumped in the shower.

Miranda longed to linger there with Parker, but there was no time.

They hopped back out and pulled on the new duds they'd bought in the Shops by the Sea.

Clean underwear. A new dress shirt and tie for Parker that they'd picked up in a men's shop that had been just about to close. Since there was no time to visit a tailor, Parker had the hotel freshen his suit and tipped them a hundred bucks to get it back in ten minutes.

Miranda wriggled into the white and teal palm tree print dress, slipped her feet into the shoes Parker had selected for her—a pair of white dress Crocs with a two inch wedge made just for the beach—and spun around in front of the mirror.

"You are a vision," Parker said, hunger in his tone.

She smiled at his handsome form. As always, he was heart-stoppingly handsome. "You clean up pretty good yourself."

With a devilish look in his gunmetal gray eyes, he stepped toward her, took her in his arms, and kissed her with a sexy intensity that took her breath. Her toes curled and her head spun and all her insides started to waltz, even though they didn't have time for any of it.

He put his cheek to hers and murmured low in her ear. "There will be more when we get home."

"Extra incentive to close this case tonight."

Finding the strength, she pulled away from him, grabbed the clutch purse with her Beretta in it, and they headed out the door.

###

As she made her way on Parker's arm through the resort's lobby and out the door to the sidewalk, Miranda's mind turned back to the case, mulling over their visit with Dr. Viotto.

"This just isn't adding up, Parker."

"What do you mean?"

He knew what she meant. He wanted to hear her thoughts. "Why go after meds if Bagitelli is on a murderous rampage?"

"A good question."

"And why did Fiona lie to us about her knowledge of Bagitelli's medications?"

"Another excellent question."

"And why wasn't Dr. Viotto sure Bagitelli was guilty? Even after that video and his attack on Estavez?"

"She wouldn't have been allowed to watch the trial."

But she'd probably seen the news coverage at the time.

Parker was holding back. "You've got a theory, don't you?"

His expression was resolute. "I have the same questions you do. And if we find Bagitelli tonight, we'll get our answers."

He refused to commit. But they were going to find Bagitelli tonight. Miranda was sure of it.

They'd round him up, hand him over to the cops, and let them sort out the details. Then they'd wash their hands of this whole crazy case, go back home, and get back to their retirement.

Feeling more determined than ever, Miranda clung to Parker's arm as they trotted up the sidewalk to the north end of the resort and out onto the beach.

The ticket booth was set up on the sand, and just now there wasn't a line.

Parker spoke to the young man on duty and secured the two tickets Fiona had set aside for them. Along with two pairs of opera glasses.

Miranda stared at him open-mouthed, though she might have known he'd be resourceful.

"I made a call while we were at Shops by the Sea and reserved these."

"Good deal." She took the one he handed her and studied it. It was a small pair of binoculars on a skinny stick.

Parker tapped the long handle. "It's called a lornette. It's collapsible."

"Fancy." She leaned in close to him. "And these will make our hunt a little easier."

"Exactly."

The sun had set, and the seating area on the beach was luminous with a soft romantic glow. A warm breeze whispering through her hair, Miranda breathed in the smell of the sea as she took in the space and the murmur of the crowd.

Wooden seats were arranged in maybe twenty rows with two middle aisles. There was a low barrier marking the perimeter of the audience area. She saw a few cops milling around alongside it. They were hunting the same prey she and Parker were.

In front of the seats, the giant seashell that was the stage was drenched in a golden glow, embellished by the matching wings of Grecian-style staircases on either side. Two ebony grand pianos glistened under the lights.

But the chairs in the audience were only half full. Or half empty, if you were a pessimist.

"Not a big turnout," she whispered to Parker.

"Perhaps the majority of Fiona and Ivan's fans are running late."

Right. Fiona could never draw the crowds Bagitelli had.

An usher handed her a program, and she and Parker made her way down the nearest aisle.

Parker leaned close to her. "Fiona gave us front row seats."

"She wants to keep an eye on us."

"You could be right."

As they made their way to the front row, she scanned the crowd, but didn't see anyone matching the photo of Bagitelli.

She sat down and looked up at the stage. Microphones had been placed near each instrument and sound monitors sat along the edge of the platform. If she leaned in just right, she could catch a glimpse of people dressed in black getting things ready backstage.

Feeling antsy already, she scanned the paper in her hand.

The names of the musical pieces to be performed were written in a fancy script. On the back was an ad for the company who'd supplied the pianos. There would be about a dozen numbers, from what she could make out what with concertos and movements and whatnot.

"How long is this concert?" she whispered to Parker.

"About an hour and a half."

Sheesh. Long enough to be bored out of her mind, but short enough not to find Bagitelli.

Lifting her opera glasses, she turned around and craned her neck as she peered through them.

There were a lot of older couples. Tourists who liked the highbrow music, she supposed. But there were groups of young people scattered among them, too. They were probably hoping for the Beach Boys.

A few families were here to listen, as well. Several rows behind her, a young boy had his head on his mother's lap.

"Yeah, I'm with you, kid," Miranda thought.

No one looked even remotely like Bagitelli.

She turned back around. "It isn't as if he's going to buy a ticket and sit down."

"No, but he might have come in unnoticed. And there are plenty of nooks and crannies to lurk in."

Parker was right.

Before she could examine them, applause broke out as Fiona came from the left side of the stage while Ivan entered from the right.

Fiona was dressed in an elegant floor length black sequin gown like the ones Miranda had seen in her videos with Bagitelli. Ivan was in black tux and tie, his hair slicked back with gel.

They met in the middle of the stage, bowed in acknowledgement of the applause, and returned to their respective piano benches.

Fiona poised her hands over her keyboard, gave Ivan a nod, and they were off.

Bum, bum, a-bum-bum. Bum, bum, a-bum-bum.

It was that peppy march.

Bright colors popped on the screen behind them in time to the music. Nice touch.

Fiona was clearly in charge, directing the tempo with her head, and Ivan kept up, though neither of them had that "bombastic" flair of Bagitelli.

The song was on the short side and over before she knew it. The audience applauded again.

Fiona waited for the clapping to die down, then began the next piece. This one was slower and not as exciting. Hazy colors drifted across the screen. Miranda felt her eyelids drooping.

She shook herself. She hadn't come here for a nap.

Once more she lifted her opera glass, but this time she scanned the pale concrete steps curving up both sides of the stage. Each had a banister with Grecian-style balustrades casting shadows that hid whoever might be behind the steps.

Once more, she leaned toward Parker. "This is a lousy angle."

Subtly he nodded and spoke under his breath. "I agree, but it would be conspicuous to move now. Let's wait until intermission."

"Okay." She let out an impatient breath that had the man a few seats down scowling at her.

What a grouch.

Fiona and Ivan were bouncing out a new tune. Miranda recognized the same ditty the duo had been playing when she and Parker had visited them that afternoon.

She thought she heard Ivan miss that G-flat again.

Fiona grimaced, then went on as if nothing had happened.

Stifling a grin, Miranda settled in, tried to listen, tried to find Bagitelli in her line of view. But again her eyes fluttered. This time they shut, and the next thing she knew, Parker was rousing her.

"Wake up, sleepyhead," he murmured in her ear. "It's intermission."

Miranda lifted her head from Parker's shoulder and straightened her back. "Right. I knew that."

Before she could cuss herself, Parker leaned in with a tender smile. "You're correct about the angle. We need to spread out and get near the back."

"You mean separate?" She was surprised he'd suggested that.

"I think it's the only way. But be careful. If you see him, don't approach him. Call me first."

There was her overprotective knight in shining armor. But it was probably a good idea to be cautious. They had no idea what mental state Bagitelli might be in.

"Okay. I'll take this aisle, you take that one."

"Agreed."

"See you soon." She hoped.

And she gave him a peck on the cheek and headed up the nearest aisle.

CHAPTER FORTY-SIX

Everyone seemed to be having a jolly old time.

The music lovers were standing around in small groups, chatting with each other and relaxing, just as you would expect.

Near the front, a man in a tux was taking notes on his phone. Must be a music critic.

As she made her way through the crowd, Miranda passed women in cocktail dresses, summer dresses, and casual slacks. The guys were in suits, dark jackets and khakis, though some wore shorts and polo shirts. Most were without ties. She and Parker had overdressed.

Which was better than underdressing, he'd always told her.

Some of the patrons had water bottles in their hands, some beer bottles.

The rules were looser than Fiona would have liked, too, no doubt.

As she headed toward the back, she heard snatches of conversations. Some folks commented on the performance, but most were talking about the beach and plans for swimming or tanning or sightseeing the next day.

Miranda would have liked to ask each of them if they'd seen Bagitelli, but that would take too long. And cause a stir.

She scrolled to his photo on her phone just to remind herself what he looked like. Those dark eyes were unmistakable. And the streaks in his hair should make him stand out in a crowd. They knew he was wearing athletic shoes, a ball cap, and the casual clothes Dixie Sawyer had given him. No one dressed like that here.

A bell sounded and everyone took their seats.

There were some empty chairs in the back row, and Miranda scurried over to one and sat down. She didn't see Parker anywhere.

Applause rang out, and Fiona appeared on the stage again. This time alone. She bowed, sat down, and started to play.

Da-da-da daa. Da-da-da daa. Beethoven? Miranda glanced at her program. She'd gotten it right.

Parker must be rubbing off on her.

Fiona finished the tune, and Ivan marched back onto the stage, bowed for his allotment of applause, and sat down.

The music continued.

Using her opera glasses, Miranda craned her neck to get a good look at everyone in the audience around her one by one. Was Bagitelli hiding in plain sight among the music lovers? But there was no ball cap or funky hair three rows up. None in the next row, either.

When she got to the row in front of her, the piano duo had been through more songs than she could count.

At the moment, they were banging out another peppy one. Miranda snuck a peek at her program again. Had to be the Hungarian dance. There were only a few numbers left.

She had to do something. If they didn't find Bagitelli tonight, he might disappear into the ether.

Then she sat up as a disturbing thought hit her.

What if they had gotten it wrong? What if Bagitelli had gone back to the hospice? What if he was breaking into Rosalynd Allen's room right now?

Could that be where he'd gone?

No. If he was in town, he knew about this concert. He wouldn't be able to resist seeing it. Dr. Viotto thought so, and she knew him better than anyone.

Wait. What had she been thinking? Bagitelli wouldn't be in the audience. That would be too risky. He'd be lurking somewhere nearby.

Behind the stage?

She scanned the fencing around the perimeter of the seating area. It was pretty low. She hurried over to it. Lifting the drapey skirt of her dress, she managed to get over the barricade without tearing the fabric.

Moving quickly over the sand in her Crocs, she made her way to the side of the bandshell and around the curving steps that ascended to the platform. No one here.

She moved on. The back of the shell was painted black, but there was a patch of light revealing a door. She could see the backstage area where stage hands were doing their thing.

Bagitelli wouldn't be up there. Someone would see him for sure.

She turned her head the other way.

Maybe twenty yards or so across the sand stood an access ramp to the beach leading to a parking lot. Once again she lifted her opera glasses and saw vans parked up there. For the stage crew, she assumed.

But then, under the beam from a street lamp, she saw a patch of candy apple red behind a row of hedges bordering the lot. She squinted harder through the glasses and nearly gasped out loud.

The Gran Turismo. What was that doing here?

No time to figure it out, but Bagitelli wouldn't be up there. Too many people.

She turned around and headed across the sand and around the rear of the bandshell. No one was back here, and there wasn't much light.

But that made for good cover.

The piano music was faint. She could hear the sound of the waves in the distance.

A cold shiver slithered up her arms as a vague sensation of falling into deep water came to her. It was her experience on the Outer Banks of North Carolina last November. The one that had made just the sight of the sea give her the creeps.

Was she getting paranoid of the ocean?

Suddenly an overwhelming tingly feeling made her stop and stand on tiptoe. It wasn't the sensation Parker gave her when he rubbed her neck. It definitely wasn't the feel of a warm bath. It was the marching ants feeling. Like beetles were crawling up and down her spine. The feeling she'd had on so many cases before.

Her instincts, Parker would say.

Something was up. She couldn't ignore it. So instead, she followed it.

She continued around the contour of the building's rear, all the way over to the other side. Here the bandshell was a mirror image of what she'd seen before, but there was no activity.

Black steps led to a black stage door. It was so dark, she could barely see them. She could hardly make out the rest of the shell here. But light from the stage spilled over the matching set of curving concrete stairs just ahead of her.

Two rows of fancy Grecian-style balustrades swung out and away from the edge of the platform, and then back in, allowing performers to make a grand entrance from either side. Fiona and Ivan hadn't used them. They'd entered the stage from somewhere in the back.

But what caught Miranda's attention just now was the foot of the staircase. It formed a nice little crook where you could watch the show.

And in that crook, leaning over the banister just beyond a circular newel post stood a shadowy figure.

His back was to her. Sure enough, he was dressed in athletic shoes and baggy clothes. He had a ball cap in his hand, and his wavy dark locks hung loose down to his neck. They were dotted with greenish-blond streaks.

It was him.

Enrico Bagitelli.

CHAPTER FORTY-SEVEN

Slowly, Miranda folded her opera glasses, put them into her clutch bag, and drew out her Beretta. She inched nearer to the figure, and as she did, she realized he was watching the performance intently and directing with his hand.

Miranda could hear the music better here. She recognized the tune. *Moonlight Sonata.* Wasn't that the last number on the program? She'd left her paper on her seat.

Fiona seemed to be playing the piece by herself, but Miranda couldn't be sure.

And as she inched closer to Bagitelli, she saw his shoulders bob.

He was crying.

She raised the gun. "Don't move, Bagitelli."

"Shh," he said over his shoulder. "I'm listening. She's better. She's been practicing. And she's using the tempo technique I taught her. But she can never play the Sonata like Rosalynd did." His voice was low, tender, and had a hint of an Italian accent.

"Is that why you went to the hospice? To kill Rosalynd?"

He turned around, his dark eyes glistening with tears. He spotted the gun and his expression turned to alarm. But he managed to speak. Defiantly. "I went to the hospice to see Rosalynd. But there were too many police."

Miranda couldn't hold back a breath of relief. Their guess had been right. Bagitelli did go to the hospice. Alerting the police had saved Rosalynd.

For now.

"But you were going to go back once the cops were gone and finish her off, right?"

His eyes blazed. "No. I love her. I would never hurt her. I would never hurt anyone."

Bull. "You kidnapped Coco Estavez."

He blinked in surprise, then smiled at the memory. "Ah, Coco. What a promising musician she is."

He was making her angry. "She's pregnant and you took her from her home and made her drive hours away to your farm."

His face said he wondered how she knew that. "You don't understand. I needed to talk to her husband."

"You mean the man you attacked in court? The one you threatened to kill?"

Again he looked surprised. "Yes, I wanted to apologize to him."

"Apologize?" This guy wasn't a very good liar.

He took a step toward her.

She steadied the gun. "Get back."

He raised his hands in submission as his words turned into a plea. "You have to believe me. I wanted to beg Mr. Estavez to forgive me for that letter. I thought my father was forcing me to write it. I was in a bad way. I wanted to apologize for the way I acted in the courtroom. I wanted to ask Mr. Estavez to petition the court to reopen my case."

Oh, really? "And you think he'd do that? After you kidnapped his wife?"

"You don't understand. I wasn't thinking clearly when I kidnapped Coco. Or when I did any of those things. My medication...if it's not just right...my mind makes me do things I don't want to do." He sounded like he didn't want to admit that.

But it made sense. "I know. We spoke to Dr. Viotto. You stole medication from her."

"I had to. But she would have given it to me if she had been home."

That was probably true. Miranda thought of the things Dr. Viotto had told her and Parker about this man. His cruel father, his breakdown at the loss of his beloved mentor, the voices he heard in his head.

Suddenly she felt sorry for him. Was he telling the truth? Had he really just wanted to talk to Estavez?

She wanted to believe him, but it wasn't up to her. "I need to take you in, Bagitelli."

She needed a cop. Where was one? And where was Parker?

Bagitelli took a step toward her again. "You have to listen to me. I took the medication I borrowed from Dr. Viotto. I'm better now. And at last I remember."

She raised the gun higher. "Remember what?"

"What happened that night. The night of Rosalynd's accident."

"We know what happened. It wasn't an accident. You ran her over with your Gran Turismo."

"No, I didn't."

"There's a video that proves it."

He shook his head in denial. "I don't know how that video came to be, but I didn't try to kill Rosalynd. I loved her."

Miranda eyed the man cautiously. He looked broken, defeated. "But Rosalynd didn't return your affection, did she?"

"Of course, she did. You're not listening. It was all because of him."

"What do you mean? Because of who?"

Bagitelli opened his mouth, but someone else spoke.

"Enrico."

Recognizing Ivan's Russian accent, Miranda spun around and watched the large man's bulky frame step out from a dark corner behind her.

He stood there in his tux, his hair slicked back, his big hands fisted at his sides. His eyes glowed with what could only be a deep seated hatred.

He must have come out here when he finished his last number. He'd been standing in the shadows all this while, eavesdropping on her conversation.

On stage, Miranda could hear Fiona furiously banging out notes, but neither of these men were listening to her now.

Bagitelli's face went livid. "Ivan. This all happened because of you."

The tall man stepped in closer to Bagitelli. "No, Enrico. It happened because of you. Because of Fiona."

Bagitelli scowled. "What are you talking about?"

Ivan threw out his arm in a wild gesture. "You know perfectly well what I'm talking about. You ignored her, neglected her for years. You told her she was a mediocre musician."

Bagitelli's eyes blazed with Italian fury. "I did no such thing. Did she tell you that?"

"She told me everything."

"She lied. She seduced you. Or did you seduce her?"

Ivan moved in front of Bagitelli, blocking Miranda's view of him. "She loved me. And I love her."

"You had an affair behind my back. After all I did for you. All I taught you. How dare you?" Bagitelli shoved his palms against Ivan's broad chest.

The big man stumbled backward, but only for a few steps. "Of course, we had an affair," Ivan growled, regaining his balance. "For years. And you were too absorbed in your music to even notice."

Bagitelli stepped toward Ivan and shoved him again. "That isn't true."

"It doesn't matter anymore. She's mine now." This time, Ivan didn't budge. He shoved back. Harder than Bagitelli ever could.

Bagitelli staggered backward and landed against the wall of the staircase with an oof.

Miranda moved back and away from the pair as she steadied her weapon on Bagitelli. "Knock it off, you two."

Fiona's notes were getting faster and more intense. The concert would end soon.

Bagitelli ignored her. Eyes glowing, he leered at Ivan. "No, Ivan. It doesn't matter anymore. Because I remember that night now. I remember everything that happened. I remember someone telling me to go to the parking lot. I remember you standing out there with your phone."

Ivan pointed a finger at Bagitelli. "You're right, Enrico. I was in the parking lot with my phone. I was the one who took the video of the murder. I was the one who turned it into the prosecutor anonymously. And I was the one who made sure it would convict you."

"What?" Miranda started to turn toward the big man.

Before she could, Ivan's bulky frame slammed into her.

Somehow she managed to keep her balance, but he grabbed her arm and twisted hard.

She yelped, and the Beretta slipped out of her hand. As it fell to the sand, she reared back and brought up a knee, aiming for Ivan's lower parts.

He sidestepped just in time, and swung a bulky arm under her thigh.

Down she went, nearly hitting her head on the hard sand.

Rolling over, she got on her knees and tried to scramble for the gun, but Ivan beat her to it. He swept it up and pointed it at Bagitelli.

Breathing hard, Miranda stared at Ivan in disbelief. "What the heck do you think you're doing?"

He turned and pointed the gun in her face.

Sudden terror zinged through her, twisting her insides. But she managed to summon a cop tone. "Put that gun down."

Eyes glowing, Ivan shook his head. "You know too much now, Ms. Steele. And so does Enrico. I'll have to get rid of you both."

What did she know? What in the world had been on that video?

Miranda dared to get to her feet. "Calm down, Ivan. Let's go to the police and let them sort all this out."

Again Ivan wagged his head back and forth. "I knew everything would unravel when you and your detective husband came to see us today. But I can fix it. Just like I fixed the video. All I have to do is shoot both of you. I'll put the gun in Enrico's hand, and go find the police. I'll tell them I saw Enrico kill you and then turn the weapon on himself. Murder suicide. He has every motive in the world to do it. He's crazy, after all."

It was Ivan who looked like the crazy one now. Crazy enough to carry out his threat.

Fiona's playing stopped.

There was a pause, and then loud applause and cheers. And then a low murmur came from the crowd.

The audience was wondering when her duet partner was going to come out and take his bow.

Her heart banging away in her chest, Miranda managed a smirk. "You know, Ivan, that murder suicide thing is pretty hard to pull off. You have to get the angles just right."

"I can handle it," he growled. "I can do anything." He turned and pointed the gun at her head. "All I have to do is—"

"No you don't."

The lights from the stage above Ivan's head blurred for an instant as a dark figure appeared on the curving stairs just above him.

A muscular figure. Dressed in a classy dark suit.

Suddenly he came flying over the banister above Ivan's head and landed on the big man's back. The force knocked the Beretta out of Ivan's hand, and it soared off into the air somewhere behind Miranda as the two men toppled to the ground.

The dark figure struggled to get his arm around Ivan's neck, and Miranda caught a glimpse of his handsome face.

Parker.

Not that she didn't know that already.

Spinning around, she searched the ground for her weapon. She didn't see it anywhere.

Then she looked up and saw Bagitelli disappear around the back of the bandshell.

There was a grunt behind her.

She turned back around.

Parker was on his feet, facing the big man now. Ivan took a swing at him. Parker ducked and hit back, landing a nice jab on Ivan's jaw.

"Go after him, Miranda," Parker yelled without taking his eyes off Ivan.

He'd seen Bagitelli run away.

She didn't want to leave Parker. She wanted to help. She wanted to hurry over to the big Russian and give him a hard kick in the groin.

But there was no time. Parker could handle himself.

With their grunts and punches in her ears, she turned around again and ran to where Bagitelli had vanished behind the bandshell.

CHAPTER FORTY-EIGHT

It seemed even darker than before back here behind the stage.

Miranda scanned the sand, but couldn't see any sign of Bagitelli. Did he have her gun? If he did, there was no telling what he might do with it.

She thought about using her opera glasses, but then she realized she'd lost her clutch purse during her fight with Ivan.

She pressed on.

Along the other side of the bandshell, the stage crew was unloading lights and other equipment, carrying heavy cases over the sand to the access bridge that led to the parking lot. Members of the audience were wandering around as if nothing was wrong. Some were lingering, some heading back to their cars.

Had Bagitelli gotten lost in the crowd?

She stopped for a second to catch her breath and scanned the beach. Farther down along the sand, surrounded by tall trees, stood another access bridge. It was hard to see, but in the dark shadows, Miranda spotted a man climbing up the steps to it.

There he was.

She ran toward him, but it was slow going in the sand, and by the time she got there, Bagitelli had disappeared again.

She hurried up the steps and across the wooden planks. Her Crocs made too much noise.

Soon the bridge turned into a path that ran alongside the resort. It was fenced in, hedges on both sides. Bagitelli couldn't have veered off it.

To her left, she heard laughing. A group of folks was strolling along a distant patch of pavement, probably heading to their rooms.

Bagitelli wasn't with them.

Running hard, she came to the end of the path. She had to stop again.

Catching her breath, she saw she was on concrete now. A sidewalk that ran alongside a paved road. It headed into a neighborhood of small homes and cottages.

She peered in that direction.

There he was.

Under the streetlamps, she could make out the dark rumpled figure. He was crossing the intersection at the end of the road. She ran after him, not daring to call out. He wouldn't stop for her.

Finally, she came to the spot where she'd seen him. Turning ninety degrees, she shielded her eyes and squinted into the darkness.

Nothing.

Where did he go?

She ran along the next sidewalk until she reached another intersection. She made another turn and continued. Past a white picket fence, a pickup truck, a yard with a big beach ball lying near a garden. The hedges were thicker here, and the road started to incline.

The wind started to pick up. Clumps of palm trees swayed overhead. Palmetto leafs brushed her arms as she went along.

Her shoes weren't the best for this, and the feel of the occasional stone on the pavement went right through the material, slowing her down.

The road curved, and as she jogged along the street lamps began to reveal pricey seaside cottages hidden in the foliage. Suddenly Miranda recognized them. She'd driven this road with Parker that afternoon. Now she knew where Bagitelli was going.

Back to Fiona's villa.

He was going to wait for her there and shoot her when she got home. With her gun.

It had to be his plan. He'd just learned she'd cheated on him with Ivan. Sooner or later the police would catch him and send him back to prison. Why not make it worth his while?

If she was going to stop him, she had to hurry.

She put her head down and went for the burn.

There were no cars on the road here. All the homes were quiet and still. No sidewalks now, either. The yards ran right up to the pavement, with just a bit of sandy dirt leading to the grass. Lots of thick hedges and saw palmetto and other plants edging the tall stucco of the structures.

Her legs started to ache. Would she get there in time? Gulping in air, she thought about the desperation in Bagitelli's voice tonight. He'd said he wanted to apologize to Estavez. He admitted he had a condition. He knew he needed medication.

Something wasn't right about her theory.

The idea made her slow her pace. And then she stopped as the truth hit her.

Bagitelli was innocent, wasn't he?

She couldn't put all the pieces together yet, but she felt it in her bones. And then all at once a loud roar rang in her ears.

It came from right behind her.

She spun around in time to see blinding headlights rolling straight toward her.

Reflexes took over and she ran for the nearest hedgerow. Taking a leap, she cleared it just as the vehicle smashed into the bushes behind her, making them shiver like an earthquake.

The car came to a halt, but the driver put it in reverse and backed out. It turned around and squealed back down the street in the same direction it had come.

But Miranda had seen the car. It was the candy apple red Gran Turismo.

Drinking in air, she blinked, trying to clear her head.

No, Bagitelli wasn't innocent. After she'd spotted him in that first neighborhood she'd run through, he'd gone back to the parking lot and stolen the car that used to belong to him.

He was trying to kill her with it before she could tell the police what she'd heard tonight. And then he would take care of Fiona and Ivan.

Where had the car gone? She didn't know, but she had to get to the villa before he did.

She crossed the street. There was more yard on this side. Huffing hard, she jogged along as fast as she could, but her energy stores were running low.

She longed for a big gulp of water. Or an energy bar. Or her gun.

Suddenly she realized she didn't even have her cell phone on her.

And then a roar came from behind her again.

Once more she spun around and was blinded by headlights zooming straight for her.

Turning back, Miranda spread out her hands and was lucky enough to find a tree trunk leaning over the road. She grabbed onto it and scrambled up a few feet, just as the Gran Turismo slammed into it with a loud crunch.

She held onto the trunk with all she had as the whole tree shivered from the force, and her whole body quaked along with it.

What was she going to do now? Climb to the top and wait for daybreak?

But once again, the car backed up, the engine hissing and steaming. The front end was damaged, but it rolled away again, this time backwards.

Getting up momentum for the next attack, she thought.

Wondering what to do, she turned her face to the ocean.

The lighthouse.

Or whatever it was. The old brick building she had noticed when she'd been here with Parker earlier.

Under the moonlight and the stars and a light on a tall pole, it stood across the street as if beckoning to her. She took in the wide sandy yard, the length of the pier beside it.

If she could just get to that house, maybe she'd be safe from that car.

Without second guessing herself, Miranda scrambled down the trunk and sprinted across the road.

The house was farther away than she thought. There was nothing along the road here but thick fern-like bushes that looked like they belonged in a jungle. She wouldn't be able to jump them if the car came back. She had to hurry. The pebbles under her feet were biting into her soles, but she pushed on.

And then she heard the engine roar behind her again. Her heart pounded in her ears.

C'mon, c'mon. You can do it.

Faster. Faster.

The headlights shined on the road beside her. The car would be here any second.

Push.

She zoomed ahead as fast as she could, bolted into the sandy yard, and ran right up to the edge of the lawn.

She forced herself to stop just in time.

Over the row of hedges she could see a steep drop off. About six feet of sharp rocks to the beach below and the rolling waves beyond. Going over those bushes wouldn't be pleasant.

But the Gran Turismo was right behind her.

Bracing herself, she spun around and watched it surge onto the sand with a growl, heading straight for her. The beams of its headlights bobbed as its hood rocked up and down. It rolled a few yards, sputtered, and then came to a halt and stalled.

The tires were stuck in the sand. It was an older model and didn't have four-wheel drive.

Reeling with relief and gasping for breath, Miranda watched the driver's door open. She raised her hands, about to call out, "Don't shoot" to Bagitelli.

But what she saw next made everything suddenly click into place.

CHAPTER FORTY-NINE

The long sequined gown shimmered in the moonlight as the elegant form emerged from the vehicle.

She took a few steps forward in the sand and stopped, making a silhouette in the car's headlights.

The figure glared at her.

Miranda glared back. "Fiona."

"Miranda Steele," Fiona sneered. "Prominent successful private investigator along with your prominent successful private investigator husband, Wade Parker. Our performance tonight would have gone so much better if Ivan and I hadn't had to spend time researching who you were. When we found out, I told him we were in trouble."

Miranda swung a hand toward the Maserati. "What were you trying to do with that car?"

She snorted as if that was the silliest question she'd ever heard. "I have to stop you."

"From doing what?" But Miranda had a pretty good idea.

"From going to the police, of course. After the concert I found Ivan with your husband's arm against his neck. It took two officers to pull them apart. And when they did, Ivan told me you know everything. I had to do something."

But she didn't know everything. Not yet.

Miranda took a cautious step toward her. "And so you came after me the way you did Rosalynd that night."

Fiona only stared at her with a satisfied smirk that told Miranda her guess was right.

"It was you who got out of that car the night of the accident, wasn't it? The same way you just got out of it now."

Her lips thinned.

"How could you run over your own sister?" Miranda remembered how emotional Fiona had been about Rosalynd that afternoon. It was all an act.

Fiona's eyes glowed as her face twisted with emotion. "Half sister."

"What?"

"Rosalynd is my half sister. My father was Gregory Smith Allen. He was a composer and music teacher in Yonkers, where I was born. He gave me my first lessons. But when I was seven, he left, and I never saw him again."

Miranda could relate to that. Her own father had deserted her at five.

"On my sixteenth birthday, I demanded my mother tell me what happened to my father. She told me he'd fallen in love with someone else. She divorced him and he married the woman. They had a daughter."

"Rosalynd."

She nodded. "I was curious, so I looked her up. I discovered she was playing concerts at eight in Paris, where my father was living with his new family. Rosalynd was the one who went to the Conservatory there."

That explained a lot.

"He never supported us. My mother was too proud to take money from him. All the time I was growing up, we had to scrimp and save just to make ends meet. While he made sure Rosalynd had the best of everything. My mother had to work three jobs to afford piano lessons for me. I had to work, too. Even when I went to Juilliard."

"Where you met Bagitelli."

Her face softened. "Enrico was a wonderful tutor. He told me I had talent. He restored the confidence I lost when my father left."

"And you fell in love with him."

Fiona gave her a condescending smile. "We were student and teacher, and then later colleagues. When we started touring together, it was for our careers. We thought marrying would only further our success."

What was she saying? "You never loved him?"

She laughed. "Women always flocked to Enrico. Of course, he loved the adulation, and as far as I know he was never unfaithful. Still, if I was in love with him, how could I have put up with that?"

Miranda managed something like that with Parker. Different case entirely.

Fiona's chest began to rise and fall. While she fumed, Miranda stepped gingerly out of the headlights and got a little closer to her.

"And then *she* came into our lives," Fiona snarled.

Rosalynd.

"All blond and pretty and young."

"And more talented."

Fiona's eyes flashed with anger. "My father had spoiled her, doted on her, like he never did with me. He made sure she had piano lessons from the best teachers, so of course, she became a virtuoso. She never had to sacrifice for her career like I did. I only prayed our paths would never cross."

"But they did."

Fiona closed her eyes and pressed a hand to her head as she moved to the side of the car and out of the headlights. "In Paris, ironically. She was playing at Saint Germain. We were at the Philharmonic. She had a day off and came to hear us. She told the stage manager she was family, and Enrico invited her onto the stage. They played the *Moonlight Sonata* together. Our song. He made such a fuss over her. He said it was because she was my long lost sister, but I knew he'd fallen in love with her. He asked her to join our troupe, and lost all interest in me. Just the way my father had."

"And so you turned to Ivan."

Again Fiona smirked. This time with a wicked glint in her eyes. "Enrico had been tutoring him for years. He wasn't the best musician in the world, but he was a wonderful lover."

Miranda recalled what Ivan had said tonight. Fiona had been cheating on Bagitelli with him long before Rosalynd came along.

"Why didn't you just divorce Bagitelli?"

"Rosalynd would have loved that. She would get a fabulous career and Enrico's money. You asked me why I never went to see my sister in hospice. I'll tell you why. Because I didn't think I could keep myself from strangling her with my bare hands. 'Be patient,' Ivan kept telling me. 'Eventually she'll be gone.' But it's been years, and she refuses to die. She took everything from me. I hate her. I hate her. I hate her."

She sounded like a spoiled teenager. "And so you came up with a plan to kill her and frame Bagitelli for her murder. You manipulated Bagitelli's medications until he didn't know which way was up, didn't you?"

"Enrico was ill."

"And you made him worse. You made sure no one else was in the parking lot that night. You got Ivan to video the scene while you ran Rosalynd over with that car. You knew Bagitelli would rush to her broken body on the pavement."

But was she right? The video had clearly showed Bagitelli getting out of the car.

Miranda played the footage over in her mind, slowing it down, going frame-by-frame. She remembered Ivan's words to Bagitelli tonight. "I was the one who made sure it would convict you."

A chill went through her as she recalled a little blip in the recording.

It was subtle, skillfully done. You almost didn't see it.

The door of the Gran Turismo opened. You could see a well-dressed man's leg and foot appear under it. You could hear the door close. And then Bagitelli ran past the car and over to Rosalynd. That was where the blip was. That leg was from some other video.

Ivan had spliced it in.

The defense attorney had been too green to catch it. She and Parker had been too focused on saving Estavez and Coco to notice it.

But it was there.

She could hardly believe it. "And after they took Rosalynd away and arrested Bagitelli, Ivan edited the video to make it look like Bagitelli was the one who got out of the car. But it was you. Wasn't it?"

Fiona's smile was as cold as a corpse. "He's very good, isn't he? He started out on our promotions team. He had tons of videos of Enrico to use. Splicing the video was easy for him. So now you know it all. Aren't you clever? But I've just started my new life. I can't let you and your husband ruin it. You're not going to stop me from putting Enrico back in prison."

Fiona was too far away to grab. But all Miranda needed was a little more time to get close enough.

She took a few steps forward. "And how are you going to do that?"

"With this."

Miranda rushed toward the woman, but Fiona was faster.

In a swift, graceful move, she bent down, reached under the hem of her gown, and straightened again.

In her hand was a gun.

CHAPTER FIFTY

Fiona pointed the weapon at Miranda with both hands.

It was hard to see the details in the glare of the headlights, but it wasn't her Beretta. Too small. A Pink Lady was her guess.

She decided to go with sarcasm. "Where'd you get that thing? A toy store?"

Fiona didn't even flinch. "Ivan bought it for me. Along with a very chic ankle holster. He said we should never be too careful while performing. There might be a lunatic in the audience. Turns out he was right."

Except Ivan and Fiona were the lunatics.

Miranda's heart began to pound again as she watched the woman shift her weight back and forth trying to aim the barrel at her.

She wasn't close to her, and she looked like she didn't know what she was doing. Couldn't have had much practice. No, she spent her time practicing piano.

"You don't know how to use that thing, do you? Put it down before you hurt yourself."

"It's you I'm going to hurt."

Not if she could help it. Her stomach in a hard knot, Miranda tried to reason with her. "You don't want to go to prison for murder."

"No, and I won't. I'll toss your body in the sea and the waves will carry you far away. No one will find you."

She'd put some thought into her plan. Still, it would be hard to pull off. There'd be too much evidence. But Miranda wouldn't be around to point that out if Fiona managed the first part.

The tough act wasn't working. She held out her palms and softened her voice. "We can work something out, Fiona. I'll help you get the Maserati out of the sand, and you can go home. I'll keep quiet about everything you told me."

Fiona's laugh rang in the air. "And you expect me to believe that?"

Right. It was too much of a stretch. She went back to the weapon. "Have you ever even fired that thing before?"

The look of surprise on Fiona's face told her she hadn't.

"You know, even at close range, there's a good chance you'll miss. Look. The safety's still on."

It wasn't, but the trick worked. Fiona glanced down at her hands.

Instantly Miranda lunged forward, clutched her wrists, and twisted hard. Fiona snarled in surprise, but her grip loosened, and the weapon fell to the sand just under their feet.

Miranda pivoted and booted the thing away with the heel of her Croc.

"No!" Fiona cried and kicked out at Miranda's shin with a sharp-toed dress shoe.

It landed right on the bone. "Ouch."

Miranda let go of Fiona's arms and kicked back with her knee.

She must have been exhausted from so much running. Her reflexes were dull. Fiona stepped back and instead of her thigh, Miranda's knee hit air. She lost her balance and started to drop to the ground.

She wasn't going down alone. Grabbing onto Fiona's sequined gown, she tumbled forward onto the moist sand and landed right on top of the woman.

"Get off of me!" Fiona's dark eyes glowed like a demon's as she reached for a wad of Miranda's hair and yanked.

Miranda's neck jerked around and she heard some of her roots tear loose. This lady was strong.

"Yow, you bitch." She threw a punch at Fiona's face but only grazed the side of it.

Fiona swung back. Miranda blocked her and tried to pin her arm.

Fiona grabbed onto her shoulder and squeezed.

Wow, that hurt. Those strong piano-playing fingers dug into her flesh.

Fighting through the pain, she reared back and socked Fiona in the side of her head.

Fiona absorbed the punch, leveraged her body, and suddenly was on top of her.

But Miranda had the advantage of a shorter skirt. And martial arts. She lifted her leg and wrapped it around Fiona, trying to stand. Fiona grabbed her arms and pulled her down again.

And now they were rolling over and over on the sand, getting farther and farther away from the Maserati and closer to the bushes and the rocks on the other side.

She had no idea where Fiona's gun was.

Her back hit the bushes and she felt the branches sticking into her ribs. With all the strength she had, she shoved Fiona off of her and got to her knees.

She raised her arm, about to give Fiona's jaw an elbow thrust, but the woman wiggled away and began digging under the bushes.

"Stop," Miranda yelled when she realized what she was doing.

Fiona twisted back around—holding her gun again. How had it gotten this far?

Breathing hard, Fiona scrambled to her feet.

Still on her knees, Miranda raised her hands as the woman pressed the barrel to her temple.

"I can't miss at this distance, can I? And the safety is off."

Gasping for breath, Miranda heard a siren in the distance. The police were hunting Bagitelli. They might be going house to house. Or they might be heading to the villa and pass this way. She hoped so.

"Hear that, Fiona? The police are coming."

"Shut up."

"You won't get away with killing me any more than you're going to get away with killing your sister."

"Half sister, I told you."

"Whatever."

"I said, shut up." She pressed the barrel harder.

Miranda knew she was going to pull the trigger any second. She had to think of something.

And then the bushes across the yard began to rustle, and a figure stepped out of them.

"Fiona. What are you doing with Ms. Steele? And with my Maserati."

Italian accent. It was Bagitelli. And he had Miranda's Beretta in his hand.

Miranda could feel Fiona jump. "Enrico. What are you doing here?"

"I was trying to get to the villa to get money and my passport. I was hiding in the bushes down the road when I saw my Gran Turismo speed by. You tried to run her over, didn't you?"

Fiona sputtered in shock. "She's trying to put you back in jail, Enrico. Don't you want to see her dead?"

Bagitelli wasn't buying it. He aimed the gun at his ex-wife. "Get away from her, Fiona."

"She tried to kill me, Enrico. Help me."

"I don't believe you. You've lied to me so many times."

"She told me everything, Bagitelli," Miranda said to him. "I know you're innocent. You were wrongly convicted."

"That's what I was trying to tell you before," he said to her. "That's what I remembered. I wasn't in the car that night. Fiona was driving it."

It was true.

Fiona spoke gently. "You need your medication, Enrico. You're imagining things again."

"No, I took my medication. I'm in complete control of my senses." Taking a step toward her, he aimed the Beretta. "And I said drop the gun."

Miranda could hear Fiona's heavy breathing. She dared to turn her head just a little and look up.

Her attention was on Bagitelli. She had to act now.

Raising her arm, she reached out and pushed down as hard as she could.

Fiona shrieked. Once more the Pink Lady fell to the ground.

This time Miranda snatched it up.

But before she could get to her feet, she saw Fiona glaring at Bagitelli with a wild look. "Fiona Delacroix does not belong in jail. Fiona Delacroix will never go to prison."

And she spun around and ran.

Where did she think she was going? Then Miranda saw she was heading for the pier at the edge of the yard.

"Stop, Fiona, or I'll shoot," Bagitelli yelled after her.

"No, you won't, Enrico," Fiona called over her shoulder. "You're too much of a coward."

The sirens were getting louder, but Miranda couldn't let her get away.

The gun still in her hand, she tore after the crazy woman as fast as she could go.

CHAPTER FIFTY-ONE

It wasn't a pier.
It was another one of those access bridges to the beach, Miranda realized as she clattered down the steep wooden ramp.
Fiona was already out on the sand, moving ghostlike toward the water.
"Fiona," Miranda shouted. "What the heck are you doing?"
"Leave me alone, Miranda Steele." She kept going.
The full moon illuminated the rising tide as the waves washed against the shore.
Birdlike, Fiona spread her arms and headed straight for them.
"Stop. That water's dangerous."
Miranda stared at the waves, heart pounding, chills rippling through her, the memory of the ocean washing over her playing in her brain.
Fiona's full-throated laugh rang out into the night. "I will walk into the sea and die before I reach forty. Like Chopin and Schubert and Mozart."
The waves were already swirling around her legs.
The prima donna wanted a tragic ending. Miranda wasn't going to let her have it.
She kicked off her Crocs and sprinted over to her.
The water was up to her knees now, and Fiona's gown began to billow in the waves.
Miranda stepped into it. The water wasn't freezing, but it was a lot cooler than the air.
"Hey, it's cold in here. Let's get out and get warm."
"You're growing tiresome." Fiona was getting away.
Miranda let go of Fiona's gun, bent down, grabbed the train of her dress, and held on tight. "I said stop."
"My fate is mine to choose. No one shall take that from me."

Good grief. This wasn't the time to get poetic. Miranda dug her toes into the sand and clung onto the hem of the gown. For a moment, she stopped Fiona's progress.

Then a wave came in and swept both of them up and off their feet. It peaked and receded, moving them out farther into the water.

Miranda couldn't feel the sand beneath her toes any more.

Breathe, she told herself. She hoped Fiona was doing that, too.

The skirt of her own dress was ballooning around her. She wished she could tear it off.

And she'd lost her grip on Fiona. Where was she?

"Help."

The voice seemed to come from a long distance.

How did she get so far away?

Miranda dove into the water and swam over to her. It seemed like half an hour before she reached her.

She was dog-paddling now. Frantically.

Miranda grabbed Fiona's arm, but it slipped out of her grasp.

"Leave me alone," she screeched. "Leave me alone." The woman was panicking.

"Calm down, Fiona. Just relax."

"How can I relax? I'm going to die."

Miranda fought the rippling water and tried to grab her under her chin, lifeguard like.

Fiona fought like crazy, batting her hands away. Miranda settled for the neckline of her gown, but that wasn't easy. The sequined fabric was form fitting and clung to Fiona's body like a mermaid's scales.

At last, she managed to get hold of some of the cloth just under her collar bone.

"Let go of me."

"Relax." Miranda turned back, trying to swim toward the shore, dragging Fiona with her.

There was activity on the beach. Was that shouting? Lifeguards? She thought she saw an ambulance, but it looked like a tiny toy. The figures on the sand were pin dots.

How did they get so far out?

If they caught a rip tide, they'd be swept out to sea. She could feel her own panic welling up inside her.

Fiona wriggled under her grip, flailing her arms against the water. "Help me. Oh, help me."

"Be still and relax. You're going to be okay."

But just as the words were out of her mouth, a huge wave crested over their heads and crashed down on them. The force of it pulled Miranda deep under the water. Down she went, terror engulfing her.

She was going under again. Just like in the middle of the ocean last November. She thought of her half-brother who'd been swept out to sea.

She was going to join him this time, wasn't she?

She wanted to sob, but she didn't dare. I'm sorry, Parker, she thought. I'm sorry I always act before I think.

And then suddenly, her body was propelled upward and her head popped up on the surface. She spat out water and gulped in air as her hands searched for Fiona.

"Miranda."

She knew that voice.

Turning around she saw Parker swimming toward her. He was wet and bare chested and beautiful. And he had something orange in his hands.

An oblong piece of plastic. A rescue buoy.

And then his hands were pulling her up and onto it. "Hang onto this."

Sucking in air, she clung to the thing as hard as she could, though her arms were shivering.

She could barely speak, but she managed one word. "Fiona."

Parker nodded over her shoulder. "He's got her."

She turned her head and saw a buff young man heaving the pianist onto another buoy.

As soon as she was secured, the lifeguard grabbed a rope attached to the device and began to swim to shore.

Parker did the same.

They began gliding over the waves as if they were butter.

She was safe. And so was Fiona. For now.

CHAPTER FIFTY-TWO

It seemed to take years to reach the sand, but when at last they did, there were blankets and hot coffee, electrolyte drinks, and a warm ambulance with EMTs to check her out. While Dr. Viotto's friend, Officer Briggs, took her statement.

Miranda didn't think she'd ever stop shaking, and she felt more tired than she ever had in her life.

But the sight of Parker's handsome face and the touch of his strong hand on hers was enough to revive her a little.

She grinned up at him. "I got a full confession from Fiona."

"So Bagitelli told us."

She blinked at him. "Bagitelli?"

"After I subdued Ivan at the bandshell, and an officer took him into custody, I rode with Officer Briggs to look for you. My guess was that Bagitelli would head for the Villa."

"That was my guess, too."

"I surmised as much, so we headed that way. Just before we reached our destination, Bagitelli ran out into the road and flagged us down."

"He did?"

Parker nodded. "He told us everything, and that you had followed Fiona into the ocean."

Parker's expression was serene, but his tone told her he had been rattled. But he wasn't angry. He was the one who'd told her to go after Bagitelli, after all.

She looked up and saw the man himself coming across the sand to her, an officer at his side. As they approached, the officer drew a weapon from his duty belt and handed it to Miranda. "I believe this belongs to you, ma'am."

Her Beretta.

She took it from him and held it gingerly. Bagitelli had saved her life with this tonight. She didn't know what to say. She handed it to Parker for safekeeping. She was too wet right now.

"Please let me speak to her," Bagitelli said to the officer in his Italian accent. The officer nodded.

Bagitelli stepped forward and took both her hands in his as if he wanted to kiss them. He still had on his rumpled clothes, but now free of his ball cap, and his thick dark hair fell in waves around his good-looking face.

His dark, deep set eyes glowed with intense emotion. "I am so sorry for what Fiona did to you tonight, Ms. Steele."

"It wasn't your fault."

"No, but I apologize for her. And I want to thank you, both of you, from the bottom of my heart. Especially you, Ms. Steele, for getting Fiona to confess what she did."

"I'm glad we got the truth."

"That's all we were after," Parker agreed.

"And finally, I know the truth, as well." Meaning what he'd seen the night Rosalynd was run over hadn't been a hallucination.

The officer led Bagitelli away, leaving Miranda feeling numb, but gratified.

"We both owe that man a debt of gratitude," Parker said.

"Yes, we do."

She was about to ask Briggs what would happen next, when a bright light had her squinting and shielding her eyes with her hands.

A production light.

Someone stuck a microphone under her nose. "How does it feel to be a local hero, Ms. Steele?"

She glared up at a young man with gelled hair and a waxy grin as Parker raised an arm to block his access to her.

"No comment," she growled.

And she got up and headed across the sand.

CHAPTER FIFTY-THREE

A few hours later Miranda awoke in the warm bed of the resort hotel to the murmur of Parker's voice.

Dressed in a white luxury bathrobe that revealed too much of his sexy muscular body, he sat in a nearby armchair murmuring softly into his phone.

She spotted her own phone and her clutch bag on the nightstand near her head.

"I agree that would be best. Very well. We'll see you tomorrow, then." He hung up.

She narrowed an eye at him. "What are you up to?"

Drinking her in with his gaze, he came over to the bed, stroked her hair, and gave her a hard kiss. "Thank God I didn't lose you tonight."

Yeah. Feeling tingly all over from the touch of his lips, she let herself moan a little. It wouldn't take much to sink into that mattress with him and indulge in a frenzied love fest.

Instead, she sat up. "You didn't answer my question."

With an amused smile, he kissed her cheek. "That was Antonio. He's going to contact the DA in Fulton County and have him request Bagitelli's attempted murder conviction be overturned. And that he not be charged with his escape."

"Can he do that?"

"As you know, Antonio can work miracles in the courts. In light of the confessions you secured tonight, he believes Bagitelli will be released in a few days."

Miranda let out a breath. "That's great."

"Meanwhile, the local police are allowing Bagitelli to be held under house arrest in his Villa. They know he's not going anywhere. And he'll be under Dr. Viotto's care, as well."

"Good to hear. Though that place probably has a lot of bad memories for him."

"Good ones, too, I think. His first request to the officers was to be allowed to see Rosalynd."

"Do you think that will happen?"

"I hope so." Growing quiet. Parker drew a thumb over her fingers.

She looked down at their entwined hands. "We got it wrong, Parker. We went after an innocent man."

"We followed the evidence we had. He had been convicted, after all."

"Wrongly convicted. If only I had looked at that video more closely." She looked into his beautiful gray eyes, her heart in a jumble. "Am I—losing it?"

Parker regarded her intently, his heart burning with love for his dear, brave wife. He had almost lost her tonight, but once again she had survived. They had to stop tempting fate like this.

Then he smiled. "A woman swims into the ocean fully dressed at night to bring in a killer? That doesn't sound like someone who's losing it to me." He took her in her arms and drew her close, breathing in the scent of her ocean washed hair. "Would you like to stay here overnight?"

Miranda wasn't expecting that question. They had planned to leave as soon as the case was closed, but it was late.

The bed was warm and comfy, and Parker's arms around her were delicious. But this was Fiona's resort. And the room Fiona had given them.

The idea kind of gave her the creeps.

She gave him a saucy peck on the cheek. "Think you can get us a red eye back to Atlanta?"

The glow in Parker's eyes told her he had been hoping for that answer. "I'll make the reservation now."

CHAPTER FIFTY-FOUR

At nine o'clock the next morning, a county police car rolled up the driveway to Island Oasis Hospice Care, and an officer escorted Enrico Bagitelli inside.

On the third floor, Dr. Hart gave him a summary of the patient's condition and told him he could see her for only a few minutes.

"You must be very quiet," he warned.

"I understand."

"And don't mention the accident or anything that might disturb her."

"I understand."

Dr. Hart hesitated another moment, then opened the door.

Enrico stepped into the cool dimly-lit room, and the sight took his breath.

There was his Rosalynd encased in tubes, her pretty blond hair in a tangle on the pillow, machines everywhere beeping softly. He approached the bed and felt so very helpless as he watched her chest rise and fall as she breathed with the help of some contraption.

She looked so frail.

He dared to whisper to her. "Rosalynd. Rosalynd, my darling. It's me, Enrico."

Of course, there was no response.

He put a hand to his mouth to hold back the tears. "I'm so sorry, my darling. So very, very sorry this happened to you."

He drew in air, tried to compose himself. "I wasn't able to come and see you for such a long time. They thought I had—"

"Mr. Bagitelli."

Enrico looked up and met the doctor's scowl. He was right. Talking about what had happened wouldn't help. There was nothing he could do here. He should leave.

He bent his head to say goodbye, hoping a gentle kiss might comfort her. And then he froze.

He could see her eyes moving under the lids.

"Don't upset her," the doctor warned.

"She can hear me, can't she?"

"From the response on the monitor, that may be the case."

Enrico glanced up and saw lines moving on the screen. indecipherable as a page of Beethoven's sheet music.

He couldn't help it. As tenderly as he could, he took her hand in his and whispered to her, at long last baring his soul. "Oh, Rosalynd. Please know I love you. I have never stopped loving you, and I will until I take my dying breath."

The doctor cleared his throat. "Mr. Bagitelli, I'm going to have to ask you to leave now."

"One more moment, Doctor." He dared to stroke her face. "Rosalynd, if you could just give me a sign that you forgive me."

"Please, Mr. Bagitelli."

It was too much to hope for. He was being selfish. He had to go. He had to leave her in peace.

But suddenly he felt pressure on his hand. "Wait."

The lines on the monitor seemed to be getting stronger.

He looked down again and watched Rosalynd's eyes flutter. Was she dreaming?

And then slowly, they opened.

She stared up at him as if he was a ghost. "En—rico?" she said in a hoarse dry whisper.

His heart skipped a beat. "Yes. Yes, it's me."

The pressure on his hand grew a little stronger. "Enrico. Where have you been?" Blinking, she turned her head as if her eyes were adjusting to the low light. "Where am I?"

"You're in a hospice."

"How did I get here?"

"I don't know where to begin to tell you."

"Mr. Bagitelli, please step back."

The doctor eased him aside and spoke softly to his patient. "I'm Dr. Hart, Ms. Allen. I've been treating you for some time. Let me assure you, you're in good hands. You've had the best of care. And it seems to have worked." With a smile, he glanced at Enrico. "Or perhaps it was something more than that."

The doctor went on to explain this case was highly unusual, but that there was a protocol to follow. Tests, rest, nutrition, rehabilitation, and all the rest.

It would take time and recovery would be gradual. But Rosalynd was young and otherwise healthy. If everything went well, in his opinion, he saw no reason not to hope for the best.

Rosalynd wasn't able to process all of the new and bewildering information. Instead she turned her head to Enrico and lifted her arm just a bit.

The doctor stepped back so he could take her hand again. "Oh, Rosalynd. Rosalynd. I love you so."

"Enrico?"

It was hard for her to speak. He didn't want to force her, but he answered, "Yes, my darling?"

Slowly she spoke each word. "I love you, too."

And her words brought tears to his eyes.

Rosalynd was alive. She was awake. She was going to recover. His heart soared with joy.

After the charges against him were dropped, he would be a free man. He would be at her side as she went through her rehabilitation and make sure she had everything she needed. She would grow strong and well. And then, perhaps some day soon, she would be released. He would have his Rosalynd back, and he would do everything in his power to take care of her for the rest of her days.

No one would ever hurt her again.

CHAPTER FIFTY-FIVE

Gen managed to pull off the double baby shower after all.
Or maybe it was Sybil.
It was held in a room on the fifth floor of one of Mr. P's buildings in downtown Atlanta. A space big enough for the hundred people who actually showed up, despite the short notice.
Gen—or Sybil—must have decided to go with a balloon theme, Miranda thought as she entered the hall on Parker's arm. There were tons of pink and blue balloons forming fanciful archways, arranged in artistic patterns along the walls, and floating in the air.
Gen—or Sybil—couldn't get a band on such short notice. Instead soft music was piped in from a playlist.
Probably a better idea for a baby shower than hard driving rock. Or piano music, in this case.
There were about a dozen round tables covered with pink and blue tablecloths all around the room where the guests chatted and mingled. It was another formal affair, and the men were in suits, the women in nice dresses or pantsuits.
Miranda had pulled a ruby red knee-length thing out of her closet to wear. It kind of clashed with the pink and blue, but she was looking forward to taking it off afterwards.
Even after the lovely "no clothes" morning Parker had given her in their own bed in the penthouse.
The food was terrific. All kinds of appetizers were laid out on a long table. Miranda eyed them greedily. Avocado and shrimp, crab cakes and hummus, smoked salmon and imported cheeses. And then there was the dessert table laden with chocolate espresso cups, cream puffs drizzled with ganache, mini brownies, and fruit tarts.

After her recent calorie deficit, Miranda let go and stuffed herself, making Parker smile. He wouldn't have to work too hard to fulfill that promise of putting fifteen pounds on her.

After playing a few silly party games, Coco and Fanuzzi were led to the front of the room where two large tables were piled high with gifts.

Wearing a shimmering pale pink maternity dress, Coco sat at the table on the left. In a pale blue maternity dress Fanuzzi sat at the table on the right. She looked puffy, and like she wished she were in jeans. Or back home.

Miranda felt for her.

One by one, they opened the presents to a never-ending chorus of oohs and aahs. There was everything from teddy bears to teething rings. Pacifiers, bottle warmers, blankets, and booties. A newborn carrier. A baby carriage. A bassinet. A nursery caddy.

Lots of onesies. Lots and lots of diapers.

Antonio stood behind Coco, helping her with the wrapping and bows, and thanking the guests. Miranda spied him stealing kisses on her cheek between packages.

The sight made her smile. They were okay now. Clearly back in love with each other. What a relief.

Becker was playing the same helper role for Fanuzzi, but he wasn't having as smooth of a time of it. He kept dropping the ribbons and paper she handed him. Mostly because she was tossing them over her shoulder. It was obvious to Miranda she didn't feel good and was still pretty crabby. She was trying hard not to look too fussy, but she couldn't help herself.

Poor Becker. Poor Fanuzzi. Maybe this party was too much for her. She worried for both of her friends.

After the gifts were opened, it was time for the cake. The big one. It was a huge five-layer deal with white icing, blue and pink sprinkles, and lots of frosting in the shape of bows.

Miranda murmured to Parker that she needed to pass on that one. She'd already eaten too many sweets.

Before Parker could change her mind, Coco scurried over to her. "Oh, Miranda. Thank you so much for what you did for Enrico."

Estavez must have told her everything that had happened in Saint Simons. "Don't mention it. I'm glad the real truth finally came out."

"I knew he was innocent. I just knew it."

"You were right. I'm glad you were."

"As you know, Fiona and Ivan were taken into custody last night," Estavez said. "They're being transported to Atlanta to stand trial for the attempted murder of Rosalynd Allen."

Miranda could only nod as she took in the news.

"Enrico could be free as early as Monday," Estavez added. "I flew to Saint Simon this morning to get the paperwork expedited."

Miranda glanced at Parker. He seemed as surprised to hear that as she was.

She gestured with her finger. "You mean you flew there and back again? In your Cessna?"

Estavez gave her a smooth lawyer smile. "Yes. It was a short flight."

Uh oh. Was he getting back into his old workaholic habits already?

Coco squeezed her husband's arm. "It's okay with me if you tell them, honey."

"As you wish, my love." Estavez flashed a happy white toothed grin. "We flew together."

"Together? You and Coco? In your Cessna?"

"Yes. In fact, she assisted me."

"Assisted?"

"She helped me keep track of all the documents and what was said at the police station."

Coco let out a little squeal of joy. "It was just practice, but Antonio says he can always use the help. I'm going to start taking paralegal classes right after the baby's born. We're going to be a team."

Miranda didn't know what to say. Coco, a paralegal? Assisting Estavez in his practice? Well, she did just prove she had good instincts about clients.

"That's wonderful," Miranda blurted out. Of course, there'd be diaper detail coming up soon, as well. She had a feeling she and Parker might get roped into some of that.

But Parker would probably enjoy it. At any rate, he was beaming as he laid an affectionate hand on Estavez's shoulder. "I'm so happy for you, son. For both of you."

Miranda knew his heart was overflowing.

Coco was beaming, too. "And we've started writing a new song. It's all about love and new life and happiness."

Back to normal, Miranda thought. Whatever that was.

Estavez held up a finger. "I almost forgot. You'll never guess what Enrico told me when I saw him at his home."

"What?" Miranda wasn't sure she wanted to hear it.

But Estavez's dark eyes twinkled with joy. "He went to see Rosalynd today. She woke up."

"She did?" Miranda couldn't believe it. The doctor was right about her brain activity.

"That's amazing, son," Parker said, looking a little astounded.

"Enrico swears it was a miracle."

"It was the power of love," Coco sighed.

"She needs a lot of rehabilitation, and the doctors aren't sure she'll ever play piano again, but Bagitelli is hopeful. He wants us to all come to their first concert."

"We'd be honored to attend." Parker turned to her. "Wouldn't we?"

Miranda couldn't help grinning at the idea. She might even stay awake for that performance. "We'll be there with bells on."

CHAPTER FIFTY-SIX

Everyone started to get ready to go.
"I need to say goodbye to Fanuzzi," Miranda told Parker. But as she scanned the room, she didn't see her friend anywhere.
She spotted Becker near the gift table. He was packing everything up and thanking the guests for coming.
But he was alone.
Miranda hurried over to him. "Hey, Becker. Great job on the Bagitelli case."
"Yeah. I heard he's going to be set free. Antonio told me the whole thing. You're a hero, Steele. Again. Both you and Mr. Parker."
She gave him a punch on his sleeve. "We couldn't have done it without your help."
He blushed.
"Say, where's Fanuzzi?"
Becker's smile disappeared. "When she was opening presents earlier she got kind of emotional and had to excuse herself."
"Was she, you know, getting sick?"
"Hard to tell, but I didn't think so. She should be back by now. Could you go check on her?"
So he wouldn't get a tongue lashing? "Sure."
Miranda headed off to the back of the room where the appetizer and dessert tables were. Hired staff were putting away leftovers and cleaning up. Some of the guests stopped her and said how nice the party was before heading out, but Fanuzzi wasn't with them.
Miranda made her way down a hall and found the Ladies Room. She checked every stall, but Fanuzzi wasn't there.
She took another turn and finally found the kitchen.
And there she was. Might have known.

Wearing an apron she must have snatched off a hook, Fanuzzi stood behind a stainless steel prep table with a plastic spatula in her hand. She was mixing chocolate in a glass bowl. Evidently it didn't make her barf any more.

Her face looked puffy. Her expression was a mixture of an angry scowl and intense concentration.

Miranda tiptoed up to the edge of the table. "Fanuzzi?"

She knew Fanuzzi had heard her because her scowl deepened.

"What are you doing?"

"What does it look like I'm doing, Murray?" she snapped in her Brooklyn accent. "I'm making ganache."

The ganache she'd learned how to perfect in Paris. But why?

"You don't have to do that. You need to get off your feet. You're the co-guest of honor. Somebody else did the food for the party."

Fanuzzi made a noise like a wounded beast in the jungle. "Polly Driscoll did the food. Ha. She thinks she's so good, but she doesn't know how to make a ganache if her life depended on it. Not one like mine."

Miranda recalled there had been ganache on the creme puffs, and on some of the cupcakes she'd scarfed down. Seemed all right to her. "Okay. So what if her ganache isn't as good as yours? It's still your party. Yours and Coco's. You're supposed to relax."

Still swiping her spatula around the bowl, Fanuzzi glanced up and glared at her. "Relax? How can I relax? While I'm busy puking and running to the john, Polly Driscoll is stealing my business."

Was that what was bothering her? Professional insecurity? But she was the best. Everybody raved about her edible creations.

"Well, like you said. You're better than Driscoll. Once the baby's born, you'll get back to catering and give her a run for her money."

Fanuzzi let out a snarl of frustration. "You don't get it, Murray."

"What don't I get?"

She kept beating the defenseless chocolate. "If my business goes under, Becker and I go under. We can't support four kids. And now we've got extra medical bills because my body decided to swell up like one of those balloons out there. Things are getting rough. We can barely make our house payments." Her voice almost broke.

House payments. The words were like an arrow that went straight through Miranda's heart.

As if realizing the guests were nearly gone, Fanuzzi stopped stirring and hung her head over the bowl. Then she picked it up, turned to the sink, and began washing it down the drain.

Miranda watched her in silence, her heart aching for her friend. And for Becker.

Fanuzzi was in a really bad way or she'd never waste a perfectly good ganache. And it was all about money?

She could fix that. She had fixed it. She and Parker and Mr. P. But they had agreed to keep it secret. Not to be revealed until some future point when Miranda thought the time was right.

Parker didn't think she should tell her until the new baby was grown.

But she couldn't let her friend go on worrying and stressing about finances, and hurting herself to try to make ends meet. That could be one reason this pregnancy was so hard on her.

The time to tell her was now.

Miranda stepped a little closer to the sink and ran her hand over the stainless steel counter. "Did I ever tell you about the Parker mansion?"

Looking annoyed, Fanuzzi shook her head. "What about it?"

"When I moved in, Mr. P arranged for me to buy the place."

She stopped rinsing her bowl. "He did what?"

"It was just so Parker would move in and take over the house. It worked." She let out a little laugh.

Fanuzzi just stared at her.

"Anyway, I made my payments every month. They were ridiculously low. And when I—left the mansion—I told Mr. P I'd make the last payment as soon as I could."

Fanuzzi knew all about Miranda's break up with Parker and why she'd left the Parker estate.

"And that was when Mr. P told me he'd been keeping my payments in an investment account. He gave all that money back to me plus what they'd earned. It really helped at the time."

Fanuzzi's bloated face was a study in anger and insult. "And you're telling me this why?"

She must have thought Miranda was rubbing her financial situation in her face.

Miranda felt her stomach quiver. She wasn't sure how Fanuzzi would react. And once the cat was out of the bag, there was no going back. But it was the right thing to do.

She was sure of it.

She took a deep breath and blurted it out. "Because we did the same thing for you and Becker."

"Huh?"

"Mr. P had all the paperwork drawn up and set up the accounts. Parker and I contributed the funds. Of course, he put up most of it." She let out another awkward laugh.

Fanuzzi didn't get it. "The funds for what?"

"For your house."

"*My* house?"

"Didn't you get a letter about your mortgage being sold last December?"

"Yeah. We had to send payments to a different place."

"That was Mr. P's investment account. We paid off your mortgage and he's been holding the payments you've been making. All that money is yours whenever you need it."

"You did what?" She didn't sound happy.

She was in shock.

"We paid off your house," Miranda said again more slowly. "You don't have to come up with money for mortgage payments anymore. And the payments you've made since December are in an investment account. They're yours."

Fanuzzi's face took on the look of an Italian hit man about to make a kill. "And you did this why?"

Miranda blinked. She wasn't expecting that question. "You were so worried about finances with the new baby. Becker was going crazy about it, but he still worked the case we were on at the time. We wanted to help."

Fanuzzi looked around the kitchen as if she had just landed on another planet. "You think Dave and I can't handle our own finances? You think we're children? That we're stupid or something?"

"No. That wasn't it at all. We just wanted to help. I wanted to help. I hate seeing you so miserable and stressed out all the time."

Her upper lip began to curl. "It's my business if I'm miserable and stressed out."

"But aren't I supposed to be your friend?"

Glaring at her, slowly Fanuzzi shook her head. "I don't think I can be friends with you anymore, Miranda Steele."

She never called her that. "Fanuzzi."

She took a step toward her, but Fanuzzi put up a hand. "Get away from me. I don't want to speak to you. I don't want to see you again." She put a fist to her mouth. Whether to choke back tears or to keep from upchucking, Miranda wasn't sure. "I need to find Dave and get outta here."

She turned off the faucet, tossed her apron onto the prep table, and hurried out the door.

Miranda stood staring after her, completely stunned.

What had she done?

For a long moment, the silence around her seemed to swallow her up. Then another door opened behind her. She turned at the sound of footsteps and saw Parker coming into the room.

Breaking down, she ran to him, dug her face into his chest, and sobbed.

Automatically Parker's arms went around her. "Miranda. What in the world is wrong?"

It took a few sniffles before she could speak. "It's Fanuzzi. I told her about the house. About paying it off and saving her mortgage payments in an investment account. And now she hates me for it. She says I must have thought she was too stupid to handle her finances. She says she never wants to speak to me again."

Parker's chest expanded in a slow breath. "I was afraid that might happen."

"She's been so upset and so sick. She's driving herself crazy with worry about money. Why won't she just accept my help? Our help?"

He stroked her hair. "She's a proud and stubborn woman. A little like someone else I know."

Relishing Parker's touch, Miranda thought about that.

It wasn't so long ago that taking care of herself was a big deal to her. More than a big deal. A very sensitive point. It still was. Maybe she should have thought this through more. But she couldn't stand by and do nothing.

Tears began to roll down her cheeks again. "Oh, Parker. I think I've lost the best friend I've ever had."

Parker wiped her cheek, then took her chin in his hand and turned her face to him. "Fanuzzi isn't herself right now. Once the baby's born and things settle down, she'll come to her senses."

"Do you think so?"

"I do. She just needs time to get used to the idea."

And Becker, too. What in the world was he going to think?

"I hope you're right, Parker."

"I am. You'll see. Just give her time and space for now."

She nodded, and he bent his head and kissed her. It was a gentle kiss. His lips were soothing, and his warm arms felt good around her. But even Parker's love might not be able to take away the hurt raging inside her. She'd never had friends before she came to Atlanta. Not until Fanuzzi.

No, Parker was right. He had to be. Things would work out. The babies would be coming in about a month, and everything would be joy and happiness.

It had to work out that way. It just had to. It would.

Because if it didn't, Miranda didn't know what she was going to do.

CHAPTER FIFTY-SEVEN

He stood at the sink washing the blood off his hands.

He washed them twice just to make sure there was no trace of the woman. Then he reached for the knife he'd used to create his masterpiece tonight and carefully rubbed soap over the blade, the handle. He held it under the faucet until the water ran clear.

He used paper towels to dry the knife and his hands. Towels he could easily burn. He was good at getting rid of evidence.

He thought of the woman. Her smile had been so provocative, so eager as he'd tied her up. Until she saw his knife and realized what he was really going to do to her. Then her smile had turned to an exquisite expression of horror. It was so delicious to hear the sounds she was capable of as he carefully sculpted her body, creating beautiful wound after wound.

It was his best work ever. Not in style, perhaps. But in execution. And all the evidence was hidden or destroyed. When they found her, the stupid Chicago police would be as baffled as they were about his last work of art.

He put the knife away in its secret compartment and changed his clothes. They would have to be burned, too.

After pulling on a fresh T-shirt and jeans, he switched on the small TV on his dresser. The news.

He sat down on the end of his bed to watch.

That chubby woman police detective was giving an interview about the slasher case. The one he'd done a week ago. Watching her made him excited.

She said they had released the name of the med student and several other details that told him he had nothing to worry about. They weren't even close. Then the victim's parents appeared, pleading for anyone who knew anything about their daughter's murder to come forth.

He watched the mother sob into the camera and felt nothing.

No one had ever felt anything for him when he had been in pain.

He stood up to turn the TV off, then he froze as a new story came on.

This was on the national front. A familiar image appeared. He recognized the dark hair, the angles of her face, those blue, blue eyes.

She'd solved another case?

He listened. Apparently, some classical muscian had been set free due to her efforts.

He sneered at the screen. "Doing good in the world again, are we? Isn't that sweet?"

She hadn't done any good for him.

He switched the television off and turned to his wall of photos. All those possibilities. They made the blood rush in his veins. He'd just gotten started. He moved the photo of his latest work to the right where the other two hung, and pressed the thumbtack into the wall. He had planned for at least two more. Blondes. According to his mentor, they had to be blondes.

Should he change his plans? He wasn't sure. He was rather new to this game, compared to his mentor. He needed more practice.

He studied the photos on the right.

Three victims. Three weeks. He was killing too fast. He knew it, but he had to learn quickly. Too much time had already been wasted. Still he needed to learn how to make them last longer.

He would scour his notes tonight. All the research he'd done, everything his mentor had left him. He would master this craft.

Looking up, he moved over to the central photo on the wall. The one he saw every morning when he woke up.

The photo of Miranda Steele in her news interview after she solved a case in Chicago less than a week ago.

His breathing grew shallow as his rage began to stir inside him. He eyed the same dark hair and sharp features that had just appeared on his TV.

He knew she'd been injured several times while going after killers. He'd researched her, too. And her husband.

Oh, she thought she was so good. But he would show her. He would make her feel more pain than she ever had during those cases. Than she ever had felt in her entire life.

He needed more skill to do that. He needed time, but it would happen. He would make it happen.

Lifting a finger he jabbed it at the picture. "And then, Miranda Steele," he hissed, the anger pounding in his temples, "then you will get exactly what you deserve."

THE END

ABOUT THE AUTHOR

Linsey Lanier writes chilling mystery-thrillers that keep you up at night.

Daughter of a WWII Navy Lieutenant, she has written fiction for over twenty years. She is best known for the popular Miranda's Rights Mystery series and the Miranda and Parker Mystery series. Someone Else's Daughter has received several thousand reviews and more than one million downloads.

Linsey is a member of International Thriller Writers, and her books have been nominated in several well-known contests.

In her spare time, Linsey enjoys watching crime shows with her husband of over two decades and trying to figure out "who-dun-it." But her favorite activity is writing and creating entertaining new stories for her readers.

She's always working on a new book, currently books in the Miranda and Parker Mystery series (a continuation of the Miranda's Rights Mystery series). Other series include the Maggie Delaney Police Thrillers and the Wesson and Sloan FBI Thriller series.

For alerts on her latest releases join Linsey's mailing list at linseylanier.com

For more of Linsey's books, visit her website at **www.linseylanier.com**

Proofreaad by

Donna Rich

Copyright © 2021 Linsey Lanier
Felicity Books
All rights reserved.

Made in the USA
Coppell, TX
04 December 2023